W. T. Wallenda

Fields of Death

The Battle of Hürtgen Forest

Information – original Photos - Novel
contemporary history of the Second World War

W. T. Wallenda

Fields of Death

The Battle of Hürtgen Forest

Information – original Photos - Novel
contemporary history of the Second World War

Impressum:

©2024 - W. T. Wallenda

Titelbild und Rückseite:

war-game-7662264_1920
panel-1451328_1920
re-enactors-2199350_1920
https://pixabay.com/de/service/license-summary/

Fotos/Bilder im Buch:

ai-generated-9141406_1280
https://pixabay.com/de/service/license-summary/

Mit bestem Dank an: Deepai
https://deepai.org/terms-of-service/terms-of-service

sowie Privatarchiv d. Autoren
© Copyright auf alle privaten Fotos

Weitere Mitwirkende:

Umschlaggestaltung und Verlag:

BoD · Books on Demand GmbH
In de Tarpen 42, 22848 Norderstedt

Druck:

Libri Plureos GmbH
Friedensallee 273, 22763 Hamburg

ISBN: 978-3-7693-1550-9

German Edition, BoD, 2015 - ISBN: 978-3-7347-9746-0

Western Front 1944 - In the fall, American troops meet fierce resistance in the Hürtgen Forest as they advance toward the German Reich.

The world-famous author and Nobel Prize winner Ernest Hemingway (1899 - 1961) was a war correspondent for the US Army in the Hürtgen Forest.

The harshness of the fighting and the cruelty of the war traumatized him so much that he wrote a novel about it.

"This was an area where it was extremely difficult to stay alive, even if you did nothing but be there," the author wrote in Across the River and into the Trees, published in 1950.

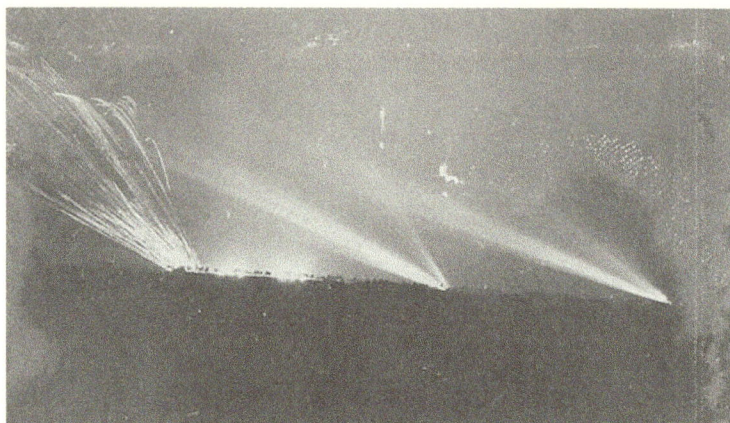

Author's private archive: PA-e-001 - Shelling, rocket launchers/artillery

Preface

After the invasion of Normandy on June 6, 1944, Allied troops advanced at a rapid pace. In September 1944, American units reached the Düren area. At the Siegfried Line, the advance came to a halt due to supply problems. This situation was used by the beleaguered German troops to reorganize.

In the Hürtgen Forest, a wooded area of about 140 square kilometers northeast of the German-Belgian border, they found an ideal defensive terrain with sparse population.

Treeless hills surrounded by dense forest and deep ravines provided natural obstacles. In addition, the Rur dam behind the Hürtgen forest could be opened at any time to flood the Rur valley.

Together with other units, the 275th Infantry Division occupied the Hürtgen Forest and dug in. The US troops met with unexpectedly strong resistance.

In the coldest autumn in decades, the inexperienced American units not only had to contend with battle-hardened Russian veterans, but also fought against the early onset of winter without proper clothing.

In the vast forested areas of the Eifel, every square meter was fought over, and in the villages, every house.
The occupation of villages changed up to 28 times.

The battles in the Hürtgen Forest (Eifel) went down in history as one of the longest and bloodiest battles ever fought on German soil and is also known as the Verdun of the Eifel.

It would be the bitterest and largest defeat American troops had ever suffered.

Key dates of the Battle of the Hürtgen Forest:

Period of fighting:

October 6, 1944 to February 10, 1945

Location/Scenery:

Hürtgenwald - a sparsely populated wooded plateau of approximately 140 square kilometers, consisting of dense forest growth, treeless hills, and deep valleys.

Geographically, the highly defensible area lies northeast of the German-Belgian border, west of the Rur and its dam, and south of the city of Aachen.

The Westwall, built in the 1930s, was located at the edge of the Hürtgen Forest. This old, partly dilapidated fortification system was part of the defense.

Defenders

German Reich - under the supreme command of Field Marshal Walter Model.

Bandages used:

- 12th Volksgrenadier Division
- 89th Infantry Division
- 272nd Volksgrenadier Division
- 275th Infantry Division
- 344th Infantry Division
- 353rd Infantry Division
-    3rd Parachute Division
- 116th Panzer Division "Greyhound

Strength:

Approximately 75,000 men (although this is only an estimate, as some of the divisions had been "bled dry" and could not be replenished to their original strength).

German losses:

- 16,000 wounded
- 12,000 casualties

Author's private archive: PA-H-106 march to the front

Attacker

United States of America - under the supreme command of General Courtney Hodges.

Bandages used:

- 1st US Infantry Division "Big Red One"
- 4th US Infantry Division "Ivy Division"
- 8th US Infantry Division "Golden Arrow" or "Pathfinder"
- 9th US Infantry Division "Octofoil"
- 28th US Infantry Division "Keystone"
- 78th US Infantry Division "Lightning"
- 83rd US Infantry Division "Thunderbolt"
- 104th US Infantry Division "Timberwolves"
- 82nd US Airborne Division "All American"
- 3rd US Armored Division "Spearhead"
- 5th US Armored Division "Victory"
- 7th US Armored Division "Lucky Seventh"

Strength:

about 120.000 soldiers

US losses:

- 21,000 wounded
- 12,000 casualties

https://de.wikipedia.org/wiki/Schlacht_im_H%C3%BCrt-genwald

https://creativecommons.org/licenses/by-sa/4.0/deed.de

army-6164896_1920

Combat Operations

First Battle

On October 6, 1944, the advancing 9th US Infantry Division clashed with the German 275th Infantry Division.

The terrain made air and heavy armor operations nearly impossible. Grueling positional and trench warfare followed. Artillery shells, mines and booby traps caused heavy casualties. In addition, the use of snipers took a psychological toll on the American fighting spirit. Just ten days into the battle, the 9th US Infantry Division had suffered 4,500 casualties, while the defenders had lost about 3,200 men. As a result, the fighting subsided.

Second Battle - Nicknamed the "Battle of All Souls"

The exhausted and discouraged 9th US Infantry Division was relieved by the 28th US Infantry Division. Supported by engineer, armored, and artillery units, the 28th US Infantry Division attacked the strategic village of Schmidt on Thursday, November 2, 1944 (All Souls' Day).

Meanwhile, the area had been further developed into a "fortress" by the German defenders. In addition to the 275th Infantry Division, the 89th Infantry Division and the 12th Volksgrenadier Division were deployed. The 116th Panzer Division "Greyhound" served as a reserve.

All German units were severely decimated and far from their original strength.

After fierce fighting and heavy casualties, the U.S. troops captured the village of Schmidt on November 3, 1944, and barricaded themselves inside. German artillery fire continued. German snipers in the woods around Schmidt kept the enemy demoralized.

Two days later, the German counterattack, led by the 89th Infantry Division and the 116th Panzer Division, followed. Schmidt was retaken after a fierce battle. The US troops again suffered heavy losses and withdrew in a hurry.

In the following days, the German troops followed up and pushed the Americans back to their starting positions in fierce fighting and extremely bad weather conditions. Both sides suffered heavy casualties, with the 28th US Infantry Division losing about 6,200 men, about twice as many as the Germans.

Third Battle - Codename: "Operation Queen"

Operation Queen was the US Army's final attempt to win the Battle of the Hürtgen Forest on November 16, 1944.

While in Phase 1 the 1st US Infantry Division and the 9th US Infantry Division attacked the German positions in the Hürtgen Forest head-on, in Phase 2 the 4th US Infantry Division fought its way through the northern half of the Hürtgen Forest with the goal of reaching the Rur.

The 275th Infantry Division, now slightly reinforced but still exhausted, was still in its positions in the Hürtgen Forest.

Heavy artillery and machine gun fire pulverized two U.S. regiments right at the start of the fighting, forcing them to retreat. Once again, the fighting was fierce and the resistance tougher than the attackers had expected. Three days later, the fighting was halted for two days to recover the wounded.

While the US troops regrouped during this time, the 344th Infantry Division and the 353rd Infantry Division were sent to the HKL to support the German defenders.

From November 21 to December 12, 1944, the American units were able to make successive territorial gains, eventually advancing to the villages of Straß, Gey, and Brandenberg, against fierce resistance.

The German defenders managed to keep the enemy away from the vital dams of the Rur valley. The area of operations for the Ardennes offensive was also kept clear of the enemy.

This major German attack began on December 16, 1944 and ended with the failure of the offensive on January 21, 1945.

By mid-January, U.S. troops were advancing again in the Hürtgen Forest. The exhausted and damaged German defenders were unable to stop the advance. The village of Schmidt was finally taken by American forces on February 8, 1945.

The battle for the Hürtgen Forest was over.

By opening the Rur dam, the Germans flooded the area around the Rur. This delayed the American advance to the Rhine for two weeks.

Note

Hazardous ordnance, including mines and grenades, are still suspected in the former combat zone.

The remains of soldiers have been found again and again. The last time was in 2008 - two US soldiers from the 28th US Infantry Division.

The museum "Hürtgenwald 1944 and in Peace" in Vossensack commemorates the events of the war. It is run by the Hürtgenwald Historical Society.

Dates

275th Infantry Division

Structure and history of the unit

The unit was reorganized in Western France in November 1943 as the 22nd Division. The backbone was formed by the staff and remnants of the 223rd Infantry Division (Army Group South), which was reduced to battalion strength during the fierce defensive fighting in southern Russia and eventually disbanded.

Initially designated the 352nd Infantry Division (until December 1943), the new unit was eventually renamed the 275th Infantry Division.

Reinforced by the XII. Luftwaffe Fortress Battalion and the XX Luftwaffe Fortress Battalion, the troops were deployed to the Hürtgen Forest, where they were involved in extremely heavy fighting in October 1944.
Again severely weakened, the losses were supplemented by the integration of the remnants of the 344th Infantry Division in December 1944.

The 275th Infantry Division was finally reorganized at Flensburg in January 1945 with the existing staff units and sent to the Eastern Front. It was finally destroyed during the fighting in the Halbe Kessel (Guben area).

Commander of the division

Dec. 1943 - April 1945 Lieutenant General Hans Schmidt

Deployment of the 275th Infantry Division

1944

February – May:

- Brittany

June – July:

- Normandy (Contentin, Falaise, and Mons area)

August:

- All Belgium

September – December:

- Hürtgen Forest

1945

January:

- Reorganization in Flensburg

February - April

- Halbe Kessel (Guben area) - Destruction

War Crimes

While researching this book, I was unable to find any war crimes explicitly attributed to members of the 275th Infantry Division.

It should be noted, however, that the relevant literature shows that during the fierce fighting in the Hürtgen Forest, at times no prisoners were taken by either side.

This raises the suspicion that both German and American soldiers may have killed their captured opponents out of desperation, anger, fear, hatred, or other motives, contrary to the international agreements in force at the time.

However, I have not been able to find a detailed report documenting such acts.

Words about the novel part

Along with other units, the 275th Infantry Division also occupied areas of the Hürtgen Forest, digging in and using the remaining old bunkers of the Westwall for defense.

When the relatively inexperienced US troops attacked in the coldest autumn in decades, they were largely without aircraft support due to the weather.
They met battle-hardened Russian veterans and were engaged in the fiercest fighting ever seen.

In addition to the unexpectedly high resistance, the American units had another problem to contend with. They were not equipped for the early onset of winter and did not have the proper clothing.

In the vast forested areas of the Eifel, every square meter was fought over for months, and every house in the villages.

Artillery fire, booby traps, minefields, numerous machine gun nests and finally German snipers demoralized the attacking US troops. But the German soldiers also experienced hell on earth in the combat zones of the Hürtgen Forest and spoke of apocalyptic battles.

The novel tells the story of one of these snipers, a Russian veteran who has returned to the front, and an assault gun crew.

With the exception of historical figures, all names are fictitious. Any resemblance to real people is purely coincidental.

Author's private archive: PA-M-100 anti-tank barrier (Dragon's Teeth)

Fields of Death

The Battle of Hürtgen Forest

"We have been digging trenches for days. I wonder why we need more trenches and foxholes back here, when the fortifications of the Westwall are already in front of us," grumbled Eduard Hofman as he hefted his spade into the ground. The german soldier encountered resistance again. "Another root. That's enough for me!"

Sweat dripped from the soldier's forehead, his cheeks were flushed. "And I don't have anything to drink either," he added, visibly angry.

"Stop grumbling, Eduard. We'll be through soon anyway," Franz Huber reassured him, reaching over to his side, pulling out his canteen and holding it out to his comrade. "Here, take a sip, it will make the world look better."

"You're right, Franz," the thirsty Hofman replied, sipping at the cool water. With his thirst quenched, the soldier's mood improved. He took out his snuff box and tapped it twice on his thigh, as usual, before opening it and sprinkling a pinch on his left hand, right in the little hollow between his thumb and wrist. The hand went under his nose, then the soldier sniffed the tobacco in completely. Then he puffed hard. "Ahhh," he groaned with pleasure. "You should switch from smoking to snuff, too. It's much better."

"You're just imagining things," came the prompt reply.

Huber inhaled the smoke from the cigarette he had now lit with relish and blew it out with equal relish. The blue cloud of vapor first danced over the two men's heads, then dispersed and dissipated in no time.

"I remember when you talked Keller and me into trying this stuff." The private laughed as he spoke. "Ha, ha. We blue-eyed rookies took a good pinch and sneezed for minutes."

Now they both laughed.

"I hope Keller gets back soon. It's been almost a year since he left. It's really boring when the old boy isn't around."

"It's almost exactly ten months! He got it pretty bad in Russia. I'm surprised he survived at all."

"We dragged him far enough back then. I'll never forget that day."

"Me neither! Our comrade Franz. Keller saved our lives in the end."

"And we his!"

Silent nods. The recalled memories of Russia made me ashamed. The times were too cruel and merciless, the circumstances too hard.

"Is it true that he's on a sergeant's course?"

Hofman nodded. "The Master Sergeant told me."

Author's private archive, PA-H-102- entrenchments

All Josef Keller knew was that the Russian T-34 was rolling toward him and his comrades. The steel colossus had come out of nowhere. The rattling of the chains sounded like a thousand hussars drawing their sabres to plunge them into the bodies of their enemies. The eyes of the two young soldiers lying beside the lance corporal in the foxhole were filled with sheer mortal fear. The other men of the squad sat in their cover holes a few meters away. Their position to break through the tank was even worse than his own.

The Russian tank's mounted machine gun rattled in their direction. Shells whirred above them. As if in a trance, Keller had grabbed the last T-mine and crawled out of the hole. Miraculously, he had escaped the machine gun's bullets. At first he crawled out on his stomach, then he hoisted himself up and ran crouching toward the rolling fortress.

A David vs. Goliath battle awaited the soldier.

With the experience of a veteran front-line soldier, Keller tried to stay in the blind spot of the on-board machine gun. The staring eyes of his comrades rested on him as if spellbound. Deadly brave, he approached step by step. The lance corporal knew he didn't have much time. In a moment, the heavy chains would roll over his comrades' foxholes and bury them beneath them.

This is it, he thought coldly.

He got close enough, ran along the massive chains, clamped the mine between the turret and the chassis, and pulled the safety cord. Keller immediately turned away and ducked for cover. Just as he was about to drop to the ground, the charge detonated.

Boom!

The lance corporal felt a powerful blow to his back. He was thrown through the air and hit the ground hard. The noise of the battle, the roar of the tank's engine, and the screams of the men around him were muffled. Gradually it became black and silent.

When the Landser *(Author's note: Low-ranking German army soldiers were occasionally referred to as Landser in the First World War, more commonly in the Second World War.)* opened his eyes again, everything was blurred. A monotonous clacking combined with a constant jerking. He knew it. Keller had to clear his mind. He was lying in a train. When he tried to sit up, the lance corporal felt pain. An almost unbearable pain that started in his back and made him sink back down immediately. His mouth was dry, his lips chapped and cracked. The stench in the wagon was terrible and indefinable. Powerless, Keller sank back into delirium. The next time he awoke, a nurse was standing beside him. She wiped his lips with a wet cloth. He greedily soaked up the wetness.

"Where am I?" he forced out in a hoarse voice through his cracked lips.

"Rest! You're on a hospital train. We're going home."

Home!

The word sounded reassuring. No more trenches. No more Ivan *(Author's note: Ivan = nickname of the Russian soldiers.)* storming in. No more tanks to crack. He was safe. Keller looked up at the ceiling with satisfaction, but a few moments later he was overcome by doubt.

Why am I lying here in the hospital train?

Fear crawled through his battered body.

Do I still have all my limbs? Did the armor roll over my legs?

The image of the T 34 kept coming back. The wounded corporal thought he could hear the rattling of chains. Everything replayed in his mind.

The front-line soldier was overcome with self-doubt. The nurse seemed to sense his feelings.

"Don't worry! You're still fine. You were badly wounded, but the staff doctor operated on you immediately. I was there myself when your comrades brought you in. It was a miracle that you were still alive after all that blood loss. Dr. Frenzel said you

24

would make a full recovery. The shrapnel didn't hit any vital organs. You are a lucky man! All you need is rest and recuperation."

Perfectly healthy.

These words had a relieving effect. The badly injured man fell asleep again.

Keller had to stay in the hospital until well into the spring. Then came the cures, a long vacation, and then the NCO course in Wörgl/Tyrol (Austria) for the recovered war hero.

At the end of the course, Josef Keller was asked to come to the office of the course instructor.

"As you have learned in the meantime, your old division has been completely routed in southern Russia and has therefore been disbanded. The remaining members have been integrated into the newly formed 275th Infantry Division. Including you, by the way! Your new unit is located on the German-Belgian border, in the northern foothills of the Eifel. Your company is in an area called Todtenbruch. Here are your marching orders," said Captain Klingenberg to the newly commissioned Sergeant Josef Keller, congratulating him on his promotion. "The NCO's braids match your decorations perfectly," the officer said, alluding to the medals he had been awarded.

Keller was awarded the Iron Cross First Class and the Silver Wounded Badge during his military hospitalization in Gars am Inn (Austria).

"With your commander's best wishes for your recovery. For exceptional bravery in the face of the enemy ...", it said at the time.

Both medals and the assault badge were pinned to his field blouse. The captain's gaze wandered from the insignia to Keller's upper right arm, where it lingered on the sewn-on tank destroyer patch. A gold tank was emblazoned on it. Klingenberg knew immediately that Keller had destroyed at least five tanks as a lone fighter. A true war hero stood before him.

"Do you happen to know which of my comrades came out of southern Russia?"

Klingenberg shook his head. "I'm sorry. I'm not informed about that. I wish you all the best."

It was that time again. Josef Keller was sitting on a train, rolling to the front. This time, however, he was not going east, to the hated Russia, but to the Western Wall. The seat next to the Russian veteran remained empty until Heilbronn. The train reached the small town in the Aera called Baden early in the morning. A one-hour stop was announced. Keller decided to get off the train to buy a newspaper and a soft drink. When he got back on the train, a lance corporal was sitting in the seat next to him. They looked at each other and nodded in greeting.

"Josef Keller," the sergeant introduced himself.

"Georg Honnige," the lance corporal said curtly.

Keller sat down, drank the rest of his lemonade and read the newspaper. The train rolled on again. Half an hour later, the sergeant folded up the paper and offered it to his neighbor to read.

"No, thank you. I read it at the station. I had to wait two hours for this train. I was told it would arrive at 5 o'clock in the morning. It was a short night for me," he politely declined. Honnige spoke with a slight Baden accent.

"Where are you going?"

"First to the Düren station, then on to the 275th Infantery Division. There I'm in the 983rd."

"Man, that's my regiment. I have to go there too."

"What battalion?"

"I. Battalion, 2nd Company, 1st Platoon, 2nd Squad, to be exact," Keller gushed.

"That's something! I'm with I./2 too, but I've never seen you before."

"No wonder. I was wounded in Russia and spent a long time in the hospital. Now they've ordered me back to my old gang. I'm curious to see who else is there."

"Second group? Wait a minute..." Honnige pondered. "I know Hofman and Huber from the old days," he began to report.

"Eduard and Franz," exclaimed Keller at once. His eyes flashed. "Great guys. Is young Burger still here? And what about Schoner, Kleemann and Reiz?"

"Yes, Burger is also with Hofman. I don't know the others, sorry."

"Three out of seven," the Russian veteran exhaled. "That's tough!"

"Wait a minute," Honnige groaned suddenly. "Now I remember. You're Josef Keller. The wounded lance corporal who got it bad on the Eastern Front. And that happened when you cracked a tank. Is that true?"

"I introduced myself by name earlier."

Honnige smiled sheepishly. "But I couldn't place the name then."

"Who is our boss?"

Ignoring the question, Honnige continued. "The tank stopped three meters in front of your comrades. They had their pants full. The T 34 would have flattened Hofman and Huber!"

"Three meters?" Keller exclaimed in amazement, frowning.

"I know the story well. They tell it at every group meeting. I've been there three times. When you ran towards the tank, your comrades first thought you had gotten battle fatigue and were trying to kill yourself. But then they saw the T-mine you were carrying. It blew the turret off, by the way. Boy, if you believe the stories, you had about a thousand shrapnel in your back."

Keller smiled a little. "It wasn't that many, but it was enough to keep me away from the troops for ten months."

"I see they weren't too stingy with decorations up there," Honnige alluded to the divisional staff.

"It's all just tin," the decorated soldier dismissed.

At the same time, he glanced at the Baden-Württemberg soldier's blouse. The silver sniper badge was clearly sewn onto the sleeve. A jolt went through the battle-hardened sergeant. Sitting next to him was a soldier with whom contact was generally avoided.

Snipers were generally unpopular, and for a long time they were considered to be sneaky snipers. It was only as the war got tougher that they gained respect for their successes, but also for the risk of dying a hero's death faster than the others.

The propaganda machine turned them into hunters and feared lone wolves. To this day, Keller had never met a sniper. To be honest to himself, he had learned to fear them. Some of his comrades had been killed by Russian snipers. Fear and terror ran through the limbs of even the oldest front-line pigs when an enemy sniper struck.

There were many ways to risk one's life on the front lines. Keller had certainly experienced some of them. But one of the most dangerous ways was to lie down somewhere in no-man's-land as a sniper. Once the enemy located him, he went from hunter to hunted. All too often, entire companies would mercilessly hunt him down. There are even stories of entire strips of land being plowed up by artillery simply because a sniper was suspected. But Keller never checked to see if this was true.

"Sniper?" the sergeant asked, almost rhetorically.

Honnige nodded. "I'm with the company. That's what Captain Retzer wanted."

"Retzer?" the corporal inquired. "When I was in the troop, Captain Stein ran the company. What about him? Did he make a career for himself?"

The man from Heilbronn shook his head. "I never got to know him. Stein fell. Must have been the same day you were wounded. Anyway, he was buried in Russia."

Keller sank back on the bench thoughtfully. "And what about our platoon leader?"

"If you mean Lt. Drexler? He's feeling very much at home right now. He's from near Düren and knows the Eifel like the back of his hand."

At least Drexler made it, the sergeant thought. What will the Westwall bring? What will it be like in the Hürtgen Forest? They were no longer fighting in enemy territory. They fought on German soil. At home. Cursed war!

"Cigarette?" Honnige held a pack of American Camel cigarettes and offered one to his neighbor.

"Where did you get these?"

The question and the grab for the cigarette came at the same time.

"You'll laugh. We swapped them. We officially met. Some of the gum-chewing Yanks and some of our people. It was after a skirmish. Armistice to get the wounded and the dead. We brought Juno cigarettes, wine from the Pfalz and good grain. The Americans had Camel cigarettes and Whisky. You can't imagine the amount of black goods that showed up for the exchange. I managed to get four cartons."

"Lucky bastard!"

"They call themselves GIs and they call us Krauts."

"Krauts," Keller repeated, grinning.

The sniper grinned, too. "Because we eat so much sauerkraut," he explained.

The remaining hours of the train trip passed quickly. Keller and Honnige got along well. They talked about many things, but not about the ruined Germany they were passing through. The looks said it all. Neither front-line soldier wanted to criticize in public as they passed the ruins of bomb victims. At Düren, the journey was over. They had reached their destination and got out.

"Where exactly is our company located?" Keller asked again.

"Somewhere in Todtenbruch. The battalion is near Vossensack. I think we'll find them somewhere between Vossensack and Lammersdorf."

"How far is that?"

"A good 20 kilometers from Düren."

"Then we should look for a ride."

"Not a bad idea, Josef, but how are you going to do that?"

"There's a chain dog there. I'll go and find out."

Author's private archive, PA-H-105 replenishment

The field gendarme (*Author's Note: german Military Police*) showed the two compatriots the way to the trucks heading for the HKL . Shortly thereafter, they marched to the other side of the Düren train station, where the trucks were being loaded.

"As long as supplies are going to the HKL (*Author's Note: HKL = Abbreviation for Main Battle Line*), the war is not over!"

"Honey, I'd like to have your enthusiasm," Keller said, astonished.

"Or humor," he finally replied dryly.

They reached the trucks and asked to pass through. The first two soldiers just shook their heads. The third driver could help. "Go two trucks over, there's a Henschel. The driver's name is Kurt. I think he must be from the I. Battalion."

"Thank you."

"You're welcome."

They walked straight on and stopped at a Henschel truck. The tailgate was closed, no driver in sight. Honnige lit a camel.

A Landser approached and stopped in front of them. "Are you Kurt?"

"Why?"

"We have to go to I./2."

"I'm sorry. I'm not traveling alone. The cab is full."

"Then we'll get in the back."

"Unhappy! I have a lot of ..." He didn't get any further because the sniper had three camels in his hand. The driver quickly grabbed them. "Get up, but I didn't see you. I was loading mines and stuff. The shipment is going to the engineers. I'm following two other trucks later. We'll get a group of infantrymen for protection. Just don't let them see you. You know how it is. When transporting ammunition, it's strictly forbidden to take anyone in the back."

"It's all right."

The cigarettes disappeared into Kurt's breast pocket. Honnige and Keller climbed onto the loading aerea and made themselves comfortable.

An hour and a half later, they reached their destination.

"I'm sure we'll see each other again. I'll go to the WuG *(Author's note. WuG = abbreviation for weapon and equipment sergeant)* first and get my rifle. I feel more comfortable with my equipment," the sniper said goodbye.

Keller walked to the company office alone. He stopped in front of the house, which had a wooden sign outside the front door. A dispatcher came out, looked the sergeant up and down, got into his DKW *(Military Motorcycle 350 cc)* and roared off. The Russian veteran took a deep breath.

Now things are really getting going again.

The Landser knew what he was in for. It would certainly take him some time to get used to a bunk again. If there was one at all. He was also prepared for the lice that would inevitably come. "Everyday soldier, you've caught me again," he whispered and entered the writing room.

31

Author's private archive, PA-H-107 writing room

"Can't you knock?" someone shouted immediately.

Keller recognized the dark, gruff voice and approached the desk without a word. Only then did the Master Sergeant, alone in the room, raise his head. Glowing red with rage, he unleashed a torrent of abuse: "You three-day soldiers must first be shown respect..." The sergeant major, who held the rank of first sergeant by virtue of his position, trailed off in mid-sentence. That he was the company sergeant was also evident from the two cob rings sewn onto the sleeves of his uniform. "The monkey's pissing me off," the sergeant exclaimed in amazement. "Josef! Is it really you?"

"In the flesh, as you can see."

"Good to have you back. The NCO stripes look good on you," greeted Sergeant Major Radomski, standing up and extending his hand across the desk to Keller. A firm handshake followed.

"You're the Master Sergeant of the company now? Where did the old Miller go?"

"He no longer exists."

"I can't believe it. Miller has fallen? He was always miles behind HKL. At least I never saw him with a submachine gun in the front lines."

"He had bad luck. When it came to the end in Russia, Miller had somehow snuck on board an old Auntie Ju *(Author's note: Aunt Ju = nickname of the Junkers 52 transport aircraft.* No one knows how he did it. In any case, the plane was shot down."

The Sergeant Major reached behind him, pushed aside a folder, and pulled out a green bottle. "Cognac? It's really good. I brought it from France. It's nothing like the potato brandy we drank in Russia."

"Gladly."

In no time, two glasses were in front of the two soldiers. Randomski carefully filled them with brandy. After a welcoming sip, the Master Sergeant pointed to a chair. "Have a seat," he asked Keller, refilling his glass.

"I thought I'd landed with the mountain troops, the wooded hills here are so steep," the returnee said.

"The terrain is really amazing. Ahead of us is the Siegfried Line ...", the sergeant began to explain, "... with its anti-tank barriers and bunkers. Well, one or two of the bunkers have been empty for years. Why occupy them?" he laughed before continuing. "But after that comes the forest. At least 140 square kilometers of pure forest," he pointed out. "There are practically no paths suitable for tanks. The valleys and hills are barely passable on foot, and beyond them is the Rur dam. Whoever occupies the dams controls the whole area!"

"And where will I find my group in this hostile jungle?"

"Josef, as always! I'm already raving about our Eifel and you want to go back to the trenches."

They both raised the second glass of cognac, toasted each other and drank it down. The brandy went down their throats. Warm and velvety. A pleasant sensation spread through their stomachs.

"Really good," Keller praised as he set his glass down. "So?" he followed up. "Where are my people?"

Radomski laughed. "They're here at Lammersdorf. It's the highest point in this area and it's called Todtenbruch. There's also a second row of bunkers near you. A fallback position after the actual Siegfried Line, so to speak!"

"Bunkers?"

"Yes, but as I mentioned earlier, those things have been empty for a long time. You can't even fire an MG 42 in the concrete positions."

"I'll be surprised."

"And one more thing, Josef."

"I'm listening."

The Sergeant Major lowered his voice. He went on almost in a whisper. "The new soldiers they send from the barracks to the front are still children. You'll be shocked at how young the guys are. Sometimes I have the feeling that the boys don't come from the barracks yards, but from the school yards. Take care of your men."

Keller nodded. Now they were his men. He was the squad leader. That was new, too. He had even more responsibility. His orders could mean the difference between life and death for his group. "I will, Radomski!"

"Now you'd better go to the Sergeant at Arms and stock up on ammunition, then come back here. I won't let an old Russian comrade go on foot. I'll see to it that you're brought back to your men in a bucket. The field post has arrived anyway, it has to go to the front."

"Thank you."

"Honnige, I've got something for you," the weapon sergeant said, almost beaming with joy, as the sniper picked up his weapon, a K 98 k with a telescopic sight.

"What have you got for me? Did a Russian Moisin Nagant 91/30 come for me?" joked the corporal.

"No, but I finally got you some special ammunition. There was a package in the last transport. I put it aside right away."

"Special ammunition for firing or B-cartridges?"

A broad grin spread across the sergeant's face. "I think your rifle is already accurate enough. I got 50 rounds of the good B cartridges. You can chop down trees with that!"

The WuG handed over the sniper rifle and placed the Hensoldt scope next to it. "I took it off. I thought it would be better not to break it," he added by way of explanation.

"That's good."

Now he placed two more boxes of ammunition on the table. "The two 7.92s should be enough for you. That's all you have now," he said, placing another handgun next to it. "And here's your 08 pistol with two full magazines. Now you're all set."

The sniper picked up his gear and left.

After his sniper course, he was free to choose his weapon. Many of Honnige's students opted for the new Walther G 43, a self-loading rifle with a pleasant recoil and a magazine capacity of ten rounds. The man from Baden-Württemberg, however, swore by the classic Wehrmacht *(Author's note: Wehrmacht = German Army)* carbine.

During the course, he received a personal rifle, which was numbered in his course book. The lance corporal was impressed by the very good telescopic sight, which was mounted on the turret mount. Here Honnige put his trust in the Hensoldt. He thought it harmonized best with the K 98 k. After only eight shots, the weapon was set to one hundred meters.

The B cartridge was an explosive projectile originally used in fighter aircraft machine guns. The small explosion allowed the pilot to correct the trajectory in case of a hit.

However, due to the complex production process, the B cartridges were only issued to the snipers in small numbers. Honnige was very pleased with his gunnery sergeant. "You're just a great guy," he said goodbye and went to the company office to report in. After that, he planned to check on the current situation and patrol the forest tomorrow, unless Captain Retzer had an assignment.

A few minutes after the sniper left, Sergeant Keller also collected his weapons. As a squad leader and sergeant, he received an 08 pistol and an MP 40 with ammunition. As he stepped back out onto the street, the promised bucket truck pulled up.

"To the positions in Todtenbruch?" the driver called to him. "Are you Sergeant Keller?" he added to his question.

"That's me," Keller confirmed, throwing his luggage onto the back seat and getting in.

"It's a nice area here. Enjoy the view. I think I'll take a vacation here someday. After the war," the driver bellowed in a cheeky Berlin dialect.

Keller looked at the corporal. "How long you been a soldier?"

"Since '42. I volunteered then and ended up here. When the Yank comes, he'll get a good kicking!"

The Russian veteran smiled. He estimated the bucket truck *(Author's note: Bucket or bucket truck = Light, all-terrain military vehicle made by Volkswagen)* driver to be between 19 and 20 years old.

"The way you talk, you've already achieved something."

"How to take it. I was in coastal defense."

"Have you ever been in combat?"

"Unfortunately not."

Keller considered telling the young soldier a few stories from the Russian campaign to cure him of his euphoria, but then decided it would be better to keep quiet. He let the conversation fade away and enjoyed the scenery. The road wound like a snake through dense forest.

"Lammersdorf is up ahead, but we have to get up there," the corporal explained after a while, turning into a passable forest path. "Todtenbruch is the highest point here. You have to be very careful, it's partly moor."

Finally they reached the position of Keller's platoon. The sergeant thanked him for the ride and got out.

Then he looked for his engineer and reported back.

"Finally, an experienced man again," Lieutenant Drexler greeted him. "Keller, you will take over the second group immediately. You still know Hofman and Huber, you'll get to know the other six men."

"I hear the squad strength is 1/8. That's almost like in peacetime, when we went on maneuvers with 1/9, Lieutenant, Sir. I remember we ended up with half that many men in Russia."

Drexler took a deep breath. "It's good that those times are over. But let's not kid ourselves. There's still a war going on here on the Western Front - with everything that goes with it. You can't forget that."

"Death lurks on every front!"

"It's a little different here than in Russia. The Americans are fighting us mainly with their equipment. He seems to have tons of tanks, planes, and artillery. His infantry usually shows up quite late in the battle."

"I will prepare for that."

"Go to your group first. The men will arrive any minute. Today was the last time they were used for entrenchment work."

Lt. Drexler explained the way, then the sergeant saluted as instructed and set off. Keller's heart pounded a little. Hofman and Huber had been good friends. He owed them his life. He had something in his pack for each of them.

Some of the soldiers who crossed the convalescent's path were very young. He casually noticed this as he looked at the position on the road. It was in the middle of a wooded area and could hardly be seen from the air, if at all. The pioneers had dug deep holes in the ground, reinforced the walls with logs, and built a flat roof of logs on top. The sloping terrain lent itself to this type of construction. As a result, a good two-thirds of the shelters, occupied by four to six men, were protected from the enemy.

Evening was approaching. A group of three men approached from the woods. The sleeves of their field shirts were rolled up. Their carbines hung from their backs, and they carried spades and hoes over their shoulders. The soldiers were sweating. Keller made eye contact.

No, none that I know of.

They passed in silence. Another group approached. The sergeant stretched to get a better look. Almost at the same moment, he recognized the unmistakable voice of one of the speakers.

"When I say I won't pick up the spade again, I mean it!"

"You know the old saying, Franz! He who dances stays alive!"

"If I were a born to work, I'd be working for the Todd organization, not doing entrenchment work for the Wehrmacht."

Keller was not wrong. Hofman and Huber were ranting as wildly and violently as they had in the Ukraine. The two veterans were followed by a couple of young soldiers.

These must be the new comrades, the returnee thought.

The sergeant took a deep breath. He wanted to greet his two friends properly. He wanted his voice to sound loud and aggressive.

"Who are these bastards? When I was in the group, we marched in formation. We sang and even whistled a soldier's song during hand-to-hand combat!"

Huber and Hofman immediately fell silent. Their companions stopped and looked at the decorated sergeant standing outside their quarters.

Author's Private Archives, PA-H-101 Quarters

"Josef?" Huber exclaimed in surprise. His expression changed from one of astonishment to a toothy grin. "Son of a bitch! That's Josef Keller! Comrades, come here, all of you. We have to greet our squad leader!"

The two Russian veterans took a step forward, threw their spades to the ground, and embraced Keller.

"You made it! I was really afraid you were going to die when we dropped you off at the military base," Franz Huber said bluntly.

"That's right! You had lost so much blood that there was no difference between your face and the snow. You were as pale as my mother-in-law's sheets after Saturday's laundry," laughed Eduard Hofman.

One by one the new comrades introduced themselves. Two of them were corporals and had been in the German Army for two years. Keller immediately thought of the bucket truck driver. The two privates might also have served in the Coast Guard. Then there were four very young enlisted men. Three were straight out of high school, and one had just finished an apprenticeship as a painter when they received their orders to enlist.

"You can all call me Josef," Keller introduced himself. "I don't know what those two said about me, but whatever it was, forget it! Starting today, you'll have a real group leader again!"

Amazement. Unbelieving looks. Only the Russian veterans smiled. "The pigtails suit him," whispered Hofman.

"How long have you been away?" asked one of the two privates.

"Ten months, one week and three days, to be exact. And I didn't come back empty-handed."

"Shall we go to our living room first?" suggested Huber.

"Good idea. Which of the homemade nature hotels is ours?"

"The one you're standing in front of. And the one next to it. Franz and I are each in a cabin with three men. The one on the right is empty. Especially for you. Even a single bed."

"I hope it's lice-free too. I'm not used to those bastards anymore."

The clunky wooden door was held open. "Come in and bring luck!"

The room was a good twelve square meters. Two homemade bunk beds stood against one wall. Opposite was the single bed. To the right of the door was a cannon stove. There was a wooden table in the middle of the room and four benches around it. Everything was homemade. A recessed window could be closed with a wooden shutter. A kerosene lamp hung from the ceiling above the table. There were also a few Hindenburg lights scattered about. *(Authors note: named after the former Reich President*

Paul von Hindenburg = a small bowl filled with fat or tallow in which a wick was inserted. It was used for emergency lighting. Its modern successor is the tea light.)

"The place is really tidy and looks clean. Respect," Keller exclaimed in admiration. "In Russia we only dreamed of a villa like this."

"So you like it?"

"Sure," said the group leader, placing his luggage on the single bed. "Straw sack, blanket, and if it's cold we'll light the stove. Somehow I missed that."

The small shelter was quickly filled. The whole group gathered around Sergeant Josef Keller. Eduard Hofman lit the kerosene lamp.

"Today we have festive lights in honor of our group leader."

Keller reached into his coat pocket and pulled out the field post. "It's not as far away as it was back then, but I think you're always glad to get mail."

He sat down at the table and read out the addresses.

"We have something for a Ralf Fischer."

"Here," one of the high school graduates squeezed through.

"Heinz Grossmann."

"Here."

"Waldemar Hassel."

"That's me," said one of the corporals.

"And here's one for you, Franz."

"For me?"

"Sure, take it."

A lump formed in Huber's throat as he accepted the letter. His hands shook as he tore open the envelope.

"What's the matter? I've never seen you so nervous."

Huber did not answer. He began to read the letter, which was double-sided. When he finished, he looked at the photograph that accompanied the letter. The soldier withdrew and sat down on a bed.

41

"Is something wrong?" Keller asked anxiously.

"On the contrary," Huber replied. "I have become a father. My wife gave birth to a healthy baby girl. Her name is Magdalena, like my mother, and she's perfectly healthy. I'm a father now."

"Congratulations!"

"But they had to leave the apartment. It was bombed out. Helga and the little girl are now living with Aunt Erika in a little village."

"That's a good thing. In the country your Magdalena will get all the milk she can drink. I'm sure she'll be fine there."

"Gosh, I'm Dad!" Huber cried enthusiastically and jumped up happily. "If old Radomski has any market goods *(Authors note: Goods and services for everyday and private use; and also alcohol or tobacco. The term comes from the medieval military system)* left, I'll buy everything I can get from my next paycheck and invide you to a party."

"You can save your daughter's wages, Franz," Keller thundered in between. "I brought you something. When I was in Tyrol, I went shopping. Three bottles of red wine and two bottles of Liquor. All from the same winegrower. "

"Let's celebrate! To Franz and his daughter and to Josef," shouted Eduard Hofman.

The comrades immediately joined in. They sang together: "Long may he live … long may he live ..."

The next morning, the returnee began the almost forgotten daily life of a Landser. With nothing out of the ordinary on the duty roster, Sergeant Keller inspected his squad's weapons and equipment. Lieutenant Drexler had gone to a meeting and was expected back around noon.

The autumn sun was high above the pale green of the northern foothills of the Eifel, providing another pleasant temperature.

"I'm very pleased," the team leader announced after checking the tube of the last carbine for residual powder smoke and flash rust. "You can start oiling."

"We're right on schedule. If we hurry, we'll be the first at the field kitchen. My stomach's already rumbling," Huber urged his comrades.

"For waking up a little hung over this morning, you look fresh and alert. How do you do it?" asked Fischer, one of the newcomers.

"As a father, you can't show your face," laughed Hofman, who joined the conversation. "My big boy took me to the fair last year when I was on vacation. He had just turned fifteen and wanted to show me that he was a man. So I bought him a beer. You can't imagine my wife's face when I came home arm in arm with the drunk boy."

Everyone laughed.

"The next day, of course, I got up early to chop wood, he was still sick. He just said he would never drink beer again."

"One pint of beer?"

"Well, yes. There were also two or three shots, but I didn't tell Traudl."

After cleaning their weapons, the group set off in the direction of Lammersdorf. Just outside the position, centrally located between the platoons scattered across the terrain, the field rations wagon arrived daily. The large field kitchen with its 150-liter kettles remained with the company's supply train.

In fact, they were the first. It smelled of sauerkraut and sausages.

"This is just the thing for daddy's little ones," said Waldemar Hassel, who joined the line behind Keller and Hofman.

"I smell it. Today it's like home cooking."

The kitchen bulls distributed the food. The smell did not deceive. The sauerkraut and sausages were accompanied by potatoes and bread.

43

The author's private archive, PA-0-G - field kitchen, also called goulash cannon in soldiers' jargon

"Divide the bread. This is also your dinner and breakfast. In the back there's canned sausage, lard, sugar, tea, coffee substitute and two eggs for each man."

"We're living like maggots in bacon here," Keller said happily, remembering the meager fare of the eastern campaign.

"We can still provide you with the best supplies, but more and more troops are rolling up to the Western Wall. We've also got neighbors in the form of a Volksgrenadier division. If things continue like this, we'll run out of food."

"What a load of rubbish. We are in the German Reich. This is our homeland. Surely there's something to eat here," countered Heinz Grossmann. "Our headmaster always said ..."

"Headmaster? Forget the armchair war hero! Teachers are worse than stagehands. When I tell you I've been in the war since '39, you know I'm speaking from experience."

Grossmann shook his head and turned away. "I don't think so," he muttered.

The group sat down a little farther apart and enjoyed their hot lunch. Then they marched back. Lieutenant Drexler, who had returned by now, ordered the platoon to march.

"Looks like the digging has paid off. Our reconnaissance reports that American armored units are approaching the border. They will be here in a day or two at the latest. Their speed is reminiscent of blitzkrieg *(Blitzkrieg = word for a military tactic - combined forces of air force, ground troops and artillery strike fast and hard to achieve a quick victory).*"

"And they're heading straight for the Siegfried Line?" Keller asked first.

Drexler nodded. "To Aachen and the Siegfried Line. I hope the hump line holds," the officer said, referring to the hundreds of anti-tank obstacles left in the ground.

The blocks, made of concrete with iron mesh, were triangular at the top, which is why American soldiers later called them dragon's teeth. Placed in rows of four to six at a time, they formed a mile-wide cordon along the Siegfried Line.

Author's private archive: PA-M-100 anti-tank barrier (Dragon's Teeth

"We heard we'd be reinforced here," another squad leader interjected.

The lieutenant grinned. "The Landser whisperer was probably faster than me. It's true. The OKW *(Author's note OKW = Abbreviation for High Command of the Wehrmacht)* is moving more divisions here. A couple of Volksgrenadier Divisions, Paratroopers, three Infantry Divisions, and last there was talk of the 116th Panzer Division."

"And why don't the Allies bypass the Siegfried Line?"

"A strategic decision! We could invade their flank, encircle the point and thus paralyze the advance. We also control the Rur dam. That gives us the opportunity to flush out an entire army."

"That makes sense. So we'll take the brunt of it again," groaned Sergeant Reiter, who led the third squad and was also one of the Russian veterans.

"That remains to be seen. Our artillery is in a good position and locked in. All strategic targets are registered there. The terrain is virtually impassable for armored vehicles. We control the few roads and paths that provide the necessary conditions. Air attacks are unlikely due to the dense forest cover."

Lieutenant Drexler looked at the soldiers' faces. While some of the young soldiers looked euphoric, the faces of the experienced Russians darkened.

"Let's move on to point two of the three things I want to address."

A pause of a few seconds in the conversation drew more attention. The murmuring that had begun fell silent.

"Is the shelter ready?"

"Yes," someone replied. A general nod followed.

"Good, because it has been announced that the weather is going to change. A low pressure system is moving in over the North Sea. It's going to get noticeably cooler. And just to make sure we don't get bored, we've been given our first reconnaissance missions. We'll be doing night patrols for a week, while the other two platoons have to do it during the day. I'll ask the squad leaders to stay, the rest of us can go. We're going out for the first time tonight."

Captain Retzer had informed his officers of the current situation. "Thank you gentlemen, that's all for today. You may resume your commands and pass on the news."

Except for First Lieutenant Schmalzl and a young Officer candidate who had just finished his front trial, the men left the conference room.

Retzer turned to his deputy.

"First Lieutenant Schmalzl, have the radio operators finally laid the line to the regimental command post so that it actually works?"

"I have been assured of that."

"Good?"

"But I am worried about the announced bad weather front. I'm worried about the supply transports getting through on the field roads. We should make sure that we get one or two additional covered field wagons. Is that possible?"

Retzer shook his head. "We must make do with what we have. But perhaps your fears are unfounded. I know that on the Eastern Front the mud prevented the troops from being properly supplied, but here we are on German soil. That's a different story."

Schmalzl bit his lip. He was tempted to tell his superior about the mud disaster, but then decided against it.

"That's one way of putting it, Captain, but you shouldn't underestimate the mud. We should be prepared," was his only comment. He preferred to concentrate on the problem at hand.

"What do you mean?"

"We have elevation changes of up to two hundred meters here in the Eifel. The terrain is densely forested. I would be very happy if we could use at least some pack animals. Porters would be the best way to get through."

The young Officer candidate listened intently. The company commander went to the map table. Retzer looked at the map before him.

"Our neighbor on the left is a Volksgrenadier Division. The men have little or no combat experience. We must keep that flank strong."

"You mean in case the enemy breaks through at the seam?"

"That's right. The dams are not far beyond Lammersdorf. It's obvious that the Americans, especially that General Eisenhower, will have a focal point of attack here. We'll definitely move our pioneers there."

"I give the order."

"I also want to order our two sharpshooters to the area. Private First Class Klevers is to cover the area here ..." the captain's finger circled on the map, "... and Corporal Honnige there." Now the index finger was in the area between Höckerlinie, Lammersdorf and Todtenbruch.

"By your command."

"Let the reconnaissance squads know that no one is to fire on our lone fighters," the company commander instructed the Officer Candidate .

"Right away, Captain," came a terse message. Then the Officer Candidate frowned.

Retzer saw it. "Is something unclear?"

"The subject of snipers was rather neglected in the officer's course. How..." he started to ask, but First Lieutenant Schmalzl interrupted him.

"Normally the snipers accompany the shock troops and let their leaders know in advance when they will be in which area. But since we have a lot of young soldiers in our division, an additional indication is appropriate."

"Thank you, that's exactly what I wanted to ask."

Retzer cleared his throat. "And one more thing."

They looked at the company commander.

"I don't want to see any of our men in Lammersdorf itself. We'll leave the village unoccupied. If the Allies scout and attack, I don't want the civilian population to suffer. Besides, the area around Lammersdorf is strategically better located and easier to defend than the village itself".

The day cooled noticeably as the sun set. Keller filled his canteen with tea, checked his firearms one last time, and finally pulled on his steel helmet.

"Let's go," he said and stepped out the door.

He went to fetch the second half of the group from their quarters, but was surprised. Fully equipped for the mission, his men were already standing in front of him. Satisfied and a little proud, he raised his right hand. "Get in line!"

Either he was lucky and his group consisted of born soldiers or, as he suspected, Huber and Hofman had taught the new recruits what was important at the front.

The moonlight penetrated the dense forest only weakly. It was almost impossible to move silently through the woods, away from the forest paths. Leaves on the ground rustled with each step, and there were many branches and twigs that broke under the soldiers' boots. The cracking could be heard from afar. There was also the danger of getting lost in the dense forest at night. For these reasons, it was clear to Keller that the only reasonably safe way to lead the reconnaissance party was to stay on the forest trails. The sergeant had a map of the area. He could use it to find his way around, and he could also mark landmarks himself.

The battalion staff had done a good job, he thought, and had thought things through.

The soldier was in his element again. He was out in the HKL, roaming the grounds. Only one thing was different. This time he was leading a group. A sublime feeling. The sergeant was glad to have two good men in his ranks, Huber and Hofman, both of whom he could use as half-group leaders without hesitation.

The forest was huge. Now that it was getting darker and darker, it exuded a certain kind of eeriness. The sergeant had warned his men beforehand. It wasn't too hard to get lost here. It was especially hard to find your way around at night.

Keller stopped and the group closed in completely. "There's one of the bunkers up ahead."

The concrete structure looked like a foreign body in the landscape.

"We'll use this as an exercise and approach it as if we were in battle! I want to know where the weak points are."

The soldiers dispersed, with Fischer and Hassel staying close to Keller and the rest of the younger ones joining Hofman and Huber.

The squad leader was satisfied. When they reached the bunker, he praised the men. "Well done!"

Fischer took a closer look at the bunker. "Looks pretty empty and deserted."

"Some of the shelters have been restored and occupied, but this one is unsuitable. Any foxhole will do," Huber explained.

"Why?" asked one of the newcomers.

"Because you can only shoot out of this bunker with your carbine. The embrasures don't allow anything else. Besides, the field of view is only moderate. Why do you ask? We inspected it the other day. We were doing some digging near here."

"He was at the dentist. You said yourself that you'd rather swing a spade all morning than sit in the dentist's torture chair for a minute," Hofman reminded his comrade.

"That's right. I forgot."

"Anyway, the bunkers further north are much better. There you can at least open a hatch and position an MG 42. The design of this one is pretty outdated."

"Go on!" Keller urged.

Now it was a steep descent. A few minutes later the group reached a path and followed it. They walked carefully.

"If it rains or snows, you're guaranteed to slide down there like on a toboggan run. You have to be careful," Hofman warned.

"But if the Americans come, we can defend ourselves very well from up here. I don't want to have to run uphill against an enemy," the squad leader said soberly.

Once in the hollow, Keller uses his flashlight to check the map. "This trail isn't marked here," he noticed, pulled a pencil from one of his pockets, scribbled a dotted line on the sketch, and decided to follow the trail. A short time later, they crossed a stream and climbed another hill. The view was both colossal and terrifying. In front of the members of the 983rd Infantry Regiment lay the incomparable, bizarre Hump Line.

"It looks gigantic in the pale moonlight," commented young Fischer. "You can't get through here."

"Like a huge black dragon opening its mouth and baring its teeth at its victim!"

"The Americans will have to give up their tanks," Hassel was also convinced.

"If our Eight-Eight *(Authors note: Eight-eight = German anti-aircraft gun (FlaK), caliber 88 mm, which could also be used against ground targets.)* comes in here, I wouldn't want to be in the Americans' shoes."

"Let's hope they're already in position."

"Speaking of being in position ..." said Hassel. "One of the snipers is supposed to be hanging around here somewhere. I haven't seen any yet. Have you?"

Heinz Grossmann shook his head. So did Ralf Fischer. "He's probably lying in some hole in the ground, sleeping."

"I don't think so. Lieutenant Drexler said that Lance Corporal Honnige patrols our area. I met him on my way here. He wears the silver sniper badge, so he knows his stuff. I'd be willing to bet that he's in our area and has already taken a shot at each of us on a trial basis.

The young soldiers glanced at each other. A feeling of uneasiness overcame them.

Keller and Hofman watched the area in front of the ridge with their binoculars for some time.

"Everything's all right. Let's go back."

Once again the soldiers followed their sergeant in single file. This time, Keller chose a different route and headed into the dense forest. Convinced there was no enemy nearby, he took the opportunity to familiarize himself and his squad with the area. To avoid relying entirely on his sense of direction and his compass, the experienced Lancer always kept parallel to the previously chosen path. Sometimes he was closer to the forest path, sometimes further away. The light was just enough to find his way. Again and again, the soldiers memorized conspicuous features in the terrain. Every time he spotted a prominent feature, such as a large rock, Keller would point it out. "If things get hot, this knowledge can save lives," he said, explaining his actions.

The group did not return until dawn. Tired and satisfied, they fell into their beds. They were awakened by the smell wafting from the field kitchen to their quarters.

Private archive of the author, of PA-H-104 comrades

After lunch, Sergeant Keller inspected the defensive positions, such as foxholes and trenches.

In the afternoon he asked his men about it. The goal was for every single Landser to know his way around. "If there's a noise, you've got to know where to run."

At night we went out again. From the fourth night on, a certain routine set in. The group became more familiar with the forest and knew exactly where each position was.

"I can't find my way in the dark anymore, Josef, I know every foxhole by name," Hofman grumbled as he had to walk back up the steep slope. "I might as well have joined the mountain troops," he puffed vigorously. His chest rose and fell much faster than before.

"You don't talk on patrol! Have you forgotten that?" Keller reprimanded him.

It had gotten noticeably cooler in the last few days. The change in the weather was clearly noticeable. In addition, a steady drizzle was keeping the soldiers in a bad mood. The squad leaders and Lieutenant Drexler had been summoned to the company. There was important news.

Meanwhile, the teams waited in the staging area. Those not on guard or post duty stayed in the barracks.

"The only cozy place there is the wooden barrack."

"But only when the cannon stove is burning."

"A few days ago we were running around with our sleeves rolled up. Now it's freezing."

"Shall we play cards?" asked Hofman, looking at the faces of his comrades.

"I'm in," said Fischer.

"I'm writing a letter. Maybe later."

"I can't. You play Skat, right? I have to learn that game."

The response was meager, but Hofman did not give up. "I see we'll have to get the third man from over there," the corporal said, leaving the simple dwelling to run quickly to the dugout of the other half. When he opened the door and entered the room, he was greeted by a mixture of smells: sweat, stale air, and coffee substitute. "It wouldn't hurt to air the place out," he laughed, closing the door behind him. "We're looking for a skat player. Who's up for it?"

"I'm not playing with you anymore. You're the lucky one, Eduard," Huber grumbled. He held a steaming cup in his hand. "I'd rather enjoy my hot grein coffee."

"I'll play along," Hassel said, jumping down from the top bunk. He quickly pulled on his boots. At the same moment, the door was pushed open again. Keller stood in the doorway.

"The American is standing in front of Aachen! Here we go! They're already in Roetgen!"

"Roetgen? They're on German soil?" one of the boys exclaimed spontaneously.

"Did you expect anything else?" another hissed at him.

"Who's taking up positions on the hump?" Hofman wanted to know at once.

Keller looked at him questioningly. "You expect the first fine contact there?"

Hofman nodded.

"The Volksgrenadiers arrived the day before yesterday. They occupied the front line, the comrades of the 353rd Infantry Division are holding the old bunker line. We're the reserve for now, but we'll take up positions right behind our comrades. If there's fire, we'll have to close any gaps quickly.

Keller paused for a moment. His seriousness was obvious.

"As far as we are concerned, we have been assigned the corridor behind Lammersdorf, the Rur dam and Vossensack. The plan is for us to occupy the entire Todtenbruch. This is exactly the interface between the regiments. We are the link. I hope the enemy doesn't attack at this weak point and break through."

"Break through?" Fischer laughed out loud. "Through the hump line? That's impossible. They can't get heavy equipment in that fast."

"I hope you're right, but when I think of the material superiority of the Anglo-Americans, I feel sick," Hofman ended the discussion. "Shall we pack up?"

"Exactly, Eduard. Get ready for action! We're leaving in ten minutes!"

"Do the boys in the other barracks know?"

"No."

"I'll go over and tell them. Then you can start packing."

Keller patted Hofman on the shoulder. "All right."

Georg Honnige had been given cold rations for three days and had moved into the woods. Most of the sharpshooters worked as a team. One shooter, one observer. Honnige was one of those men who preferred to be alone. He felt more comfortable when he didn't have to worry about a second man and was left to his own devices.

Over his steel helmet, he wore a wire netting in which he could attach various camouflage materials. Over his uniform, the sniper also wore a camouflage shirt and pants made of the same material. On top of that, the sniper had his waterproof canvas striped in a patch pattern. The belt with the equipment was strapped on the outside. The lone fighter's mission was to cover the company's reconnaissance troops, which were advancing steadily up to the ridge line.

"You can't see anything at night," the kitchen sergeant had said while serving the meal. "So why are you hanging out there? The other sniper always goes into the woods with the different groups and comes back with them."

"Everyone works in his own way. I want to know the terrain as well as I know my own garden. I also need prepared positions. I've already prepared two. I can also spend the night in them."

"In this terrible weather? You've got a screw loose," remarked the person serving the food.

"I call it experience. My instructor taught me that, and it was a good thing. In Normandy, that knowledge saved my life.

55

The Americans overran me. I stayed undetected and was able to get back to our lines after a while."

"Through enemy lines?"

"They weren't that tight. It went relatively smoothly."

The kitchen policeman turned. "Wait a minute," he said to the sniper, walking to the back and returning a few minutes later. "In my infinite kindness, I have another little surprise for you," he said, placing Esbit tablets on the table. "Do you have a stove for this?"

Honnige nodded. "I still have the thing. I wanted to get rid of it because there was no fuel left, but I see it was worth saving the Esbit stove."

He inserted the tablets gratefully.

"And here is some extra soup concentrate. When you're lying out there, something warm in your stomach is priceless."

"Thank you. Thank you," said a delighted Honnige.

The red-faced kitchen bull made a contemptuous gesture. "Come on," he said, "that stuff will just rot. I can't use it anyway."

Author's private archive: PA-H-109 food edition

The soldier from the Heilbronn area nodded to his comrade once more, then turned and walked away. The cook stared after him in silence. There was admiration and awe in his gaze.

How many have I seen leave and never return?

Only when the sniper was out of sight did the cook return to the steaming field kitchen. He rolled up his sleeves and went to work.

Meanwhile, Honnige had disappeared into the green of the Eifel forest. He seldom needed his marching compass. Determined, the private walked to his two positions one after the other. He was still satisfied with his choice. In fact, it seemed to him that he was becoming more agile and, above all, calmer as he moved through the forest. The telltale cracking of small branches was hard to avoid, but little by little, the hunter, as he was often called by his company commander, developed an idiosyncratic gait that was also paired with the intense gaze of a ranger. All in all, it could be said that he had completely adapted to his surroundings. The vast forest of the Eifel was made for Honnige's fighting style.

At noon, the lone warrior took a short break. He put down his rifle and equipment. It had been drizzling for a while. The lone soldier quickly slipped out of the tent and hung it between two trees as a rain shelter. He sat down under it, dug the Esbit stove out of his pack, placed a tablet in it, and boiled some water for tea. While he waited, he studied a map of the area. With a smoking cigarette in the corner of his mouth, the plan was laid out. Knowing that most of the scout leaders preferred the existing paths and trails, he placed his shelters near them. Although the word "shelter" was probably not quite accurate. Many of these positions were nothing more than natural cover with a good field of fire, such as a fallen tree whose canopy and high roots provided the best camouflage.

The soldier easily stubbed out his cigarette butt as the embers immediately went out with a soft hiss on the rain-soaked forest floor. As his stomach growled, the sniper whispered to himself: "Take it easy. I'll have a cup of tea first, then some tasty tinned fish."

Author's private archive, PA-H-108 break - a hot meal

After drinking the tea and eating a small meal, Honnige felt better. He poured the rest of the warm tea into his canteen, packed up, put his tent back up, and continued through the forest. His destination was the Hump Line. He wanted to explore and set up two or three more shooting positions there. From the hump line to the bunker line, he wanted to set up at least ten safe havens.

"The area can easily handle that," he muttered to himself.

In the last light of day, he dug a foxhole with a folding spade next to a tree stump, which was hard work because of the branchy roots. The man from Baden-Wuerttemberg kept encountering resistance, cursing loudly as he cut through individual root strands and then continued digging doggedly. He wanted to finish the hole before nightfall.

Honnige did it. He had made a roof out of pine branches that he had tied to a branch frame. The cover was about a meter wide, a meter and a half long, and even halfway waterproof. But more importantly, it was invisible in its surroundings.

The foxhole offered enough space for him to lie comfortably. A quick escape was possible to the back and he had the best view to the front. Once again he scanned the front line with his binoculars. There was nothing to see, so the sniper treated himself to a last cigarette, finished his tea while smoking, and then wrapped himself in the canvas.

The next morning he wanted to look for a second tree seat. He had already found one of these natural high seats. The branches of the conifer had grown so that he could climb up almost like a ladder. He was perfectly camouflaged in the dense branches, had a clear view, and could even put the rifle down for the shot. Although only one shot should be fired from one position, Honnige was sure that he could fire at least two shots from this tree. With these thoughts he fell asleep.

Shivering slightly, the sniper was rudely awakened the next morning. The sound of an engine could be heard. The soldier was wide awake at the sound. He immediately grabbed his binoculars. He lifted the roof of pine branches about twenty centimeters up and propped it with a stick he had prepared beforehand. Honnige was lying on a hill with the best view of the ridge line. He recognized vehicles at the edge of the antitank obstacles and took out his binoculars.

They are here. Two tanks.

One of the steel behemoths stood directly in front of the concrete pillars, while the other slowly drove along their edge. Platoons of infantry stood in loose formation behind them. A few soldiers were watching the forest, but most of them didn't seem to think they were in any danger.

A jeep stopped. The passenger jumped out. A second and a third jeep followed. Three soldiers, officers, were now standing in front of the concrete barriers, arguing heatedly. More infantrymen approached. Honnige counted five trucks. The men jumped off the backs of the trucks and took up positions.

Damn it, why isn't anybody firing? There's no better way to present yourself, thought the well-camouflaged Landser and swung his binoculars over to his own front line. He scanned the area slowly. Then he saw them approaching from the valley. Dressed in Wehrmacht green and without heavy weapons, a company of Volksgrenadiers marched toward the enemy. The enemy could not yet see each other.

The lone fighter turned his eyes back to the American troops. His binoculars swept over the troops and military vehicles.

"Damn! There are more of them," he groaned softly.

The soldier knew his comrades were marching to certain death. The enemy was setting up machine gun nests. They were probably meant to secure a planned advance into the forest. Sub-commanders received orders and passed them on to their teams. Assault teams were formed.

The sniper had to act. His equipment was packed in an instant. One last move and he was off to another position.

First to the tree, it went through his head.

He quickly crawled backwards and slipped out of the small one-man position through the recessed emergency exit. There was a slight pressure on his bladder. It was time to relieve himself in the morning. Honnige relieved himself. Then he grabbed his sniper rifle and ran to the tree he had chosen. The lone fighter climbed up with ease. The view was even better than from the cover hole. He wouldn't have much time. A last look through the binoculars.

Only a few hundred meters to go and the Volksgrenadier would be in the enemy's line of sight and under machine gun fire.

Honnige's thoughts raced. The binoculars were swung around one last time. Two squads of GIs were carefully slipping through the line of humps. They held their rifles ready.

"Useless," Honnige whispered. "If we were lying there, y-ou'd already be under fire."

The two tanks were still in the same place. Their tubes stuck out into the forest. The turret hatches were open and the tank commanders stood inside, smoking. They seemed to be watching the infantry.

One officer walked purposefully back to his jeep. He picked up a radio and talked.

The sniper had picked his target. The binoculars now hung in front of Honnige's chest, the K 98 k in his hands. The stock was pressed into his shoulder, the scope minimally adjusted. He was ready for action. The soldier had acquired his victim through the optical sight. His pulse was surprisingly steady.

I can guarantee that no one is expecting my shot.

The Landser was amazed at how uninhibited the US forces had been in driving so close to the anti-tank barriers.

You can't do that in war.

The time had come. The victim had been chosen. The moment the officer put down the radio, the shot rang out. The echo echoed two or three times. The American, mortally wounded, collapsed. At the same time, confusion broke out among the enemy. The Allies ran around in confusion, taking cover behind the concrete pillars.

Honnige repeated in a flash.

They hadn't considered me, he felt, and he knew that only the second, maybe even the third shot would be dangerous for him. He wanted to risk it. At any cost! His comrades' lives were at stake.

Before the American soldiers realized what was happening, the chest of a tank commander appeared in the sight of Honnige's rifle. When the crosshairs were level with the heart, the sniper fired the second shot. A small fountain of blood spurted from the hit man's torso. He was thrown backwards and lay unnaturally on the tower.

Regardless, the German moved on to the next target. This time he stopped at the sergeant who was leading the shock troops towards the Volksgrenadiers. Honnige knew he was taking a big risk and going completely against Wehrmacht doctrine, but he trusted his instincts. It was the recklessness with which the US

61

troops had approached the hump line that gave Honnige the mental support he needed.

They had not expected to make contact with the enemy. Especially not a sniper.

The sergeant was in plain sight. With the second shot from the sniper, the US soldiers had taken cover, and with them, of course, the squad leader, but the left side of the sergeant's body was sticking out from behind one of the so-called dragon's teeth. A mistake.

The hunter's right index finger moved slightly backwards. The pressure point had been reached. The target did not move. The GI did not know where the shots were coming from and felt well protected. Honnige pulled the trigger back, overcoming the pressure point, the shot cracked and the sergeant collapsed, hit.

The lone fighter paid no attention to his latest victim or the reactions of his opponents. In a flash, the private slung the carbine around his neck and climbed out of the tree as fast as he could. He ducked and ran back to his foxhole. He heard a commotion. Orders were being shouted. He also heard the shrill screams of the sergeant who had been shot. The procedure was the same in every army in the world. The medics were called. They rushed forward and tended to the wounded. Honnige had seen it many times before. He felt no compassion, wasted no thought on his victims. This was the enemy.

It's him or me!

A silent absolution for the conscience.

Rumble

The two tanks opened fire. They fired their shells blindly into the forest. The bullet holes were far from Honnige. A good sign. They didn't know where his shots were coming from, hadn't seen him or his position.

Suddenly, dozens of projectiles crashed into the surrounding trees.

Rrrrrrt ... rrrrt

Wood splinters, twigs, leaves and needles were thrown around and swirled through the air.

MG carbines.

The soldier immediately dropped to the ground.

Have they spotted me after all? Damn it! You shouldn't fire two shots from one position! Especially not three! No matter how sure you are that it will work. I'm such an idiot!

Compared to before, the shooter's pulse was now racing. He covered a few meters at a crawl. During a pause in the shooting, he jumped up and rushed through the forest.

Get out of here!

The machine-gun fire had shifted. The incomparable sound of the bullets flying around and hitting the bark of the trees was no longer audible. The Landser raised his head.

No, they haven't spotted me. They spread fire all over the hillside. They don't know where I was.

Honnige reached his cover hole and crawled under the cover of pine branches from behind. As he had done in the morning, he used a stick to lift the front part up and support it.

Binoculars. Get an overview. Hurried thoughts.

Beads of sweat dripped onto the damp ground. Breath mist was visible in the cool morning air. The noise of battle rose. Honnige was pleased to see that the Volksgrenadier had scattered. The first firefights took place. The opportunity was good for him. If he fired now, his shots would be drowned out by the fighting.

The sniper fired again. Shot after shot, he chased the enemy. He counted more than ten hits before he finally had to retreat. The Americans had long since realized that a German sniper was in position opposite them. The hunt for him had begun. The hillside had already been plowed with grenade launchers. More American units were arriving. It was only a matter of time before the first shrapnel whizzed around his head.

Time to retreat.

The sniper's hits would not end up in the statistics. No witnesses. Besides, kills made during a fight do not count. The corporal was not a fan of these evaluations anyway. He didn't want to brag about how many enemies he killed. He just wanted to save the lives of his comrades. It was war! Another excuse for his actions.

After landing in Normandy on June 6, 1944, the Allied forces advanced with tremendous speed. By September 1944, the 1st U.S. Army was at the gates of Aachen and occupied the village of Roetgen on September 12th.

With neighboring forces lagging far behind due to fuel shortages, the commander of the 7th US Corps decided to bypass Aachen for the time being and advance through the Düren area into the Rhine Valley.

On September 15, 1944, the 3rd U.S. Panzer Division, part of the 7th U.S. Corps, encountered the Siegfried Line near the village of Rott and its distinctive hump line, which quickly earned the nickname "Dragon's Teeth" due to its appearance. The concrete anti-tank barrier was no great obstacle to the US troops due to their enormous material superiority. Heavy bulldozers laid wide tracks in no time at all, and the US tanks were able to roll on.

But suddenly the American units were faced with a new problem. The northern foothills of the Eifel, the Hürtgen Forest. It blocked the direct route to the Rhine Valley and Cologne. Since the German defenders were expected to launch flank attacks from this cover-rich area, the Allied commanders did not want to bypass the gigantic jungle, but rather march through it. The 9th US Division was ordered to take the highest point of the Hürtgen Forest. The so-called Todtenbruch.

Captain Retzer stood in front of the company. "Roetgen fell three days ago, and at Rott the Americans are overcoming the anti-tank obstacles with ease. The enemy's material superiority is beyond words! It is clear that General Eisenhower intends to march through the middle of our Eifel forest."

Pause. Retzer looked at the faces, some of which were petrified. The company leader clarified the last sentence once more.

"They will not go around. No way! They want to go right through the middle and will head straight for the important Rur dam. That must be prevented. In plain language, this means that we occupy an area of the Todtenbruch. The terrain is ideal for defense. It is the highest point in our combat section and is also flanked by a line of bunkers. This was partly occupied by the neighboring 353rd Infantry Division".

The usual slogans followed.

It was that time again. For the first time in almost a year, Sergeant Josef Keller found himself under enemy fire. He was glad that his company was not on the bunker line Retzer had mentioned. The Russian veteran suspected that it would surely become a target for the American troops. The Landser had great respect for the US Air Force and Allied artillery.

The Keller group lay in their dug-out foxholes, keeping an eye out for the enemy. The place was indeed ideal for defense. Prepared positions. Dense forest. Sloping terrain with a view of the only road that could be used by larger vehicles like trucks or tanks. Keller had no intention of trading places with the enemy. German artillery barrels were well aimed at strategic targets. The engineers had also planted mines and booby traps everywhere. There were many warning signs on trees in this area.

Death lurks, waiting for its victims like a fat spider in a web.

The increasingly cold west wind not only pushed heavy, dark rain clouds in front of us. It also brought something else. It was the sound of thundering cannons. It was as if the wind was pushing the war back to the land from which it had left five years ago to spread fear and terror across the world.

Huber cleared his throat. With an almost stony expression, he began to speak. "The Víctory won't last long. The Americans will bomb the old bunkers nonstop. When the planes are gone, there will be hours of aerial bombardment. I bet my next military paycheck on it. I feel like I did in Russia. Remember that? The great winter offensive of the Red Army?

It had grown dark. The weather had been cold and wet for days, and the men's spirits were correspondingly low.

"And what do you want to tell me?"

"We had snow in October and it was at least ten degrees below zero. Winter took us all by surprise, and it came with a vengeance."

"What now?" grumbled Keller.

"What I mean is, it's not so bad here."

"You can die here just as easily as on any other front in this war."

Keller scratched the back of his head.

"But I also think the Volksgrenadiers are poor bastards. I wouldn't trade places with them," he added.

Huber fumbled around under his canvas tent, which he had set up as a rain shelter, and pulled out a pack of Juno cigarettes. He took out two of the cigarettes and handed one to the sergeant. "Here ..." he said, "... maybe this will cheer you up a bit. It's unbearable, as grumpy as you are today. It's been like that all day."

Keller put the cigarette into his mouth. A moment later he picked up his storm lighter and lit Huber's cigarette, then his own. "Thanks," he replied. "I'm upset about the weather. I'm hungry, I want something warm in my stomach, and I'm tired, too."

"I think it's more the uncertainty before the fight. The Yank is coming. That much is certain. We just don't know when and how strong. And that's what makes you so nervous."

"I heard from the food carriers that the front line of the grenadiers didn't last long. The Americans marched through as if our people were soft as butter. That scares me. It's only a few kilometers from them to us.

"You can't compare the Volksgrenadiere to us."

Keller took a drag on his Juno and blew out the smoke with relish. In the twilight of the falling night, the sergeant's face glowed orange-red for a few seconds. "Sorry if I snapped at you."

"Already forgotten."

Irritation was common. Cold nights out in the open, fatigue, hunger, and the constant fear of a surprise enemy attack wore down the soldiers.

Josef Keller was his old self again. He was a Landser again. A pig at the front. Sitting in the foxhole and holding out. He suffered with his comrades, laughed with them and fought with them. The severe wounds had left no psychological damage. At least none that he could consciously name.

The very next day there was a roar in the sky above them. Enemy reconnaissance planes, protected by fighter planes, searched the area and got a picture of the situation.

Hofman, Hassel and Fischer had just brought the food. Although they were well protected by the forest canopy, they hurried and were extremely careful. The group had been taken out of the trenches in the morning. They were able to catch up on sleep in the morning. There was hot food and they finally had time to wash and change their clothes. The joy of being back on duty did not last long. A shock troop operation was scheduled for the afternoon. Nevertheless, the food carriers were greeted with joy. The containers were eagerly opened.

"I'm in the mood for monkeys. Pork chops with boiled potatoes. I haven't had that in a long time," Huber said happily, shoving a piece of potato into his mouth.

"And for cold food, sardines in oil and Edam cheese."

"What a strange mixture," stammered Huber, his mouth full. He swallowed the bite. "But I don't care. I'll eat anything I can get my hands on," he added more clearly. As soon as he said it, the fork went back into his mouth.

After lunch, the time had come. The report of the American breakthrough had been confirmed. The Allies had literally over-run the front line of defense and were now moving toward Lammersdorf and Todtenbruch.

"That is why the reconnaissance party. We have to find out where the Americans are," muttered several compatriots.

Dressed in camouflage, the soldiers blended into the forest and its autumn colors. If they hid in the thicket, they would be invisible. The squad followed Sergeant Keller in the line of fire. Huber was Rifleman I and at first carried the MG 42 with the drum slung loosely over his shoulder. Later it hung from the belt at his side. It was rather unusual to carry a machine gun in a reconnaissance company, but you wanted to be prepared for any eventuality.

The last man to march behind Huber was Waldemar Hassel, who acted as Rifleman II. He carried the spare barrels, tools, and two spare belt drums. The position of Rifleman III was elimina-ted. Keller felt that everyone should help out as needed. If there was enough ammunition, those who were strong enough should help carry it. This approach had worked well in Russia. It had also worked well during the previous exercises. The reconnais-sance unit itself did not carry an extra ammunition box anyway.

The forest smelled of damp wood, moss and rotting leaves. They had been walking for over an hour. It was unusually quiet. No hasty fluttering of birds, no chirping and no wildlife. Keller took the safety off his submachine gun. He didn't like the silence. After another half hour, he stopped.

Hofman caught up with the group leader.

"What do you think? Is the Yank here yet?"

"If their reconnaissance is as good as ours, there are bound to be some storm troopers in front of the bunker line."

"Is that far from here?"

"No! And that makes me nervous. It's different than usual."

Huber and Hassel had caught up. The group had surrounded Keller.

"What is it?" the machine-gunner inquired.

"Nothing. I just have a feeling in my stomach, Franz," Keller replied.

"Oh, dear. I know your feeling. It doesn't mean anything good."

Keller ignored the statement. He knelt down, took out his map and set the compass beside it. "We're right about here," he pointed to a spot on the map with his index finger. "We roamed this exact area on one of our first days."

"I know," Hofman shot out. "There was also the path in the valley cut, you know," he tried to explain, "where the stream flows. Fischer slipped, and water ran down the shaft and into his right boot. The boot was wet for two days."

"That's right! He swore like a groom whose horses lost all their shoes," Huber confirmed.

"And that's what worries me."

Keller emphasized the word "that" and began to explain. "The trail is wide enough for tanks. It leads to the bunker line and from there past our current positions."

"This is the same road?" asked one of the younger soldiers.

"When the Americans attack, the planes come first, then the Ari hammers, and then the tanks roll in. The infantry comes at the end of the line," Hofman tried to reassure.

"I don't think so, Eduard," Keller countered. "Neither an Allied bomb nor a US artillery shell will find its target here in the forest. At least those who open the bomb bay or the men who pull the triggers of the guns can't aim at a specific target. The forest hides everything."

"And the tanks?"

Keller thought about it. "They're advancing a bit anyway. They marched into Lammersdorf yesterday. Every place you can drive to is in danger, but behind the bunker line, where we are, is dense forest. No vehicle can get through it."

Huber nodded in agreement. "They'll have to send in their infantry, and by the time they do, there could be masses of American soldiers milling around."

"And that's what we're here to find out. We're going to increase the distances. Be as quiet as possible and report anything that looks suspicious!"

The sergeant looked urgently at his men.

"Forward!" he finally gave the order.

They moved on. Keller oriented himself with the compass. A quick glance at his wristwatch followed. In three hours it would be dusk, in four it would be pitch dark. Now the experienced soldier recognized a prominent rock. He had memorized this prominent point and marked it on his sketch. The bare rock looked strange in the forest. A short thought.

How and when did the stone get there? Ages ago? Concentration!

From the stone, it was a good kilometer and a half to the wide, easily passable forest path. The word "route" was written on the map. Keller thought of lumberjacks.

They must have worked hard to cut the track into the forest.

Engine noise. Powerful engines!

Was that chain rattling?

Keller's hand shot up. He gave the tactical signal to halt and made a hand signal for the squad to follow in a wedge, with Huber closing in on the sergeant with the MG 42. The central position of the rapid-fire weapon meant that everyone could provide cover fire in an emergency.

Suddenly everything happened very fast. Two or three violent detonations tore the air apart.

Wham Wham

The echo echoed through the forest several times.

Wham

Machine gun shells rattled.

Rrrrt Rttt

Wham

70

There was another bang.

"They're attacking the bunkers!"

"No, the bunkers are higher up! They must be individual fighting nests of ours."

"We must go back and report it," said Hofman.

"Or help the comrades from our flank!"

Keller looked at Hofman and Huber. "Neither of them! We'll get a quick overview, then try to find out if the Allies are advancing through the forest on our side as well. Then we'll go back as planned. We have a mission and we must accomplish it."

"But the comrades in the positions?" asked Huber.

"First, they've probably already reported the attack to their battalion by radio or field telephone, and second, as a small group we can't do anything. Especially not against tanks. Third, we're just a small cog in a big machine. When we do our part, the cog turns and drives a bigger one. Namely that of society. That in turn drives the regiment, and so on. Do you understand what I am saying? We must not act from the frog's-eye view, but leave the action to the men with the bird's-eye view."

"Did you learn that in the NCO course? That sounds really pompous."

"So you can ..." he started to answer, then was abruptly interrupted.

Shots rang out. Bullets drilled into trees. The sound of the impact in the bark was inimitable.

Chinng - fatsch

"Take cover!"

The Landser immediately melted into the forest floor. Everyone made themselves as small as possible. There was no enemy to be seen, but their voices could be heard clearly. Orders were shouted in English. Everything sounded hectic.

Hofman, who as a lance corporal was armed with a submachine gun like his squad leader, fired a volley.

Huber had not yet found a target with his machine gun.

The MP volley was returned by the enemy. This time even harder than before.

"Bloody hell. Must be at least half a platoon," Keller whined to his neighbor, trying to drown out the noise of the battle.

He strained to see past the tree he had taken shelter behind. He only risked a glance for a few seconds. Nothing happened. No direct fire. The second time he looked around longer. There was still no shooting at him. The enemy shooters had moved on to another target and probably hadn't even spotted Keller yet. The sergeant pushed the barrel of his MP forward. At the same time, he motioned to his neighbor, Heinz Grossmann, to take aim as well. Grossmann took aim with his carbine. Shadowy American soldiers darted between the trees. The two Germans fired. A long scream was heard.

Hit.

Keller checked his grenades. Both stick grenades were ready to go in the paddock. At the same time the unmistakable rattle of Huber's MG 42 could be heard. Burst after burst was fired. Again and again, ragged shouts in English echoed across the paddock.

Instinctively, Hofman and two other comrades had separated themselves from the others. Unnoticed by the enemy, they crept through the underbrush.

Keller noticed his Russian comrade's maneuver and guessed what the lance corporal was up to.

This Sky Dog wants to fall into the enemy's flank. He relies on Huber and his machine gun.

Since the American fire seemed to be focused on Huber, Keller decided to imitate Hofman. He motioned for the young Grossmann to follow him. The two soldiers retreated slowly. They crawled almost silently across the leafy ground. The plan worked. They managed to avoid the enemy completely unnoticed.

Rumble

Two hand grenades exploded. Screams could be heard again.

"That must be Gollman. He's falling into the Yank's flank," groaned Keller.

There was another crash.

Thud

His next thought was of the enemy. Would the Americans make the fatal mistake of throwing grenades blindly?

If you were untrained in forest warfare, it could happen that, in the stress of mortal fear, you threw hand grenades that hit tree trunks and, in the worst case, bounced off them. The effect was often devastating.

"Come on, Grossmann, let's get the enemy from the other side!"

Grossmann was panting with effort. He crawled out from behind a huge tree trunk. He could see them. The Americans. The enemy had been evaded.

Three GIs lay in what appeared to be safe cover. A fourth US soldier was off to the side, firing his rapid-fire rifle until there was no ammunition left in the magazine. He fell back to the other GIs to reload. The Anglo-American soldier's face froze when he saw Keller and Grossmann standing in front of him. Keller pulled the trigger of his MP and swung the barrel. After a few bursts, the weapon fell silent. Grossmann stood motionless, staring at the dead US soldiers.

"Go on," the Russian veteran ordered, but the young compatriot could not take his eyes off the shot Americans.

"We've got to take out Huber!"

Keller ran on, crouching. He used the trees for cover and turned around briefly. Grossmann followed. Rifle fire from the other flank.

This is Hofman. I wasn't wrong earlier.

Because of the echo in the forest, the direction of the shots could not be clearly determined. Confusion began to spread among the Allies. As if from nowhere, they suddenly came under enemy fire from three sides. Suddenly the German machine guns fell silent.

Did they take out Huber?

Keller's insides rumbled. Anger and desperation spread. Two enemies reappeared in front of him. After a short burst of fire from the MP 40, a GI fell to the ground, hit.

Clank

Empty! Take cover behind a tree. Changing magazines.

Grossmann fired. A shrill scream was heard. A second shot followed. The screaming stopped. The spare magazine was engaged.

"Go on!"

The squad leader made sure to stay mostly under cover. The whimper of a wounded man could be heard.

Shuddering.

"Damn, isn't somebody helping him?" muttered Grossmann.

"Shut up!" came gruffly from the sergeant's mouth.

Loud cracking of branches. Quick steps.

They fled.

The noises grew louder.

"They're coming for us!"

Grossmann knelt down and fired. His superior's hand slapped the barrel of the K 98, followed by an exchange of glances. Keller just shook his head. Grossmann lowered his rifle and peered out from behind his cover. He saw two medics hurriedly carrying away one of their wounded comrades.

The soldier's next thought was, "Keller's not as cold as I thought.

The gunfire had stopped. An oppressive silence fell. Cautiously and scrupulously, they crept on. Now they were at their real destination. A few men were visible. Keller went down. He raised his binoculars to his eyes and saw that the Americans had prisoners. But the sergeant could not see who they were. Angrily, the squad leader slapped his thigh. He put the binoculars back on. Then he recognized Huber. A stone fell from his heart. His old comrade had not fallen. The Americans had obviously surprised him.

Apparently these gum eaters aren't as bad of soldiers as I always thought, it raced through his head. "We need to get closer. They've got Huber and Hassel. We're not leaving them," he whispered to Grossmann, who just nodded.

The young Landser felt sick. He was trembling with fear.

"No sign of Hofman," Keller added, making the binoculars disappear again.

He crept silently toward the group, followed by the young man.

The experienced soldier chose a good attack position. A last overview. A young lieutenant was talking to a radio operator sitting next to him. Not far from them was a sergeant not much older than the American officer. A short distance away, a GI was guarding Huber and Hassel. He pointed a gun at them. The soldiers were kneeling on the ground with their hands up. There were three other Americans standing around. One of them was smoking, the other two were apparently shocked by the previous brief firefight. They stared impassively ahead.

"You shoot the one who points his gun at Huber. I'll do the rest! Got it?"

Grossmann's stomach seemed to rebel. His expression betrayed the feeling.

"Look out! We're all comrades. I don't know if they'll shoot our men in a few minutes! Unfortunately, that was the order of the day in Russia. We take out everyone we can from enemy hands. These two would do the same for you! So pull yourself together and aim at the guard. Can you do it?"

"And if they don't shoot you?"

"And if they do, your comrades will be on your conscience. This is war. Don't forget that!"

Grossmann nodded. "I can do it!"

Keller knew there was a difference between pulling the trigger in the heat of battle and deliberately aiming at a person. He noticed that the young soldier was shaking.

"You don't have to kill him. You just have to incapacitate him!"

Seemingly relieved, the barrel of the carbine was noticeably steadier in the German soldier's hand. "I'm ready."

"Good, I'm going to the big spruce now. The big one right in front of you. Can you see it?"

"Yes."

"When I get there, you fire. Then you run to me and the rest will take care of itself."

"I understand."

Keller moved with extreme caution. When he reached the old tree, he pressed against it. The submachine gun lay in his hands, ready to fire.

What is the boy waiting for? Have I asked too much of him? He's so young, he doesn't know war. No! Certainly not! If you're a soldier and you want to survive in war, you have to do things you would never do otherwise.

The shot cracked. The echo echoed several times. Keller immediately jumped forward behind the log. The group of American soldiers was less than ten meters in front of him. The MP rattled off. The sergeant fired as he ran. His first targets were the officer, the sergeant, and the radio operator. After a long burst, he jerked the barrel around and fired bursts at the other three GIs. The three Americans jumped away.

Huber and Hassel instinctively ducked. It took them a few moments to realize what had happened.

Grossmann watched the scene, turned away and vomited. A human reaction.

"Get out of here!" yelled Keller. "Run before the others come. There are more Yanks in the woods."

Huber jumped to his MG 42, grabbed the weapon and ran. He grabbed Hassel by the shoulder, pulled him up, and pushed the soldier the first few yards in front of him. "Burger fell. They were behind us all of a sudden," he hissed.

A rapid-fire rifle rattled behind them. The wounded Americans began calling for the medic.

Boom!

The detonation of a hand grenade ended the fire.

"That was Hofman," Keller said with satisfaction.

After about five hundred meters, they came to a panting halt. Huber suddenly lay down behind the machine gun. Panting wildly, he would not have been able to fire on target.

"No one...follows!"

"Go on!" Keller ordered.

They met up with Hofman at one of the prominent points two kilometers from the battlefield.

The lance corporal and his two companions were not followed. "They stayed with their wounded," he explained, looking through the line. "Where's Burger?"

A shake of the head. Sad looks.

"Burger, of all people, had to get it. He survived Russia and fell at the first enemy contact with the Americans."

Anger spread. Disbelief followed.

Keller made a decision. "Come on. We have to go back."

As the soldiers of the 9th US Division continued the offensive from Lammersdorf, they were unable to fall back on their armored forces due to the unfavorable terrain. The U.S. infantry formed three wedges. One advance was in the direction of Paustenbacher Höhe and Rollesbroich, one directly to Hürtgen, and a third wedge was to advance through the Gieschbach valley to Todtenbruch.

The outskirts of the Todtenbruch were reached relatively easily by the forces of this shock wedge. Some of the first rows of bunkers were not manned due to their age and unsuitability.

They were immediately blown up by the following American engineer units. This was to prevent them from being retaken and occupied by German troops.

The other two shock wedges met strong resistance and encountered an enemy whose fighting spirit and ruthlessness were shocking. The encounter with the first Russian veterans literally horrified the US soldiers. They were unfamiliar with such fighting power, tenacity and doggedness. Word spread quickly about how tough the former Russian fighters were. Fear spread. No one wanted to face such opponents, but that was exactly what the Anglo-American troops were up against. Some GIs felt like the ancient, civilized Romans who had to defend the Limes against the barbaric Germanic tribes.

To accomplish their missions, the US infantrymen had to penetrate deeper and deeper into the forest, losing their technical superiority completely. Allied tanks could not get through, and air and artillery could not find targets. The infantry was on its own.

Lance Corporal Georg Honnige watched the column from a safe distance. While the Americans' all-terrain jeeps climbed the bumpy roads with ease, the Sherman tanks had a hard time moving forward. They crushed the earth with their tracks, leaving a muddy mess.

If it keeps drizzling like this, we're going to have a blue miracle, the sniper thought to himself as he continued to circle the binoculars.

He was in a tree again and had a relatively good view. The weather was cloudy. Autumnal chill. Heavy rain clouds were moving across the Eifel. The soldier had left before dawn. Alone, as was his custom. Honnige sensed that something was in the air. He had a nose for such things. The eternal west wind carried a babble of voices to him. The marksman didn't know how much time had passed when it happened.

I promised you. It had to happen!

One of the trucks had skidded on the slushy, slippery surface. It was now leaning over the road at an angle, its rear end protruding slightly over the slope. In panic, the American infantrymen jumped from the bed. Some of them tumbled down the steep slope. Most of them managed to hold on to the trees, but three soldiers could not. Their boots had no grip. Their bodies tumbled far down into the valley before they could be brought under control.

A group of soldiers clung to the cab. They tried desperately to weigh down the front of the Ford truck, but the wheels inevitably came off.

Inexperienced driver.

Honnige watched the scene calmly.

As the rear of the Ford slid further down the slope and the front wheels lost traction, the driver jumped out of the cab. The truck slid down the hill. It crashed through two or three smaller trees before finally being stopped by a large tree trunk.

Rescuers tended to the slightly injured GIs who had jumped out. Military traffic was backed up on the forest road. A few men were having a heated discussion. Apparently they were discussing how to proceed. After about twenty minutes, engineers arrived with long wooden planks to secure the danger zone.

Not a bad idea. They set up a sort of railing.

After another hour, the convoy was rolling again.

Rumble

Like the day before, violent detonations shattered the silence. They echoed through the impassable forest, breaking up several times in an echo.

They blew up the old bunkers.

Honnige felt safe. Between him and the Anglo-Americans lay one of the many ravines crossed by a stream. Three weeks ago it had been a trickle. Now, after days of rain, the stream had grown into a small river, creating an additional obstacle for the Allies.

The sniper had deliberately suppressed his first hunger pangs. Now his stomach was rumbling. He climbed down from the tree and stretched. When he put his weight on his right leg, he noticed that it was almost asleep. He had been sitting on it for too long, and the circulation needed to be restarted. Only slowly did the feeling of a thousand ants crawling in his bloodstream subside. The rifle with the scope attached was leaning against the tree. The barrel and scope were wrapped in a dark brown sack-like fabric. Twigs protruded from the wire mesh of the steel helmet. The man's face was covered in paint. The private opened his pack and pulled out a piece of sandwich and a can of liverwurst. He took one last look up. The pine trees were still keeping out most of the drizzle. There was no need to put up the canvas tent for extra protection. Satisfied, the Landser opened the can, cut off a slice of bread with his combat knife, and spread the sausage on it. He took a bite with relish. When the can was empty, he wiped the rest off with a piece of bread. Then Honnige poked a small hole in the soft forest floor with his knife, helped himself with his hands, and finally placed the tin can inside. Then he pushed earth over it. He wiped the blade of the combat knife - it was the Infantry Knife 42 - on his pants leg, examined it briefly, and slid it back into its sheath. The usual grab for the pack of cigarettes followed. It was his last pack of Camels. As the cigarette smoked, the soldier took a big gulp from his canteen. The coffee inside had cooled by now. With relish, he sucked the smoke from his next puff deep into his lungs, then slowly exhaled it.

"Damn weather," he groaned minutes later, stubbed out his cigarette, and packed up. He had two days' worth of rations. Captain Retzer had ordered him to gather as much information as possible. He was only to fire if it was tactically important or helpful to his mission. Possible defensive shots were not discussed. That was clear.

The sniper shouldered his rifle and started to move again. He decided to get a little closer to the enemy, even though he knew there were enemy scouts and shock troops on the opposite hill. It was his territory, his empire, his turf. It was not for nothing that he had roamed the woods for days and weeks, searching for and setting up positions and camps for the night. It was his world and they were invading it.

He thought back to when he first joined the snipers.

"Don't do this," his squad leader warned him. "These snipers have no friends. They don't trust them."

"If you're a regular Lancer, you'll just get burned out. Every night we go out on a raid, and every night we come into contact with the enemy," the young Honnige countered.

"Do you think being a sniper is different?"

"Yes, I see with my own eyes how Hintermeier disappears in the morning and comes back in the evening. He sleeps through the night and always gets something to eat. It can't be that bad."

"And he risks his life every day."

The budding lone fighter acknowledged the statement with a loud laugh. "And us? How many of us have died a hero's death out there?"

The group leader cleared his throat. "The real difference is that you see the faces of the people you kill."

"Tell me the difference! What's the difference if I shoot a russian, an english oder an american Soldier in the stomach with an MP round, crush his skull with a butt shot or slit his belly open with a bayonet and a well-aimed shot?"

The old sergeant just shook his head. "That's different. We meet the enemy, Georg. And when we meet him, we fight to survive. It's him or you! With a sniper it's different. You're the hunter and you're looking for your victim. He's defenseless! You'll soon find out that I'm right."

"Then let me tell you something. We were seven good friends when we joined our group. Three are missing, two next to me were shot by an enemy sniper, and one is a war invalid with only one leg left at home. I'm the last, the only one left. I've lost five friends in one year and sent one home a cripple. I'll

81

make it as difficult as possible for our enemies to put me on their list. Besides, I'll feel a lot safer if I can go out there alone instead of as part of a group."

The sergeant nodded. His face, however, was devoid of any expression. "All right then. I know how good you are with weapons. If you volunteer, I'll put in a good word for you."

It worked right away. The training was a breeze and felt like a vacation for Honnige.

The instructors were experienced frontline fighters. They knew their stuff. There were none of the typical barracks sergeants found in droves at the beginning of the war, chasing drill-dressed recruits around the grounds. There were no would-be heroes who, according to their slogans, would have held Stalingrad alone and never given up on Africa, who would have liked to have been at the front but were unfortunately indispensable here at home because their job was to turn young men into tough soldiers. And there was no one else in the world who could do that.

The Lance Corporal loathed that kind of soldier.

It's a good thing they're not all like that.

There were exceptions. Anyway, it was a load off his mind when he realized that there were actually men in front of him at the sniper course who knew what they were talking about. The instructor was a major whose right arm was stiff against his body and whose right eye was covered with a patch.

"Good morning, gentlemen," he had greeted them on the first day. "You are here because you all have a gift that can be both a curse and a blessing in this day and age. You are all excellent marksmen!"

Then, for the first time, they heard the saying that would accompany them from then on.

"The marksman is the hunter among the soldiers, and only his skill, his prudence, and his personal weapon give him the feeling of being superior to the enemy. As long as you take this to heart, you will return from your missions".

This was followed by theoretical instruction, which mainly consisted of weapons of all kinds. Various weapons, both our own and the enemy's, along with various ammunition and all kinds of aiming devices were formally internalized. Later, the participants were able to try out all the rifles presented in practice and decide which weapon and which rifle target finder suited them best.

In the field exercises that followed, the shooters had to prove their skills. They shot with normal sights and optics. All starting positions were taken into account, and some budding shooters were shown their limits.

Honnige, now promoted to corporal, found the lectures and practical exercises on camouflage interesting. He became a true master of camouflage and was very inventive in creating perfect camouflage from the simplest means.

After three weeks they used special ammunition for the first time. Even the lone fighters were enthusiastic about it.

The hit (impact) could be observed with the observation cartridge (B cartridge), as both a small flame and a small cloud of smoke could be seen on impact. Behind a phosphorus charge was a capsule containing lead azide or nitropenta. The projectile usually had a silver tip.

The use of the B cartridge as an explosive projectile was possible in principle, as the effective range of the projectile ended at about 600 meters, but its use depended heavily on the actual circumstances.

The Pr (phosphorus) cartridge was used as another incendiary projectile.

In the case of tracer ammunition, the projectile was combined with a tracer charge. This was ignited by burning nitro powder. The burning time reached up to 900 meters. A so-called glow mark was visible.

At the end of the training, each participant received a course certificate. Only a few were not or not fully qualified. A little proud of his achievement, Honnige returned to the troops.

After his first shot, he remembered the words of his former sergeant. Now he knew what his former squad leader was trying to tell him. There was no way to describe the feeling. Honnige suppressed it, as all snipers probably did. It was war, and they had become a separate branch of the armed forces. Hated, feared and revered. It was too late to stop. The sniper's career was predetermined. They were the wolves unleashed on the flocks of sheep. Hunt and kill!

Scraps of words brought Honnige back to reality. At some point, while walking through the forest, he got lost in his thoughts. He stopped to get his bearings. The soldier quickly realized that he had probably gone further than he had originally intended.

He quickly knelt down and listened. He had to find out which direction the voices were coming from. A soft whimper mixed with a stream of words. Again, only fragments of sentences reached him. Unmistakably in English. The rifle had long been in the private's hand, ready to fire. His heart began to beat noticeably faster.

I'll probably be able to turn this off completely, muttered Honnige.

"Ahhrrrg!"

The scream of pain was so loud that the direction could now be clearly determined. They were in the hollow straight ahead. Honnige waited a few minutes. The situation had not changed. Someone was talking to another man. One of them was obviously wounded.

The lone fighter crawled towards the hollow on all fours. His pulse increased visibly. His mind warned him, but his curiosity was stronger. The closer he got, the clearer the sounds became. Now it was certain. It was always the same voice. The moaning came from a second person.

Two men, one of them injured, it flashed through his mind. Just a few more meters and I'll see them.

The sniper felt safe, thanks to the perfect camouflage that blended in with the surroundings. Taking a risk, he crawled close enough to the enemy to finally see him. Two GIs sat leaning against a tree. One had a bandage on his leg, the other was crouched next to him. The nature of the injury was obvious at first glance. The injured leg was bent at an unnatural angle.

Broken!

The Landser slowly slid his carbine forward and fired. A glance through his weapon's sights confirmed his suspicion. The leg was definitely broken. The bloody bandage indicated an open fracture.

He must be in terrible pain.

The optics moved upward. Honnige was startled to see two very young faces. The American soldiers were no more than nineteen or twenty years old. The German spoke broken English, with a vocabulary of 50 to 100 words at most, but he could understand a little.

The two soldiers had lost their way during a night march, one slipped, probably fell down a slope and broke his leg. The healthy man kept repeating the words. "They will find us!"

They would find them. Surely they're already on their way, interpreted Honnige. Boy, you're a good comrade. Don't let your buddy down, the sniper thought to himself as he took aim at the enemy's head. So young.

The finger did not move back. Something stopped the man from Baden-Württemberg from firing. Honnige closed his eyes for a moment. This situation was different. There were two enemies in front of him, but they were not dangerous.

The healthy one could be shot. The next thought was that both would go to the military hospital and be eliminated.

He took aim again. The scope moved along both GIs. He saw no gun on the wounded man. But there were two rifles on the healthy one. Should he capture them? No! The idea was immediately rejected. It was nonsense. He would run into an American shock troop with the prisoners and be captured himself.

"For God's sake," he muttered to himself. "Or they'll massacre me instead of putting me in a prison camp!"

The admonishing words of his instructor came back to him. "If you fall into the hands of the enemy and they identify you as a sniper, you'll wish you'd been in my place when the grenade hit!"

At the same time, the chief instructor had pointed with his healthy arm to his right side and the broken eye.

As if someone was sitting across from him and looking at him, Honnige shook his head.

No! A sniper doesn't take unnecessary risks.

He aimed at the two Anglo-Americans again. Surely they were already being searched for. Surely one or two scouting parties had already been sent out.

"Damn," the soldier finally groaned and stood up. He held the rifle ready. No doubt! If he had to, he could pull the trigger right away. The two American soldiers turned white as a sheet when the German sniper suddenly appeared in front of them and took aim. He walked slowly downhill. He was careful not to trip or slip.

"Oh my God," the healthy man exclaimed, about to reach for his weapon, but the German's threatening stance was clear. The soldier was instantly recognized as a sniper. The GI's realized immediately that this enemy knew no mercy.

Accordingly, the healthy man's hand twitched only briefly and, instead of reaching for his weapon, slowly rose upward.

With the barrel of his rifle, Honnige motioned for the healthy man to stand up and step aside. The healthy man recognized the silent request and immediately complied. When he was a few meters away from the weapons, the sniper went to the rapid-fire rifles and pushed them far back with his foot. He placed the rifle on his hip and motioned for the prisoner to kneel. Trembling, he obeyed. The American's expression suddenly changed. The corners of his mouth pulled down and thick tears rolled down his cheeks.

Without taking his eyes off the American, Honnige lowered his rifle and pulled his .08 pistol from its holster. He approached the wounded man and pointed to his leg. Pain was a word he knew. Barely uttered in English, the young soldier nodded. "Pain!"

The Lance Corporal slipped his pack off his back, not an easy task with the tent wrapped around him. Then he fumbled around with his left hand and pulled out a painkiller. In his right hand he still held the 08, the barrel of which pointed unmistakably at the enemy. He gave the medicine to the injured man. It was probably the good-natured look in the German's eyes that prompted the American to take the pills. He then ordered the healthy man to lower his hands. Honnige pulled out his pack of Camel from under the canvas and offered them both a cigarette. The injured man refused, but the other accepted. He had stopped crying, but his whole body was shaking. They sat facing each other and smoked. Neither said a word. When they finished smoking, the painkiller slowly began to work. The injured man smiled slightly and said he would be all right. At least that's what Honnige thought he understood.

"Go home! Go back tot he USA," the german sniper said.

"No," the healthy GI's stammered. "We can't go."

A flurry of words followed, and the German sniper waved them away. He didn't understand half of what was being said.

Shouts echoed through the forest.

They came to pick up their scattered comrades.

The fearful look immediately returned to the prisoner's eyes. How would the German sniper react?

Honnige hastily packed his things. When he was done, the healthy American tossed him a full pack of cigarettes. The one with the broken leg also pulled a pack from his field blouse. He added a gasoline lighter. "Thank you," he croaked, holding it out to his enemy.

The German took the gifts, put them in his pocket, nodded, and, from the GI's point of view, disappeared as quickly as he had come.

Honnige heard shouts and footsteps behind him. Snap of branches. The rustling of leaves. They were here. The shouts were repeated. Honnige was moving fast. Only now did the two Americans respond to the calls of their comrades.

They gave me time to disappear.

It was a strange encounter. It was the first time he had come so close to the enemy in action. Without a cease-fire. He had helped. Saving instead of killing. They were not his targets.

Not these two, he told himself as he became one with the forest again.

After a few hundred meters the soldier stopped. He sat down, looked back, and realized he was not being followed.

"One hand washes the other," he said softly to himself. Then he looked at the lighter. It was engraved.

"9th US Division," he read aloud.

Below that was the number 1, a slash, and a 3.

On the back of the silver lighter was a name and a note.

"PFC Brian Lordson, Easy Company."

Honnige looked at the lighter from all sides. The company name was stamped on the bottom.

ZIPPO, Bradford, PA. Made in USA

The private turned the ignition wheel until a small flame was lit. He lit a cigarette and clicked the lid of the lighter shut. Then he opened it again and slammed it shut. The sniper liked the sound so much that he repeated the process a few times. He smiled, slipped the lighter into his breast pocket and watched the area, smoking. They still didn't follow him.

Then they stopped coming, he thought.

The Landser looked at his compass, got his bearings, thought for a moment, and continued on his way. He had changed direction and was heading back to Lammersdorf. The blasting of the bunkers had stopped some time ago.

Probably only ruins remained.

In front of the chain of bunkers the terrain was just as uneven, but only sparsely overgrown with trees. Ideal for advancing with tanks. Honnige wanted to pass by and report back to the company. If the tanks he had seen earlier were actually deployed there, he and his comrades could be in for a hot dance. Their own tank units were not there yet.

My God, now the enemy is already at the border and has occupied the first German towns, he suddenly realized. The soldier suddenly realized that he was fighting on German soil. Of course, you didn't have to be a clairvoyant to know that the war was lost, but a final battle in Germany had always been out of the question.

Panting, the man from Baden-Wuerttemberg climbed the next hill. He wanted to discuss the matter with Keller and the others tonight. He looked at his watch. Three and a half hours had passed since the meeting with the two Americans. It had stopped drizzling, but the cloud cover had not completely lifted. Upon reaching the top, the private immediately took cover. He couldn't believe what he saw. The Anglo-Americans were in position ahead of him. The whole hollow was filled with them. Honnige estimated the enemy strength to be at least a battalion. There was also a squadron of tanks. The German memorized as many prominent terrain points as he could. He had to get back quickly. His knowledge was worth its weight in gold. The Anglo-Americans were trapped. There was no way forward. The tanks had to go back. The attempt of the US pioneers to blast a route through the forest had inevitably failed.

Oh my god, if the Ari thunders in here, thought Honnige and stood up. He was so fascinated by his discovery that he stepped on a branch. The cracking sound was clearly audible.

"Crap," he groaned.

A shot rang out. A roar! Something struck the bark of the tree next to him. How could he have been so naive as to assume the Americans had no outposts?

The private took off running. He stayed on the wooded ridge, hoping the trees would catch the deadly bullets for him.

Fatsch

Another bullet ripped the bark off a tree at head height. His pulse increased explosively. The feeling of being hunted was ugly, really unpleasant. Goose bumps spread all over his back, starting at his neck. He had to get out of here.

Back to the forest.

Another hook. A machine gun rattled, but the whistling of the bullets did not materialize. Had they lost him? So quickly? Honnige threw himself to the ground, rolled to the side, and looked back. His lungs hurt. There was a stitch in his side. The butt of the rifle was right in his shoulder. A good shot was still almost impossible. His chest rose and fell too quickly. His body reacted too nervously and anxiously.

Calm down! You have to calm down, he thought.

Gradually his breathing became shallower. He kept looking through the optics. His camouflage was priceless now. They were traveling in groups and had spread out. They had actually lost him, couldn't see him. He concluded that he could make the last stand unnoticed. Someone barked orders. Another repeated the same words over and over.

A radio operator and the scout leader.

The barrel of the sniper rifle moved from tree to tree and from man to man. Honnige could have gotten two or three by now, but he wasn't allowed to shoot too often.

One shot, then change position. Only shoot when he had to.

He could not panic.

Stay calm, he repeated to himself.

Nevertheless, the tension, the slight trembling and the fear of being discovered remained.

The right wing of the Americans was visibly moving away. They were looking for him in the wrong place. At the same moment, the radio operator and another soldier appeared in the field of vision. A white bar was clearly visible on the second man's helmet. The sniper's mind raced.

An officer! A lieutenant!

So they are here, at least in numbers. They're probably spread out all over the place! He coordinates, calls them together and sends them out again. I have to finish him or they'll get me!

The project was dangerous. On the other hand, they couldn't catch him. He never wanted to be caught as an unmasked sniper. Honnige didn't know a single one of his brothers-in-arms who wore their sniper badges in the field. It was an unwritten rule of thumb.

The officer and his radio operator had stopped. The radio operator knelt down, the officer raised a pair of binoculars and spoke. A few soldiers followed them at a distance.

Honnige felt like a rabbit caught in a trap. "You're not getting my fur," he said quietly, putting his index finger on the trigger.

The American officer's head was in the center of the sight. The shot rang out, and before the lieutenant collapsed, mortally wounded, the sniper repeated the shot, swung to another target, and fired a second shot. Before the radio operator could assess the situation, he lay dying next to his platoon leader. Honnige drew his rifle, jumped to his feet, and ran, crouching. Shouts echoed in his direction. Gunshots were fired aimlessly. The pursuing GIs immediately realized that a sniper had struck and panicked.

The sniper pulled another hook, leapt over a rotten stump, and caught the tip of his boot. With a curse on his lips, he flew through the air and landed on the forest floor. Shots rang out.

Loud and close this tim. And in close proximity. Still falling, the German had seen the tips of a soldier's boots. After landing, he immediately turned around. He had seen the enemy out of the corner of his eye. The GI pointed his weapon at the German sniper, his finger on the trigger guard, but the sniper hesitated. His eyes were wide open. Honnige's sudden appearance and fierce stare had probably startled him as well. The private looked like a green gnome. The German had not let go of his rifle even when he fell. Even when he was lying down, the barrel of his rifle was pointed at the enemy. Unlike the American soldier, he pulled the trigger. He hit. The bullet pierced the stomach of the American soldier, who stood there in shock. The soldier dropped his weapon in disbelief. Both hands grabbed the wound and were instantly covered in blood. He fell to his knees. His face instantly turned ashen. His eyes were wide open, but no cry came from his mouth. Not a moan.

The sniper jumped to his feet and continued his flight. He ran farther and farther into the sheltering forest. Soon the voices faded. There was no more shooting. He seemed to have made it, but he still ran as fast as he could. He wanted to put some distance between himself and the enemy.

The image of the last victim kept reappearing in front of his eyes. Honnige had to keep pushing it away.

Damn it! What's wrong with me?

It was a good twenty minutes later when the German fell exhausted against a tree, knowing how close he had come to escaping death. Goose bumps still covered his back. The thought of his own death literally sent shivers down his spine.

It was not until an hour later, when it was already getting dark, that the private was able to continue on his way. Another hour later, he realized that it was almost impossible to return to his own ranks at night. Only the faintest moonlight penetrated the dense cloud cover. Nevertheless, he did not give up. He kept pulling his compass from his pocket to get his bearings. Honnige trudged toward his goal. His head was empty and he was freezing when he was called by a guard well after midnight.

"Stop! Slogan?"

"Edelweiss," Honnige called back. "Edelweiss! I'm a sniper!"

"Come here!"

He had made it. Completely exhausted, he passed the outpost. "I need to get to the company CP immediately."

"Go to the back first. Our sergeant will make you some coffee. You look pitiful. Like a forest goblin! Besides, they might be sleeping in the company CP at this time of night!"

"Thanks for the compliment about the goblin. Be careful, comrade. The forest is full of Americans. They'll be here soon!"

"With tanks?"

"I don't think so. Their Shermans are at a dead end. They can't get through the woods!"

"We have to lie here of all places. I'd feel safer in the woods."

"Huber's in the foxhole next to us. Behind us is the heavy platoon with grenade launchers, and we are flanked by Paks," Hofman tried to calm the agitated Heinz Grossmann.

"When do you think it will start?"

It was pitch dark. Sergeant Keller's squad was on duty in the front positions. All was quiet ahead of them. The occasional clatter of cooking utensils could be heard, but nothing else.

Grossmann pulled back his left uniform sleeve to reveal his wristwatch. Despite the glowing numbers, he couldn't make out anything and fumbled for the flashlight. Together with the watch he put it under his coat. There he turned on the light and then turned it off again. Nobody saw anything. When he looked at the watch again, the phosphorescent numbers were clearly visible. "Another hour, then we'll be relieved."

"Is it five already?"

Grossmann nodded. "Just ten minutes past five. The others should be here at six."

"I'm really tired. The weather is getting more and more unpleasant, too. If it continues like this, we'll have a hard winter."

"Nonsense. How can you be so sure? It's still September."

"It's much too cold for September. I can feel the icy winter in my bones. It was the same with my old man, and he knew his stuff. He was a winegrower through and through."

"Winegrower? You mean winemaker?"

"He always said he was a winegrower. We had two vineyards. Well, yes," he revised, "let's say two small vineyards. It was just enough for us and, in a good year, a few extra bottles to sell on the market."

"And in addition to growing grapes, you also had a farm?"

"That's right!"

"With livestock or crops?"

"Small livestock, potatoes, apples."

"Hence the term winegrower."

Silence.

Grossmann thought about the words that had been spoken. Something was bothering him. Hofman had spoken in the past tense. That didn't fit. "Why did you have them? Don't you have the vineyards anymore?" the young soldier asked.

"After my brother and I were drafted, my father was no longer able to work the vineyards. He leased them out last year to earn a few extra marks. But I promise you one thing." Hofman paused for a moment. He looked at his comrade with a serious expression. "When the war is over, I'll cancel the lease and plant the vines myself. I'll buy a few more hillsides and have my own vineyard."

"Great."

Hofman alternated between reminiscing and planning for the future. The last hour passed in a flash. The lance corporal was already packing up and looking forward to a few hours sleep when a red flare was fired into the sky.

Puzzled, he looked at the bizarre flickering light. "I can't believe it! I hope someone made a mistake," he muttered.

"That was an alarm!" Grossmann exclaimed frantically.

The fire attack began at dawn. Reflectors twitched in the sky. Enemy artillery fired, but the whistling and howling of the shells did not reach Hofman's position. The attack was directed at another section of the front.

Again, balls of light whizzed upward. This time they were white, bathing the landscape in a grotesque magnesium light. They recognized running shadows. Crouching, they ran up the flat hill. Machine gun fire began. Tracer rounds showed the path of the deadly bullets. The gaps in the trenches and the empty spaces at the barricades filled up. Sleepy, unshaven faces huddled behind their weapons and opened fire.

Grossmann's heart beat extremely fast. The young Landser studied the man next to him. With soft legs and a slight tremor in his hands, he crouched behind his carbine and took aim. Two stick grenades lay beside him. Ready to throw. Only the ripcord had to be pulled.

"Only fire when you can see a target. Otherwise it's a waste of ammo. Watch out for the tracer ammunition of the machine guns and use the light of the flares!"

He wanted to follow Hofman's advice. Absolutely. The battle noise grew. Grossmann's right forefinger twitched. A shot rang out, the stock of the K 98 slammed against his shoulder. The young Landser aimed into the twilight, fired the repeater and fired again.

"Always shoot at those closest to you," his neighbor shouted at him.

Grossmann took a deep breath. Deep and hard. His heart almost stopped when Keller dropped into the foxhole.

"Man, you scared me," he groaned.

"Eyes on the enemy!" the sergeant ordered, pulling out his binoculars. "Huuuuber!" he shouted as loud as he could. "Huuuubeeer!"

95

The machine-gunner looked for Keller. His arm shot up. His hand showed two fingers. "Two o'clock! They're coming in platoon strength! Two o'clock," he yelled.

Huber nodded. He got the hint. The machine-gunner I changed the direction of the barrel, took aim, and paused. He recognized the dark spots in the grass. It was time. He pulled back the trigger. Again and again he fired short bursts, corrected the direction of fire, and pulled the trigger again.

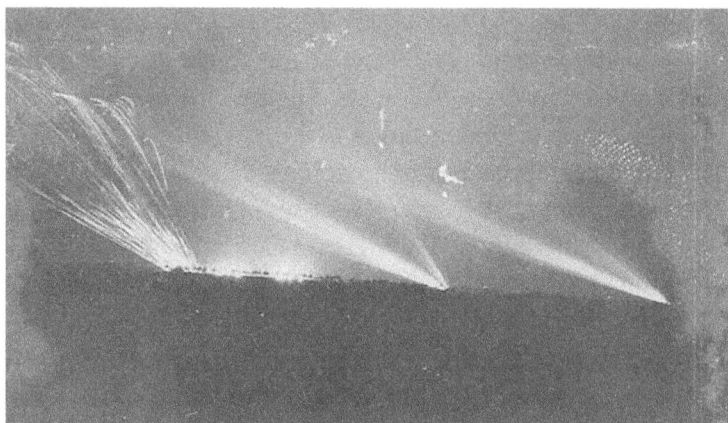

Author's private archive: PA-e-001 - Shelling, rocket launchers/artillery

As the attack of the first wave faltered, the earth began to shake. A wailing whistle announced the shells.

Huiiit - Wumm

The American artillery fire had shifted to Sergeant Keller's section.

"Barrage! Keep your heads down," he shouted, pressing himself firmly to the ground. The explosives detonated again and again in the area around the Landser. Shrapnel, rocks and earth were thrown around. It smelled of gunpowder smoke. Not far from Grossmann, the torn and mangled arm of a German soldier landed after a direct hit.

Whammm

There seemed to be no end to the horror. Nevertheless, a few medics risked their lives and repeatedly ventured out from under cover to rescue the screaming wounded. Death-defying, they went about their task.

Captain Retzer tried desperately to reach the Artillery Comander. He repeatedly demanded that his messages be connected.

"Nothing is moving."

"Keep going."

The soldier's face finally lit up. "I've got him."

Retzer picked up the field phone. "This is Captain Retzer of the 2nd Company. We desperately need artillery support. If this continues, we won't be able to repel the second wave of attacks. How? ... No! ... Damn, not even ... what? Hell, yes! Do you have the coordinates? ... ... Good! As soon as possible! Over!"

Shortly after the conversation, the roar of battle increased again. Several explosions followed each other so closely that they resembled a single, mighty, never-ending thunderclap. The shells from the German 8.8 cm guns were frighteningly accurate. The shells hit exactly where the second wave of the Allied attack was supposed to be hiding in the woods, waiting for the order to attack.

In addition, the 38 kg explosive grenades of the 15 cm Infantry Gun 33 suddenly roared into the treetops above them, detonating and discharging with a tremendous roar. Their deadly shrapnel rained down on the American soldiers like a rain of steel. The effect of the grenades was intensified by shredded and torn branches of various sizes. Some were so large and heavy that they rained down like wooden torpedoes, killing the U.S. soldiers as they sought shelter under the trees.

Others swooped down on the men like jagged spears, piercing the Americans with sharp points on their shoulders, backs, or legs.

The Hürtgen Forest seemed to have formed an alliance with the German soldiers, exacting a heavy toll in blood from the Allied fighters.

Author's private archive: PA-0050 - Haubize and motorcycle in the Ari field camp

In the blink of an eye, the strip of land intended as a protective forest had been transformed into a barbaric death zone.

Trembling, hoping and praying. They were shocked. The heroism they had talked themselves into had given way to an indescribable, naked fear. Fear had them in its grip.

When the artillery fire from both sides finally subsided and the order was given for an infantry assault, a green wall emerged from the forest and ran toward the German positions. It was almost a relief for the soldiers to hear it: "Forward! Charge!"

They jumped to their feet and charged forward. They would overrun the German positions. In the sense of relief, coupled with the expected start of Hitler's saws *(Author's note: Hitler saw = nickname for the German MG 42 = powerful German machine gun)*, the next shock hit the US soldiers unexpectedly. Instead of waiting and holding their positions, as the Americans had been accustomed to doing, the German soldiers charged at them, shouting loudly.

"Out!" the shouts of the officers and NCOs echoed through the ranks of the German soldiers. "Counterattack!"

The Landser stood up.

"Hurrah!" they shouted to encourage themselves.

Fearful comrades were swept along. They automatically fell into step and ran toward the flowing green wall.

Rrrrrrrrrrrrrr

Again and again, volleys from their machine guns in the rear tore gaps in the ranks of the US soldiers, but these were quickly closed by advancing men. The inevitable happened. The enemy charged with full force.

Keller held the MP against his hip so as not to scatter the next volley too much. He stopped and squeezed the trigger. After two bursts, he ran on. With each step, the faces of the enemy became clearer. There was fear, anger, and determination. Many of the Americans were young. The sergeant suppressed his thoughts. He became an animal, a beast.

The squad leader's neighbor fell to the ground and lay motionless. Bullets whirled through the air.

"Hurrah!"

The cry echoed over and over across the battlefield. The loud roar spurred the soldiers on, whipping them forward.

Hofman emptied the magazine, grabbed the MP by the barrel, spun him around, and swung the weapon like a club at two GIs standing in front of him. The stock cracked against the first American's helmet. Before the second, stunned Allied soldier could react, the butt of the German corporal's submachine gun slammed into his face. As if hit by a horse's hoof, the GI dropped his weapon, dropped to his knees, and put his hands in front of his bleeding face. "Ahhh!"

Only then did Hofman change the clip.

Huber had followed with the machine gun and was firing incessantly. The antitank guns positioned to the side of the group also fired explosive rounds over the heads of their comrades. The explosives detonated close to the edge of the forest in the ranks of the advancing enemy. Only when the infantrymen of both camps had become entangled in an indeterminate human tangle did the men behind the antitank guns cease their fire support.

Gunshots, metal clanking. Groaning, yelling and screaming. Orders shouted in German and English mingled into a barely intelligible panic scream! The hand-to-hand combat was hell on earth. Blood spurted, medics rushed across the battle-field. When the gruesome fighting seemed to have reached its climax, the American soldiers gave the order to retreat.

soldiers-7662300_1920
Pixabay Lizenz: https://pixabay.com/de/service/license/

The Landser were no match for their opponent. They did not feel like glorious victors. They were not shining heroes in the sunlight, but felt only fear, cold, and disgust. They had once again jumped from the brink of death. Stooped, empty-eyed, they too returned to their positions. This wave of attacks had been repulsed. The enemy was in retreat, but that was no cause for celebration. Keller knew the enemy would return.

The victory was only temporary - not for long. The sergeant immediately took stock. The emptiness in his eyes disappeared, giving way to a kind of worry. Concern for his men. Keller saw Hofman and called to him: "Hofman, where are our men?"

The corporal did not answer. He sat silently on the ground, holding his snuff box and staring into space. The soldier's uniform was covered with blood splatters.

"Hofman, is everything all right?"

The Landser answered this second call and stood up. "I don't know," he muttered. "Grossmann was beside me earlier. He must be here somewhere."

The snuff box went into his pocket. Grossmann

stretched, looked around, and spotted the two machine-gunners. "Huber and Hassel are over there. I don't see Grossmann."

The machine-gunners stopped at Keller. "Grossmann was taken to the dressing station. He was hit, but it's nothing serious. I reckon he'll definitely stay with the troops and not have to go to the rear hospital," Huber said.

The attack was called off for the day. Keller's company was pulled back from the front. Grossmann rejoined the group that evening. He wore a white bandage on his head.

"I saw Willi Klein," he told his squad leader, "you know. The blond guy who was always so quiet and only talked when you talked to him."

"Yeah, so? Where is he?"

"Badly wounded. They pinned a piece of paper with two red stripes on it."

"Crap. Poor guy. That means he's not fit for transport. Is he at least at the main dressing station yet?"

"Yes. He screamed loudly. Over and over again. When I left, they gave him a shot of morphine, and only then was he quiet."

"Good to know, I was just about to put him on the missing persons list. I still have to file a report with the company. What's wrong with him? Did you see the wound?"

"His legs are shredded and he's got a bullet in his chest. It looks like he was shot with a machine gun."

"How do you know all this so well?"

"The medic who brought me in was in basic training with us. He told me about it."

"Then all that's missing is Stober."

"Pleased," Huber said dryly. "You brought his badge earlier and gave it to the Master Sergeant. I understand Lieutenant Drexler wants to write to the next of kin."

"A bitter day for us."

"A bitter day for their families," muttered Keller.

The soldiers on both sides were going through hell. They thought the horror of the suffering and the death that hung over them could not be surpassed, but they were only at the beginning.

Again and again the Allies raced against the German lines. Death-defying officers and NCOs led their men, were beaten back, and whipped them forward again. Yet little ground was gained.

After three days of fierce fighting, the American attack wedge advancing against Hürtgen was finally ordered to retreat.

Due to the tactically sound defensive position and the incessant German counterattacks, the Americans suffered far too many casualties to achieve their planned military objective.

It was not only in this section of the front, but also in the Todtenbruch that the other two Allied shock wedges got stuck.

"Opposite us is the 9th US Division," explained Lieutenant Drexler, passing on his knowledge and the upcoming new mission to the Landser. "Their attack is bogged down. They can't get their tanks into the woods, and they're certainly being supplied by the roads and tracks we know. This leads to the conclusion that they are getting weaker and weaker. We try to encircle the troops opposite. Our 8.8 cm guns are firing into the American withdrawal area, while at the same time we are driving a wedge between the US troops dug into the forest and their supply routes.

"From defender to attacker? Not a bad tactic. The enemy certainly isn't expecting it."

"If our plan succeeds, the Allies' efforts to advance through the Eifel forests into the Rhine Valley will be thwarted. Departure at five o'clock!"

The ammunition bags were full. Cold rations were issued for three days, as fierce resistance was expected. Only when the new HKL had stabilized were the field kitchens to be brought in and the combat troops to be supplied with hot rations by food carriers.

It was still dark when they left. At last the rain had stopped.

Fischer looked up. For a moment it seemed as if he was going for a night walk. "I just missed the cold water."

The neighboring battalion would distract them with a mock attack in two hours. Then the Achtacht would begin their disruptive fire, and finally they would drive a wedge between the combat troops and their supply routes.

Ralf Fischer talked non-stop. "I just hope the Artillery knows where to shoot. I've seen enough tree breakers. Do you know how those things come crashing down on you?"

"Can you shut up for once? We're on our way to the front, there's no need to keep talking!" Hofman reprimanded. Like the others, he wanted some peace and quiet. His last thoughts before a battle were of his family. Somehow the soldier let his whole life pass him by. He thought about what he would do after the war and what he didn't want to waste time on. The chatter of the man next to him disturbed him.

"Helps me, though," Fischer replied. "Takes the edge off."

"What if the Yanks use tree shooters? They're guaranteed to hear you talking before they see us."

That was enough. Fischer was silent from then on. He had great respect for enemy marksmen.

Grinning, Hofman returned to his thoughts.

The area occupied by the enemy was largely avoided. They had taken a short break. Water bottles made their way to the top. The thirst was quenched. One or two drops were poured into the mouth. Smoking was forbidden.

The company commander looked at the glowing hands of his watch. "We must hurry. The detour was more difficult than I thought," Captain Retzer demanded. The Company Commander took hold of the leather strap of his steel helmet once more. He tightened it through a hole and raised his hand. "That was the last rest. The artillery will resume firing in two minutes. That gives us a good half hour to reach our objective. Let's move out!"

Keller stubbed out his cigarette, then motioned to his men. "It's our turn to take the lead. Our snipers are already on the left and right flanks to cover us from there. Fischer and Hassel, your position remains the same. You march right behind me. Any questions?"

No one spoke.

"Forward!"

Honnige had only ventured this deep into the forest once before. Fortunately, he had memorized a few of the more prominent features of the terrain. Relieved, he now stood in front of one of them. It was a fallen fir. A once mighty tree with an enormous girth.

How old could it be, he wondered to himself.

The sniper knew that the company would have to change direction at this point due to the nature of the terrain. He had an idea of his comrades' position, but there was still no visual contact. Honnige decided to advance a little further and then wait for the men. In the meantime it had become light. The huge fir tree in front of him provided good cover. The lone fighter wondered if he should smoke a cigarette. He held the American Zippo lighter in his hands, but resisted the temptation to smoke and rejected the idea of a cigarette. Instead, he played with the top of the lighter a few times. The metallic *click* reminded him of the engraved manufacturer's name. He heard the *zi* when he opened it and the *po* when he closed it.

Zi...po

Honnige looked for a good position and sat down. He watched the area. The company soldiers reached him faster than expected. He quickly explained the route to Sergeant Keller and then left the group.

The information was immediately passed on to the rear.

Captain Retzer's nervousness grew noticeably. "The Artillery should have fired by now, what's going on?"

He kept looking at his watch.

"Maybe they're waiting until we've reached our deployment area, so we won't come under their fire?" said Sergeant Meier, who was part of the company squad.

Retzter didn't seem to notice the remark. "Radio guys to me! I want to talk to the Artillery Comander immediately."

At the same moment the thunder started. Twenty minutes late, the German 8.8 cm guns began their planned bombardment. The whistling and howling of the shells surrounded the hitherto quiet morning atmosphere of the wooded area with an eerie infernal noise.

Huiiiit wummm wumm huiiit wumm wumm wumm

Drexler had looked for his superior and went straight to him. "The advance guard just reported that we've reached our destination. You have a good view of the road. An enemy column is approaching."

"Column? What kind? I want detailed information," the captain pulverized.

"Column is probably a bit of an exaggeration. You see three trucks and one jeep. There are tarpaulins stretched over the trailers of the trucks. We don't know if it's a crew or a supply transport."

"Who is leading the advance?"

"Sergeant Keller, Captain," Lieutenant Drexler announced.

"A good and experienced soldier," said the company commander. The officer's brow furrowed. He thought for only a few seconds before giving an order. "Tell him to stop the column! Meanwhile, we will attack our predetermined target as soon as the artillery fire is over. Have the company move into position immediately. Form up as discussed."

"Yes, Captain."

"Lieutenant Drexler?"

"What?"

"Keller, if he takes prisoners, should wait until the rest of the company is here and turn them over to him. Then he should follow us."

"Understood. By the way ..." the platoon leader noted, "... the whole group now consists of only six men."

"Then let Honnige accompany them."

"Got it."

After thirty minutes, the thunderous hell of the German guns came to an end. The company was in its positions. The Soldiers were ready to attack. On command, they charged. This time they met less resistance than they had expected.

The mission was clear. Sergeant Keller and his squad remained separated from the rest of the company. The American trucks were under constant surveillance. When the Eight-Eight began firing, the U.S. column commander ordered a halt.

Standing in the jeep, he tried to see something through his binoculars, but he could see nothing but the treetops from his position. He picked up the radio.

"They stopped," Hofman whispered.

"They don't want to run into artillery fire."

"What if they turn around?"

Keller lifted his binoculars and looked down the road. It stretched like a snake through the autumnal, wild-green jungle forest. "We won't give them that chance. They're still crouching and smoking. The boss is a sergeant. I can see the stripes on the sleeve of his uniform."

Keller turned the binoculars elsewhere.

"Three trucks, one jeep. I think they were carrying food or ammo. If it was a troop transport, the mounted soldiers would be standing around too. It's the same in every army in the world," the sergeant said dryly. "The sergeant is obviously getting some instructions over the radio. Maybe he's also being warned. The artillery shells hit a good two kilometers from here. They'll wait and see! There are two men per vehicle."

"When do we attack?"

"Now! We sneak down to the edge of the forest, get into position and fire."

Honnige joined the group and was briefed. The Landser crept up at a safe distance from the road. The sniper was the first to take position. He was still well camouflaged and literally swallowed by his surroundings. Honnige rested the rifle stock on his shoulder. Aiming through the sights would have been possible because of the short distance, but the private opted for the optical sight. Soon he had the squad leader, his driver, and five men taking turns in the crosshairs. None of these men had any idea how close to death they were at that moment.

"One missing," the sniper muttered as he swung his rifle from truck to truck. He spotted the missing GI in the third truck.

"Fire!" Keller ordered.

Huber's machine gun rattled off. The rounds bored into the sheet metal of the vehicles, punching several holes with apparent ease. The accompanying crew immediately dropped to the ground. The attack had taken them completely by surprise. Only the driver of the last truck returned fire. He was still in the cab and fired blindly into the forest.

A white cloth was waved by the soldiers behind the jeep. The sniper in the truck didn't seem to see it, or didn't want to see it. He kept firing without stopping. Huber swung the machine gun around and sent a burst of fire into the cab. The return fire stopped abruptly. As Keller, Hofman, Huber, and Grossmann stood up and walked down with their weapons at the ready, the Americans raised their hands. Huber secured with the machine gun. He and Hassel watched the enemy closely. They were ready to fire at the slightest danger.

Honnige also stayed hidden and aimed at the enemy.

The Germans approached the vehicles.

"Hands up!"

"Stand up!"

The GIs stood. When the german sergeant reached the prisoners, he waved to the machine-gunners. They went to their comrades.

"Look for the man in the truck," Hofman and Fischer were told.

Fischer held his carbine ready, while the lance corporal let the MP dangle loosely from his hip. When they were roughly level with the center of the second truck, a single shot rang out.

Everyone stopped and stared.

"Stay calm. Nobody shoot," Keller yelled, paying more attention to his men than to the American soldiers still standing in front of them with their hands up.

Moments later, Honnige stepped out of the woods and approached Hofman and Huber. All the men looked at the German sniper skeptically.

"What was that all about?" asked Fischer angry.

"Look under the truck. The driver wouldn't give up. He was aiming at you while your eyes were fixed on the cab. Another meter or two and you would have died a hero. You could have gotten a posthumous medal for that."

As Honnige spoke, Hofman bent down, looked under the truck, and turned white as a sheet. "He's right. The guy's lying there in his blood with his gun at the ready. Another two meters and we'd be in his line of fire."

"I thought Huber got him with the machine gun?"

They opened the cab. No blood.

"The Yank knew he had to get out. He played high and lost his game."

"Thank you."

The sniper nodded. "That was my job."

"Thank you," Hofman said.

The prisoners were allowed to bury their fallen comrade and say a few words. Then they crouched and waited. Huber and Hassel were guarding the road to the rear, Honnige was in position at the front. Hofman and Fischer guarded the Americans, while Sergeant Keller and Heinz Grossmann inspected the truck's cargo.

Author's private archive: PA-N-0118 - US truck loading area with tarpaulin

"Lots of food," Grossmann announced loudly as he opened a few crates from the first truck's load.

"Here's something for us. Whisky and cigarettes. Probably for the officers. Come here."

The Landser quickly jumped off the truck and ran to Sergeant Keller. He already had two bottles of Whisky in his hands. "Quick! Each of us should pack a bottle and you take it to the boys. If there's one left, give it to the prisoners. The poor fellows should have a few good minutes before they go to the prison camp. Hurry up."

Author's private archive: PA-N-0119 – Provision boxes

Then the cigarettes were distributed. Everyone got two sticks. Then came the corned beef and white bread. Two rarities.

"Hurry up! We have to throw the empty boxes into the woods. I don't want anyone from the company to find out that we took anything from here. Everything will be handed over cleanly."

Grossmann grinned. "You think of everything, Josef," he said to Keller, and ran off into the woods with the remains of a box he had broken open. There was no need to hurry, because the boss didn't arrive until almost an hour later. The covered wagons hadn't made it through the forest as quickly as they'd planned.

"The kitchen bull will be pleased," was the first sentence the group heard.

The reserve company provided complete rear cover along the road. A troop assembly area was also set up.

After the prisoners and spoils were handed over, Keller led his squad and the sniper back to the company.

"They smell like three drunken Russians," Fischer imitated the comrade who had taken the captured GIs and laughed out loud.

Everyone joined in his laughter. For a few minutes, the daily grind of war was forgotten. Their packs were full of valuable goods. They marched back to the front, but none of the men gave it a second thought. They suppressed the fact. All they cared about was this moment. The Landser enjoyed the feeling of happiness. It was like Christmas. They had captured American booty and were rich for the moment.

Only gradually were they brought back to reality. The shock came in the form of medics carrying wounded comrades on stretchers to the Field Hospital. There was no sound of battle. As a small group of captured US soldiers marched past, accompanied by two squads, Sergeant Keller recognized an old comrade.

"Erwin," he called to him. "Erwin Gromek. How's the front?"

Corporal Gromek recognized the sergeant and waved. "Keller, I heard you were back here."

When he was level with Keller, he paused for a moment. "On our side, it was easy like eating a piece of cake. We walked right into their battalion headquarters. Beyond it were some medical tents and a supply depot. The Eight-Eight really wreaked havoc. We had relatively few casualties. Our old man ..." the corporal said, referring to his company commander, "... said the neighboring battalion was hit harder."

"Does that mean the tactic worked?"

"It looks like it. The Americans are in a kettle. Well, more like they're cut off from their troops in the rear, which is like a cauldron. But one flank should still be free. But the main terrain is all downhill. There's a valley cut through it."

"Thank you for the information. If you could tell me where our people are, I'd be eternally grateful."

"Just keep going straight. Your company was at the American camp earlier. Where all the tents are. You can't miss it."

They said goodbye.

The next day began with the same hellish scenario. The German artillery, primarily their 8.8 cm guns, pounded their shells into the forest belt occupied by the Americans.

The infantry then tried to force the Allies, cut off from their supplies, to surrender with non-stop attacks. However, their own fighting strength had dwindled considerably as the 275th Infantry Division had also suffered enormous losses.

On the third day of the encirclement, the 9th U.S. Division succeeded in penetrating the sparsely occupied belt. The American supply line was reopened, but it was not until three days later that US troops were able to launch another attack on the stubborn German defenders of the Hürtgen Forest.

The German units took advantage of this three-day lull in the fighting. Requested reinforcements arrived and another regiment left.

Meanwhile, the 9th U.S. Division made one last major attack. Again without tank support, the American soldiers stormed the ridge called Ochsenkopf and the bunker lines. They put everything on one card to break through the German lines. The defenders, hardened by the Russian front, did not retreat a meter without a fight.

Keller's group breathed a sigh of relief. The battalion had fought bravely and had been recaptured. They were back where they had dug the trenches when Keller rejoined the troops. The company's fighting strength had been cut by more than a quarter, but they were not being redeployed for refreshment. They had to remain in their positions.

"This is sheer madness," Grossmann grumbled like a ragamuffin. "We're still six men, and we're supposed to provide the defensive strength of a whole squad!"

Keller lit one of the looted cigarettes. It was a Lucky Strike, the last one in the pack. The sergeant crumpled the paper and threw it on the table. Wisps of blue vapor floated above him. "You have passed your baptism of fire, and most importantly, you have survived. Now you know what awaits you."

"Why are you so quiet?"

"Ha, ha," the group leader laughed. "Why fuss unnessessarily? What's the point? The enemy is coming on foot. The Artillery is only moderately pounding, and you hardly ever see a plane, let alone fighters opening their bomb bays," he instructed his young comrade. "In Russia these would have been ideal conditions. Believe me, out there ..." he pointed to the bunkers and foxholes, "... it's a cruel war, but it's an honest one."

"Really?" Huber interrupted. "It's the same everywhere. It doesn't matter if I'm hit by a Russian, American or English bullet. Death looks the same everywhere!"

"So? Does it?" Keller's face darkened. "If it does, you can go back to Russia. Would you like that better?"

Huber was surprised at the answer. He thought about it. "To be honest, I have to say no."

"You see. That's what I mean. There's nothing to sugarcoat. Nothing at all. Still, no one wants to change places with the Eastern Front."

Hofman spoke up. "Grossmann, you mustn't get too carried away, or you'll get a case of frontal paralysis. That's no joke."

"Everybody just pick on me!"

The door flew open. Lieutenant Drexler burst in. The officer. "Heavy fighting has broken out at Ochsenkopf. The bunker line is also under constant attack. We have to get out. In five minutes I want to see the platoon ready to move out with their combat packs!"

They had been in the area for less than ten minutes when they came under heavy enemy artillery fire. Again and again, shells roared toward them, announcing the disaster with a swelling whistle and detonating thunderously among the soldiers. Once again, Death rode through the Hürtgen Forest, swinging his scythe and reaping a rich harvest.

"Heads down!" shouted Keller as he heard the telltale whistle.

Immediately, his men pressed to the ground, ducked their heads, and hoped to escape the sharp-edged shrapnel. It was an inferno. The trebuchets raged the most. In addition to the flying metal shrapnel, branches, twigs, and smaller trunks were blown from the trees. The ground shook.

Keller heard loud cracking and crashing after a detonation. The sergeant's inner alarm bells went off immediately. "Get out of here!" he yelled, pulling violently on the sleeve of Fischer, who was lying next to him in the foxhole. They both jumped up and saved themselves with a pike jump from a falling treetop. With a muffled sound, almost in slow motion, the blasted treetop slid down and buried the original position of the two soldiers under its branches. Just ten centimeters from Fischer, a branch as thick as his arm dug itself into the ground. The young soldier looked at the branch in shock. All the blood drained from the German's face. His eyes sought contact with Keller. He lay flat on the ground and remained there. Fischer immediately did the same.

When the spook finally stopped, the machine guns began to rattle again. The war knew no rest and certainly no mercy.

"Get up! They're coming back!"

Calls for medics echoed through the forest.

"Meeeeediiic," Over here!"

"Medic! Heeeereee!"

Captain Retzer surveyed the terrain before him. American infantrymen were steadily working their way toward the bunker line. Although no tanks were visible, loud engine noises could be heard all the way to the company's flank position. The officer turned to Drexler. "Lieutenant Drexler! We have to push to the enemy side. The Americans have sappers with them and are about to blow up the bunkers."

"We have a bad field of fire from here."

"Then we'll push forward."

Drexler swallowed, wondering if he should suggest a different tactic, but the unshaven face of the company commander radiated determination. Retzer was an officer of the old school. He led his men from the front, lay in the foxhole with them, ate the same meager rations, and fought the same hard battles. That earned him unparalleled respect.

After taking a deep breath, Drexler acknowledged. "By your command, Captain."

Only seconds later, the time had come.

"Attaaaaac," the voices of all three platoon leaders thundered through the ranks of their men. Despite the heavy fire from the American howitzers, the morale of the soldiers was not broken. They stood up, left their cover, and ran toward the enemy.

Within a few hundred yards, Huber found an ideal firing position. He dropped down, wedged himself behind the machine gun, and chased over the heads of his comrades, firing deadly volleys at the enemy.

Click

"Damn it! Inhibition!" he cursed as another of the enameled steel casings was burned into the barrel. "Change the barrel!" he followed immediately, pulling the machine gun closer to him.

Hassel grabbed the asbestos rag. He used a homemade tool to remove the burnt sleeve.

"Do we have another box of good ammo?"

"Yes."

"Give it to me!"

The new belt was inserted, the target was aimed, then the relentless infantry weapon fired again. The fighting was fierce. Hand grenades flew through the air, exploding loudly over the heads or in the middle of enemy positions. The enemy's hand grenades also exploded between their own ranks. The ground was saturated with blood.

Just when Captain Retzer thought he had pushed the enemy back, tank shells exploded near the bunkers. Two Sherman tanks and an M7 Priest, an American self-propelled howitzer with an open combat compartment on the chassis, rolled forward. The M7 howitzer spat out shells incessantly. The heavy mounted machine gun rattled, punching holes in the ranks of the Landser, or at least forcing them to take cover.

"Where are the tank destroyers?" Retzer shouted, throwing himself to the ground.

After days, the Anglo-Americans had finally managed to get some armored vehicles onto the ridges. Heavy bulldozers followed, again accompanied by infantry for protection. With renewed courage, the US soldiers charged forward once more.

Keller saw three tank destroyers approaching a Sherman. A smoke grenade flew through the air. The soldier used as a blender jerked his arms back after the throw.

Poor guy. He got it bad.

The man next to him flinched after taking several hits and fell forward onto his T-mine.

No!

Keller closed his eyes for a moment.

"Damn war!" he muttered and pulled the trigger of his MP.

At the same time, Honnige jumped up and ran away. He spotted a grenade launcher and dove into it. The enemy's machine-gun salvo flew over him. His weapon went over the edge of the crater. Three rounds, three hits. He pulled a fresh clip from his pocket. Someone dropped into the funnel beside him. It was Captain Retzer. The officer drew in a deep breath.

"The howitzer has to be stopped. Can you do it?"

Honnige nodded, leaving the loading strip with the normal ammunition and instead digging out a loading strip with special ammunition from another pouch. He inserted it into the weapon.

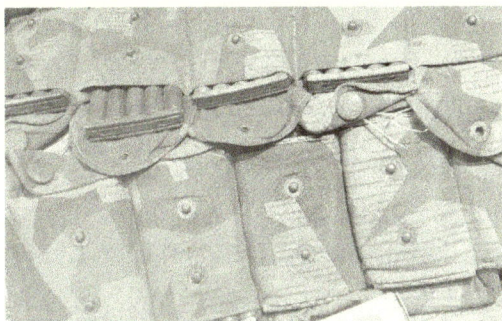

Author's private archive: PA-N-011- ammunition belt pouch - carbine loading strip

Then he tried to aim at the crew of the M7 through the hazy fog of the battlefield. For a brief moment, the machine gunner's steel helmet appeared. It was only a split second, but it was enough for the sniper, whose finger slipped back. The shot rang out, and the M7's machine gun immediately fell silent. Quick repetition, aim, aim. Another shot, another hit. After the third hit, the tank stopped.

"Get out of here!" the sniper yelled to his company commander. They both jumped up and left the shell hole. Moments later, a Sherman fired in their direction.

The captain wondered if Honnige had seen this or if it was the sniper's intuition that made him leave his position. In the end, he had no answer.

The retreat had to be ordered. The superiority was too great. American bulldozers were already filling the trenches of the first bunkers with earth. Pioneers laid explosives. Everywhere you looked there were dead and wounded on the battlefield. The line of bunkers had to be abandoned, and the trenches and foxholes dug into the forest floor were now occupied. At the same time,

German engineers mined all the open roads. New defensive positions were set up at all strategically important points in the terrain.

Even after the fighting was over, the sound of detonations echoed through the forest. American engineers blew up the bunkers.

The faces of the defenders were covered with stubble. They hadn't had a chance to wash in days, let alone change their uniforms. Those pesky lice were spreading again. They itched everywhere and got on their nerves. Fischer had fallen. He had been mortally wounded during the retreat. Sergeant Keller's squad had dwindled to five men.

Within a few days, the sparse late summer had completely vanished, and autumn had taken over with much too cold air. It was one of the coldest autumns in decades. Still dressed in their summer coats, the soldiers froze at night on the front lines.

After an endless week of almost daily contact with the enemy, the company was relieved. Since the civilian population had been evacuated from the combat zone, their homes served as housing for the soldiers. Keller's group shared a house with other comrades.

At night, the few pieces of furniture were moved aside and the soldiers slept on the floor. They covered themselves with their tents and enjoyed having a roof over their heads. Stoves burned in the living rooms. When they were finally given fresh clothes, shaved and washed, and received their daily hot meal, their vitality returned. After the medical department also deloused them, life became bearable again for the front-line soldiers.

"Where did you get your hair cut?" Hofman asked Hassel, who was cleaning the breech of the MG 42.

The young soldier grinned. "You'd be surprised."

"The skull looks pretty good for a field shave," Hofman admitted, still interested.

There were rarely good barbers among the soldiers. Most of the time, someone who thought he could cut hair grabbed a pair of scissors or a razor blade, and everyone had a standard haircut.

"His name is Ernst Krüger and he's in the first company. I went to school with him. The Krügers have a barber shop and Ernst is a trained barber."

Hofman sat down beside Hassel. "Do you think he'd give me a haircut like that?"

"Maybe."

"Couldn't you put in a good word for me?"

"Possibly."

"I see where this is going. What do you want for it?"

Hassel's grin deepened. "I'm having trouble getting all the powder smoke out of the cap. Could you..."

Hofman grabbed it at once. "Give it to me. In the meantime, you go straight to the 1st and get your barber buddy to join us."

Keller had listened carefully to the conversation. "After the lice invasion, I'll join you. I'd spring for half a pack of American cigarettes."

"Ernst doesn't smoke."

"What would he ask?"

Now everyone's ears perked up. In the blink of an eye, several soldiers had gathered around Hassel.

"Josef, when Krüger comes for his haircut, you'll have to talk to his squad leader or platoon commander. I don't know what his shift is today."

"No problem."

"And you can all get out your flasks so everyone can pour some into Kruger's canteen. If he gets enough of the Yankee booze, I'm sure he'll do it."

No sooner said than done. It took Keller ten minutes to convince the team leader to let the barber go for the rest of the day. Krüger himself didn't think twice and accompanied Keller as soon as he had gotten the comb and two pairs of scissors. The whole group waited.

"It's like Saturday morning at our village barber shop," grinned Hofman. Everyone got a haircut.

When Krüger was finally finished, he had half a canteen of Whisky and a few sundries. "I was very pleased. If you need a decent haircut again, you're welcome to come back."

Meanwhile, the fighting in Hürtgen Forest continued fiercely. Wave after wave of Allied attacks were repulsed. Both American and German soldiers experienced moments so terrible that they would be etched in their memories for the rest of their lives. The rugged woods had long since become a killing field, a bone crusher. No matter what uniform the soldier wore, he was next to be caught between their millstones.

On one of these days, American war correspondent Ernest Hemingway may have thought of the words he would later use in one of his novels: "This was a place where it was extremely difficult to stay alive, even if you did nothing but be there!"

Drexler was promoted to first lieutenant. It was dark when he ordered the platoon to line up. Next to him was the spike and seven new men, who were assigned to the squads.

Corporal Keller's group was assigned a private who had participated in the Allied landings in Normandy and had been wounded in the defensive battles there. He had now recovered.

Keller was glad that he had not been assigned one of the very young, freshly trained recruits. The new recruit's name was Günther Baar and he was from Frankfurt/Main.

First Lieutenant Drexler also reported on the current situation. The Landser listened with rapt attention.

"On October 21st, Aachen was abandoned for tactical reasons," he began. "The city was fiercely contested. House to house fighting! Anyone who has been through that knows what I'm talking about! The American superiority was enormous, and the OKW wanted to reinforce our front and not send more troops unnecessarily to the strategically less important Aachen."

There was a murmur among the men.

"Quiet please, gentlemen!"

"What does this mean for us?" asked Sergeant Grün of the third platoon, his bass voice drowning out the others.

"We expect them to reinforce the forces here, but our reconnaissance also reports that the enemy is beginning to withdraw the US 9th Division opposite us."

"I can guess what's coming next," Keller whispered to his neighbor.

"That's why we have to send out reconnaissance units. We just need more information, so we are moving forward again. You can consider the quiet phase over."

The sergeant drew the right conclusion. When the US Army stopped its offensive and troop movements took place, the Wehrmacht needed reconnaissance. For this reason, the command of the 275th Infantry Division repeatedly sent shock troops into the dense forest of the northern Eifel.

The Anglo-American troops were in the process of dislodging the badly battered 9th US Division from the front. The Germans' new opponent was the 28th US Infantry Division, based in Pennsylvania and recruited largely from GIs of German descent.

Lance Corporal Honnige had been temporarily assigned to Drexler's platoon, although he was the only sniper in the entire company. The unit's second sniper had been missing since the fighting for the bunker line.

The night was already so cold that you could see the haze of breath hovering in front of their mouths. Dressed in their winter uniforms, they once again made their way through the forest. When the clouds allowed a glimpse of the moon, visibility was reasonably good. Otherwise it was pitch black.

Keller had been right. The rest period was over and the reconnaissance companies were ordered.

"This is Corporal Dolling. He will lead us through the mine belt. We will stay close to the edge of the road and get as close to the enemy as possible. Dolling not only has the plan in his head, he was there when we laid it."

"Until I give the all-clear, stay close behind me. Preferably in a row, because we've also laid booby traps between the trees."

"And you're sure you'll find the right way?" asked Huber.

"We've marked the backs of the trees with yellow flags. Stick with me and you'll march through the mine belt like a sharp knife through a butter cake."

"Yellow flags..." whispered Huber, "... how am I supposed to see the flags when it's pitch black?"

By midnight they had passed the worst of it.

"It's all American mines from here on out," Dolling joked, but none of the men in the reconnaissance team could laugh.

The path was very hard to see. Every now and then someone would trip over a branch or a protruding root. As they crossed a former combat zone, they had to dodge shot-up trees and shell casings. At one particularly large funnel, Hofman pointed into

the hole. Just then, the moon reappeared and bizarrely illumina-
ted a soldier's boot sticking out of the wood. No one dared approach.

"He's probably been under there for days," the corporal
whispered.

They approached the enemy lines. A flare shot steeply upward. The artificial magnesium light flickered bizarrely in the
sky. Gunfire could be heard.

First Lieutenant Drexler stopped the platoon. "Third Platoon, this is over. You have enemy contact."

A green flare shot up. This time it was fired by German soldiers. Shortly after, a red flare shot into the sky.

"Those two things were fired by our people. It's the distress
signal! They need help! We must go in!"

The order was immediately carried out.

Sergeant Grunner and his squad ran ahead. The squad leader didn't hear the sound as he touched the fuse of a pedal mine,
causing it to detonate. A deafening boom echoed through the forest.

Wham

The thunder had not subsided before a second explosion
sent a shiver down Drexler's spine.

Wham

Grunner was tossed through the air. He remained motionless on the ground after the impact. Not far away, another soldier
writhed on the ground in pain. The soldier's right leg had been
torn off at the shin.

"Mines!"

"Medics, fast!"

"Form a hedgehog!"

Everything was happening at breakneck speed. The constant practice was showing. A hedgehog formation was immediately formed. In their midst were the victims of the mines. Grunner was dead. The medic tended to the serious injuries of the second mine victim.

"Radio operator to me!" yelled Frist Lieutenant Drexler. He wanted immediate radio contact with the company leadership.

Cracking and popping in the pipes. Hectic movements on the equipment. Finally the connection was made. The situation was described. Silence for minutes, then a command was transmitted.

"Hold until dawn, then drop off!"

"Got it!"

"Don't walk blindly into a minefield!" warned the radio operator transmitting from the company leadingship.

Drexler seethed with rage as he heard the words, and had an appropriate response on his lips when his own radio operator spoke. "That's Eberhard. He's out of line sometimes, but he means what he says, First Lieutenant. I know him. Eberhard is a kind-hearted man."

The officer took a deep breath and thought. "In the end, he's right. I'm responsible for my men."

The radio operator nodded.

Drexler replied: "Got it. Over."

The situation was bad. They were in the middle of a mine belt and the enemy could show up at any moment. There was really no choice but to wait until daylight brought better visibility.

The monotonous moaning of the severely wounded man became a nervous endurance test.

"I can't take this moaning much longer," grumbled one of the Landsers.

"You must be able to hear that moaning for miles," said another.

"That's true, but they can't locate it."

"I've already injected him with something for the pain. That's all I can do," the medic defended.

Half an hour later, the loud moaning had subsided to a soft whimper. The medic had some morphine with him for special cases. A field doctor had sent it to him.

First Lieutenant Drexler walked over to the injured man and knelt down. „It´s Meier ..." he recognised, „... who had recently returned from home leave."

The medic looked at the wounded Pioneer.

"What does it look like?"

"If I may be honest, First Lieutenant, bad! I've done everything I can, but if we don't get him to a doctor as soon as possible, I can't guarantee anything."

The first drops fell from the sky. The soldiers grabbed their backpacks. As the rain poured down in a short time, the soldiers were wrapped up in their tents. Time seemed to stand still.

After two hours, when the moaning of the wounded Pioneer grew louder, the medic went to the platoon leader.

"We've got to get him back. He's dying, Frist Lieutenant."

Drexler pondered. He was more than unhappy with the situation. "There are mines everywhere. They can't see where they're going."

"He's got three kids at home."

"I know it. I gratulated him to his third kid."

The medic's eyes never left the officer's, pressing for an answer.

"If I send you and two or three men back, I run the risk of losing them all."

"Or save a life. The life of a family man."

Boom

The detonation made the soldiers' heads spin. A few shrapnel bored into the surrounding tree trunks. One soldier, who was the assigned sapper, had to get out and left the hedgehog position to do so. He ran into a mine. The body lay lifeless on the soft forest floor. The water from the rain washed the blood into the ground.

"Irony of fate," Sergeant Keller whispered to Grossmann. "He laid a few mines himself and now he is a victim."

Drexler stood up. "You can see for yourself how mined the area is. If we want to get through unmolested, we have to march in daylight."

"Then it'll be too late."

The first lieutenant thought feverishly. He didn't want to be responsible for the death of the father of the family.

"All right then. You, three volunteers and Honnige! You can take turns carrying, the sniper will provide adequate protection."

"Thank you."

"I hope I won't regret it," the first lieutenant said honestly.

Keller, Grossmann and the new corporal, Günther Baar, volunteered. Hofman, the machine gunners I, and his machine gun wingmans Huber and Hassel, stayed with the platoon.

"Make sure Meier makes it. Three kids would keep their father. I know what that's worth, because my father stayed in the field during the first war. I was just five years old when my mother got the news. I will never forget that day."

"Lieutenant, don't worry," Keller reassured him. "We'll make it."

The platoon leader was secretly glad that Josef Keller was going with them. The Russian veteran had both the experience and the foresight to lead the small group back to their own positions.

If it weren't for this damn minefield. Damn it!

The officer's thoughts were abruptly interrupted.

"I think there's something up ahead. Watch out, guys."

A second voice was heard. "Alarm! They're coming!"

Drexler grabbed the flare gun, looked at Keller, and said, "When the magnesium light goes out, go!"

The sergeant nodded. The sound of the flare gun firing echoed through the forest. The projectile shot steeply upward, scattering and casting a bright artificial light over the treetops. The light flickered across the forest.

Huber saw figures and squeezed the trigger. Two or three guns fired. Then the light went out. Huber changed position to be safe.

No more shots were fired.

"They're coming," was silent repeated.

The deceptive silence continued.

"Our tactical hedgehog is standing. We will hold the fort. I wish you good luck," were the brief words with which the small group was bidden farewell by their superior.

Keller and Honnige led the way. They placed their feet carefully on the ground. They were largely based on old footsteps. Meter by meter was carefully covered.

The wounded man lay on the collapsible stretcher. He swayed back and forth with every step his bearers took.

Let's hope he makes it, were Keller's thoughts.

Unknown to the soldiers of the 275th Infantry Division, they had already been relieved by the exhausted 9th Infantry Division. They now faced the mighty 28th US Division. They, in turn, had no idea that their opponents were experienced Russians who had experienced the hardships of war on the Eastern Front. They would not surrender an inch of ground without a fight.

After the 9th US Division had gained only 2.5 kilometers of ground since the beginning of the battle, but had lost more than 4,500 men, the American Army command had to act.

General Eisenhower sent more troops into the Hürtgen Forest. He wanted to march through the northern Eifel with all his might.

Only gradually did the Allies realize that they had made a big mistake. They had forgotten to take into account both the valleys and the heights of the terrain in their maps. This oversight was to take a heavy toll.

The renewed order to attack ushered in the greatest defeat in U.S. military history.

First Lieutenant Drexler knew he had led his assault team deep into enemy territory, and he expected enemy contact, but the fact that they had run into an American minefield made the situation much more difficult.

"It's probably an American reconnaissance team," said one of the soldiers. "Otherwise they would have attacked by now."

The enemy took a wait-and-see approach.

Drexler had given the tactical order to form up, as it made little sense to march through a minefield in the dark. The risk of losing more men was too high.

Huber lay behind his MG 42 and thought. Finally he said to his Gunner II, "I don't know if I would have sent Keller and the others back. We're going to miss them in the fight."

"If you were in charge, what would you have decided?"

"Stay here! That's clear," it came with complete conviction.

"And what would you have written to the widow and children?"

Huber remained silent. He was struggling for words in his mind.

"You see, nobody wants to write letters like that."

"We can do it without Keller," he said. "I just hope they get Meier through, too. Then it will have been worth it."

They had been walking for some time when they heard the first shots echo through the forest. The firefight had begun.

"Keep moving," Keller told his comrades. He was at the front of the group and noticed that the men behind him had stopped.

"Keep moving, guys. If we're too late, he'll die," the corps-man said in verbal support of the sergeant, pointing to the mine victim.

The badly injured man lay on a stretcher. The wound had been provisionally treated, but the medic knew the soldier nee-ded surgery as soon as possible. "Besides, I am almost out of painkillers," he confirmed.

The troop moved on in silence. Fortunately, the enemy mi-nefield had only been touched at the edge and was now behind them. They had come a long way during the night. The danger of encountering an American shock troop was therefore very high. The half-darkness of dusk still provided some protection, but soon it would be full daylight.

It was raining and cold.

"I'm going to move away from the group, so I can cover you better," the sniper said, breaking the monotonous silence, which was only broken by the occasional moan of the unconscious wounded man.

With the sergeant's approval, Honnige disappeared into the woods.

Keller knew this was the only correct tactic. The sniper had his trust. "There shouldn't be any more mines buried here. But watch the ground anyway."

The soldier with front-line experience had been moving close to the trees the whole time. His thoughts were all about the mines.

Due to the dense root growth, the enemy could not dig deep, at least not without leaving visible traces. They certainly didn't bury any mines here, he thought.

He walked on. The men followed in silence. The pattering rain seemed to drown out everything. Only the occasional groan or the rattling of equipment could be heard at irregular intervals.

Keller had led them out of the kill zone. They knew that. This group leader was irreplaceable in the field.

"He survived Russia and he will survive the Western Front," the soldiers said to each other, closely following the group leader's instructions.

Their progress was slow. The weather was getting worse. The first snowflakes mixed with the rain. The frosty east wind increased. The cold ate away at their rain-soaked uniforms. The porters took turns every quarter of an hour. Finally! The wide forest path was reached. Keller stopped.

"The pioneer said our people had laid booby traps between the trees near the forest path. Watch out for wires."

"Should we wait until it's completely light?"

Before the sergeant could answer, there was a crash. First a single shot, then a whole staccato.

Honnige had moved a few hundred yards away from the small group. The sniper had not forgotten the warning words of the engineer who had pointed out the booby traps before he left. The private paid close attention to his path. A clatter, followed by an exchange of words, made him pause.

Were they his own men or an American raiding party? He tried to determine the direction. Again he heard fragments of words. Now the Landser was sure. English was being spoken. The sniper's pulse quickened. Ducking, he moved toward the path and took cover under the low-hanging branches of a pine tree. Though the deciduous trees had long since shed their leaves, the green of the conifers still provided ample cover.

The advantage of a mixed forest, he thought to himself.

Cautiously, he peered out from behind the thick trunk. His hands were cold and clammy. He put the rifle down and rubbed his palms together. Then he blew warm air into his clenched hands. He reached for the rifle routinely. Honnige felt the stock against his cheek. He was lurking, waiting. He often compared himself to a spider, waiting in his web for his victims.

He heard movements an quiet conversations. The enemy appeared in his vision. They were walking in loose formation

130

along the edge of the forest on the other side of the trail. A radio squawked. The sniper tried to spot the scout leader through the scope. The dim light of the cold, rainy morning made this difficult. The soldier cursed the weather. The American GI's were hard to make out.

Sleet and twilight are not good conditions. Damn it, they're heading right for Keller and the men. This is not going to end well.

The lance corporal quickly realized that his comrades were about to run straight into the enemy. At the very least, the enemy would be able to hear the moans of the wounded. There was no time to go back and warn them.

I have to shoot to draw attention to the danger.

With his rifle at the ready, Honnige waited for the right moment.

They felt safe. They didn't suspect any enemies this far back. Or did they? Surely they had been informed by radio that a German attack force was ahead of them.

The Americans stopped. One of them used binoculars to watch both the trail and the wooded area. The German sniper had no fear of being spotted. He had complete confidence in his camouflage. He knew he had become one with his surroundings. Honnige had him in his sights. Just as a GI raised his hand, obviously to order his men to follow, the sniper pulled the trigger.

The shot rang out. The muffled echo echoed through the forest several times. The goal of the lone fighter was to wound the selected American soldier with a shot to the stomach. They would have to take care of their wounded man and thus have fewer men available for the fight. A tactical hit.

Accompanied by the screams of pain from the man he had hit, the private immediately changed position. Several volleys rang out. Bullets whizzed through the dense forest, tore through branches, and were lost somewhere in the Hürtgen Forest without hitting the invisible target. Orders were shouted.

131

They would certainly not follow him right away. Their situation was far too uncertain.

They would shoot aimlessly for a while.

The Americans had no way of knowing where he was hiding. The soldier ran quickly through the trees. He had to get back to the group as soon as possible. When he saw a mark on a tree in the morning twilight, he remembered just in time. Booby trap!

He jumped as high as he could.

Hopefully the wire is only stretched just above the ground, was his only thought.

He landed awkwardly on the wet forest floor and banged his knee against a protruding root. The pain was sharp, but the feared explosion didn't happen. He had done it. The booby trap had not been triggered. The gunfire behind him faded. The pain in his knee grew.

"Damn it!" Honnige cursed, gritted his teeth, got up, and limped on.

When the private heard the click of a pistol lock, he announced his arrival to be on the safe side.

"It's me, Sergeant!"

"Get over here!" he was told.

The sniper hobbled over to his comrades.

"What's going on?" Keller asked immediately.

"Yanks! I've wounded one of them. They're on the forest trail. I don't know how many," replied the man from the german federal state Baden-Wuerttemberg, who came from a village near Heilbronn.

"Are they following you?"

"I don't know."

"You're limping. What's wrong with your knee?"

"Open up."

"Let me see," said the paramedic.

The stretcher with the badly injured man was set down.

Honnige pulled his pant leg up awkwardly. A swelling the size of a chicken egg had formed next to the kneecap.

"Can you move your leg?"

The injured man waved his leg back and forth. His face was contorted with pain.

"I don't think it's broken, but there's a bursa next to the kneecap. The swelling is pushing against it, and that causes a lot of pain. If you're unlucky, a piece of the bone has splintered off. That's just as painful," the medic explained. "I can give you a pill. It will ease the pain for now."

"Give it to me."

"I think they're coming," a comrade warned.

Boom

Loud screams were heard in the midst of the detonation.

"That was one of the booby traps the pioneer told us about. I crashed into that tree root."

"Swerve to the right. I'll cover you and draw them off," Keller ordered.

"I'll stay with you," the sniper insisted.

"That's out of the question! You can't run away when the going gets tough."

"I'm just ballast for the others. They can't move fast enough if I'm with them. The only way we can save Meier's life is if they move as fast as possible. I would only slow them down."

The sergeant looked at the medic. He looked at the mine victim, then at Keller. "Time is of the essence. He needs surgery," he pointed at Meier.

"Get out of here," Honnige confirmed.

Keller nodded. "All right, then. Get going. We'll get out somehow. Straight ahead here and then keep a wide berth. Grossmann, you go ahead and watch out for mines and booby traps! We've come this far. It would be a disaster if we were to die from our own weapons. You and Baar take turns carrying the medic."

"All right."

133

While the men set off with the stretcher, the group leader and Honnige looked for good positions and waited for the enemy. Heart pounding.

How many are there?

The wet uniform was clinging to my body. It was more than uncomfortable. Only the rush of adrenaline coursing through her veins made her unaware of the cold.

When there was still no sign of an enemy after a quarter of an hour, Keller crawled over to his comrade, who was about ten meters away.

"Looks like they've had enough. Nothing's moving."

"Possibly. Now they have to drag the shot GI and the IED victims with them. It's getting light and they don't know how strong we are."

He was right. The American force had retreated, avoiding the battle.

The rain and snow clouds were whipped across the land by strong gusts of wind. The wind picked up to storm speeds. Trees swayed in the strong gusts as if they were thin bushes. The wood creaked. The soldiers froze. Shivering with cold, they held out. They had to be sure that the enemy would not return. When no enemy appeared after half an hour, the sergeant crept through the underbrush to scout the situation.

Twenty minutes later, he was standing next to Honnige, who was shivering with cold. "Get up! I'll support you. They've retreated. There are no casualties near the booby trap and no grave has been dug. But there's a lot of packing material lying around. Almost too much for one man. I guess they've bandaged up the poor devils and are dragging them along. They've had enough."

"Great," the injured man replied, getting to his feet with a groan. "Ahhrg," he puffed out. "I think the medic gave me glucose instead of a painkiller. My knee hurts like hell," the man from Baden-Wuerttemberg added, forcing a grin on his face.

"You never lose your sense of humor, do you?" the sergeant remarked. "Grit your teeth."

He helped the sniper by shouldering his pack and taking the rifle.

"When we get back, put some ice packs on it and you'll be walking around tomorrow," Keller tried to cheer him up, draping the sniper rifle around his neck and supporting the limping private.

"Believe me ..." he pressed, "... when we get back, I don't want to see, hear, or feel anything more of the ice and cold."

They made slow but steady progress. They finally reached their positions without incident. Keller immediately took the sniper to the medics. As the squad leader left the medical tent, he met Grossmann. After the usual greetings, in which everyone had to describe the way back in a few words, the decisive question came.

"How is Meier? Can you tell me anything yet?"

"The doctor said it was high time. Meier is in surgery right now, but tell me, where is the sniper?"

"Don't worry. Honnige is also being treated right now."

Two hours later, First Lieutenant Drexler returned with the rest of the platoon. The officer's face was stone-faced. He was visibly tense. They had lost four men, two were lightly wounded.

"... and then the Americans suddenly retreated," Huber said, reaching for the cup of hot tea. A warming fire blazed in the cannon stove. All around, wet uniforms were hung out to dry.

"There's something in the air again. I can almost smell it. The Americans have brought new troops to the front and the forest is crawling with shock troops. I say they're attacking."

"Not in this filthy weather!"

Josef Keller put the oily rag aside and looked at the breech of his submachine gun. "Ready! What's for dinner today? Does anyone know what the goulash cannon *(Author's note: Goulash cannon = nickname for field kitchen)* spits out?"

135

"Whatever's been available for days. Either sauerkraut or green cabbage."

"Just right for me. I love home cooking."

The next day, Sergeant Major Radomski came by. He stopped the bucket and got out. The slamming of the driver's door sounded tinny. His shiny black boots were dirty in no time, but the sergeant major didn't seem to mind. He whistled the tune of Lale Andersen's *Lili Marleen* and trudged to First Lieutenant Drexler's quarters.

Keller's group returned from lunch just then.

"This is the first time I've seen Radomski up here, and he knows exactly where our boss has set up camp. How is that possible?" Hassel wondered.

"Quite simply," Corporal Hofman explained. "If you look closely, you'll see that the radio car is parked in front of the house."

"I'm more interested in what Radomski is doing here."

The Master Sergeant had disappeared into the house.

"I'll find out. You go to the shelter, I'll catch up with you," said Sergeant Keller, walking toward the bucket truck.

The requisitioned house, where First Lieutenant Drexler had set up quarters for himself and the platoon, was no different from the other buildings and could only be recognized as the platoon leader's quarters by the radio truck with its long antennas.

Keller knocked, waited for an answer, and entered. A signalman met him, greeted him, and stepped outside. A detector followed. Keller walked down the hallway of the former apartment building. Radomski's loud voice was impossible to ignore. When Keller stood in the doorway, Drexler invited him in.

"I've got news," the officer told his squad leader immediately.

136

Author's personal archives, PA-H-111 - a bunker after the onset of winter

Radomski nodded at Keller. "I've got something for you," the Master Sergeant quickly interjected.

"Radomski just gave me a message. He wants me to report to the battalion immediately. I'll probably have to hand over command of the platoon to Sergeant Giessenmeier, since I'm taking over the company."

"And Captain Retzer?"

"He will lead the battalion. He has been promoted to Major and at the same time appointed to the Battalion Staff."

Pause.

The officer looked at his subordinate skeptically. "What brings you here? Do you have a request?"

"Do you know what happened to Meier?" the sergeant asked, evasively referring to the mine victim. He could hardly explain his curiosity about Radomski's visit.

"I visited him this morning. He is doing well under the circumstances. Afterwards I spoke with the staff doctor, Dr. Pfeiffer. The surgery went well. But it was very close. In fact, his life was saved by the quick action that was taken. As soon as Meier is ready for transport, he will be transferred to a hospital.

Keller was visibly relieved.

"Honnige is already fit again. He got a traction and is sitting with the sergeant. He should take it easy for two or three days. In addition to his bad knee, he's also suffering from a bad cold."

The front door opened. Sergeant Giessenmeier and a Corporal came in.

"Then I'll go to my group and tell them the news."

"Just a moment," Radomski asked him to wait. "I have some cutlery and field mail for you."

Keller waited outside the door. He pulled out his cigarettes, lit one, and stood next to Radomski's bucket truck, smoking.

The Master Sergeant arrived about ten minutes later and handed the things to Keller. Keller gladly accepted. "This will put you in a good mood. The last few days have been very tiring."

"I know, Josef. I met with the other sergeants when we turned in the casualty lists. The whole division was decimated."

Radomski was referring to the master sergeants who wore cob rings on the sleeves of their field blouses, identifying them as company sergeants. Although they carried the title of sergeant major (or master sergeant), the supposed rank was merely a service position.

"Is that why we're in the ready room?"

The *Mother of the Company*, as the Major Sergeant was known, looked around. Realizing they were alone, he continued.

138

"I heard there was a big exercise going on nearby. At least three divisions, including an armored division, are right behind us. That gives us hope. I'll bet my entire year's salary that something really big isn't in the air."

"Your word in God's ear."

They said goodbye. Keller brought his group the mail and the goods from the welcome market. There were drops and *Scho-Ka-Kola* (*Author's note:* Caffeinated round chocolate packed in a tin)

The atmosphere in the shelter was great, and the trials of the last raid were forgotten. They sat together and drank the last of the Whisky. There were no seats left in the saloon. The haze of blue cigarette smoke hovered over them in the form of a thick, constantly billowing cloud.

Author's private archive: PA 66 – Landser celebrating

"Let's belt out a few songs," Hofman suggested, joining in. "The rotten bones are trembling ... the world before the Red War ... we have broken the terror ... for us it was a great victory ..."

Now everyone joined in.

"... We will march on ... when everything falls to pieces ... because today Germany hears us ... and tomorrow the whole world".

After all four verses of the Baumann song had been sung, Hassel immediately continued to warble. "We are the old Landser ... we know half the world ... from north to south, from east to west ... we travel without money ..."

The singing and laughing gradually attracted the whole platoon. The place was packed, and every soldier conjured up some black stuff from somewhere. Later in the evening, when one of the comrades took out a trumpet and played the *Florentine March*, everything was perfect.

It was to be the last carefree get-together for a long time. Only two days later the earth shook. It was All Saints' Day. It began in the morning, just before 8 o'clock. Sergeant Keller was about to announce the duty roster when the American artillery pounded the German positions with thousands of shells. The staging area was not spared, although it was not as badly hit as the HKL itself.

Enlisted soldiers raced around. Field telephones rang.

"Yes, General," the battalion commander confirmed the order. "We're moving out immediately!"

"Alaaaaarm!" they shouted.

Steel helmets on and strapped. Weapons to the man.

Does the paddock fit? Don't forget your haversack.

"Did you bring the tent?" they asked.

Hustle and bustle! In between, the howling of the grenades and the crash of the shots. We moved forward again. The enemy attacked. This time with artillery preparation.

First Lieutenant Drexler sat in his bucket truck, tossed from side to side by the rapid movement. Still, he tried to study the map. After an hour, the hellish spell in the sky was over. The latest situation was relayed by radio. American units were making a massive push against the front lines.

The 28th US Division of the Pennsylvania National Guard sent its regiments into battle.

The 109th US Regiment stormed towards Hürtgen, the 112th US Regiment over the Vossenack to the heights of Kommerscheid and the 110th US Regiment towards the Ochsenkopf and the bunker line there.

First Lieutenant Drexler's objective was Vossenack. He and his company were to support the troops in the village. The rest of the battalion was to be deployed in the surrounding area.

As they moved into the area, they expected the worst, but aside from a few grenades falling to the left and right of their route, the company remained largely undisturbed.

When they reached the Eifel village, the German soldiers noticed the effects of the artillery attack. Ambulances were rolling toward them. Smoke was rising. Hardly a house had been spared. Almost all had been hit. Some houses were burning. Comrades ran through the debris-strewn streets. They had survived a hellish storm of steel. Orders were shouted. Tank destroyers on a self-propelled gun, followed by towing vehicles with a Anti-tank guns attached, roared past.

"They will cross the main road and rush Schmidt!"

"The road is in the area of our figure eight."

"So they will be looking for another supply route, and the only possible supply route there is a paved forest road through the Kallschlucht gorge," said the newly appointed company commander at the last muster.

The map reading had paid off. It had to be that way. His military experience left no other alternative.

"It's steep and narrow. No tank can get up there."

"I hope not! We must send scouts to find out! Occupy the houses."

The company swarmed out. At the same moment, the roar of heavy engines could be heard. The first tank shells whizzed through the air, descending and exploding with a crash.

Wham

Drexler watched as the Shermans pulled off the main road onto the large meadow in front of the village and spread out to attack on a broad front.

Boom wham

More and more explosions ripped through the air. The burning village took the brunt of it, but the meadow in front of the village was also hit hard. Through the binoculars, Drexler could see that the two US tanks in front had hit mines. Broken tracks. The two giants were unable to maneuver. The heavy rollers had been pushed deep into the ground.

"Our pioneers have mined the meadow," he said triumphantly, then ducked his head as a tank shell exploded near his position.

Infantry followed the tanks. Machine guns rattled. Grenade launchers fired.

Anti-tank gun crews searched for their targets. The battle for Vossenack had begun.

Sergeant Keller ran crouched through the streets, leaped over some rubble, and pressed himself against the wall of a whitewashed house.

They made it.

Grossmann and Baar were right behind him. Keller ran to the end of the house and peeked around the corner. His left hand shot up. He waved his men to him and took off. His target was the shot-up house across the street.

"We'll find the best cover in the ruins. They'll have to pass through here if they want to get to the center of the village," he shouted to drown out the noise of the battle.

Again and again, grenades exploded around them. When Huber and Hassel were the last to cross the street, bullet fragments whistled around their heads. Both took cover behind the fence of the ruined house. Her nerves were on the verge of collapse. They were shaking and scared to death. Only the deep-seated military drill and the urge to survive gave them the strength not to cower and give up.

Hassel lost an ammunition box when it hit the ground. It hit a large stone and burst open.

"Shit," the gunner II of the MG 42 whined, picking up the belt.

"The machine gun on me!" Keller's voice thundered over to them.

Grossmann and Baar fired the first shots.

"The Yank is coming!"

Huber quickly reached Keller. A grenade had blown a large hole in the wall of the house next to a window. The private placed the bipod of his weapon on the wall.

The machine gun was ready to fire. Hassel joined him, panting heavily. Huber tucked the butt into his shoulder and ran his eyes over the sights. They were coming in groups. He crooked his right forefinger. The rattle began. Muzzle flashes flashed. Shell casings were ejected.

Hassel held the belt with both hands to keep it moving smoothly and without inhibition. The first Rifleman fired into the middle of the line of attackers. Some of them jerked their hands up, and one or two immediately collapsed, mortally wounded. It was as if they were running into an invisible wall of steel.

"They're taking cover," said the sergeant who had observed the machine gun's effect. "Stay on them!"

The enemy fire intensified. Huber's machine gun had stopped the flank attack. The open field in front of them and the road leading into the village were directly in the machine gun's field of fire. There was no way around that side without being seen. The Russian veteran fired his volleys at the enemy again and again, then the first grenades exploded at the house.

Wham

Shrapnel and dust were thrown up. Huber instinctively pulled the machine gun into the house.

"They've taken us out and are sending in the tanks."

143

Panic was visible in Hassel's eyes. "Should we run?"

The rattling of chains, followed by the dry firing of machine guns, confirmed our suspicions.

Boom

The shells burst into the wall of the house, tearing more holes.

"Ahh," a death scream echoed through the room.

One of the new soldiers lay bloodied under the remains of a wall. Any help came too late.

"Damn, I've been hit," Baar cried as well. His cheek had been grazed. His face was completely covered in blood.

Keller immediately attended to his comrade. "It's nothing," he tried to calm Baar, holding a handkerchief to the wound. "It's just a stupid place for a bandage."

"Thank you", he breathed, relieved.

"We need to get out of here."

The group quickly gathered and slipped out the back, out of sight of the enemy, through a window into the garden. Another gauntlet was thrown. They hurried to the fence and jumped over it, while Huber stayed in front of it with the machine gun, taking up position. "I'll cover you. Get out of here!"

Hassel took his place next to Shooter I.

Three small detonations were heard from the house. "They're there. Those were hand grenades," Huber said. "They're coming around the corner."

They came with full force. On the street, the tanks rolled toward them one by one as the first American soldiers appeared at the ruined house. Despite the danger of the tanks, Huber pulled the trigger. At the same time, the first GI automatic rifles barked.

Hassel thought he was watching the shells fall in slow motion. He was afraid, terribly afraid, which made his knees weak and shaky. The enemy was overpowering, the shells were getting closer and closer, and he felt helpless. Then his hands began to tremble.

"The time has come. Come on, get up! Get up! Get out of here!" shouted Huber, jumping up and pulling Hassel with him.

But as soon as they had jumped over the fence and covered a few meters, they had to throw themselves back to the ground. A volley of machine-gun fire came right over their heads.

First Lieutenant Drexler saw two Shermans, followed by infantry, making their way around a house. Only then did he notice the group of fleeing soldiers. A machine gun seemed to be covering their retreat. The Shermans opened fire with their mounted machine guns. The company commander looked around quickly. There was a towing vehicle only twenty meters from him.

"Where there's a towing vehicle, the anti-tank-gun is not far away," he shouted, running to the towing vehicle. The officer was lucky. The anti-tank-gun was indeed not far. The target was quickly identified. The gun was turned and a tank grenade was loaded.

The gunner took aim.

"Ready!"

He became a sign.

"Fire!"

The firing sound was loud. Muzzle flash flashed on the barrel.

Boom

While the anti-tank-gun operators wore earplugs, Drexler covered his ears with his hands.

"Shoot them," he yelled, and ran back to his starting position, where his reporter was waiting for him.

Keller paused. He took cover and fired in the direction of the pursuers until his magazine was empty. He quickly reloaded.

Author's private archive: PA-N-0113 - Sherman tank

Huber and Hassel were pinned down. A Sherman rolled toward them. The American infantry kept their heads down for the moment, but the damn tank kept firing. Then there was a crash. The first shell had gone over the tank and detonated in the wall of the house. Screams!

It must have hit the GI's in cover.

Another detonation followed.

Boom

This time a grenade hit the ground near the tank. Stones and metal shards drummed against the steel. The force of the explosion broke the track with a crash. The Sherman rolled another meter, braked, and was forced to stop. The pipe swung with the turret. The second steel colossus had also stopped and was already firing at the helpful 75 mm anti-tank-gun.

Boom

"Hit!" shouted Keller as a loud explosion sent a jet of flame shooting out of the unmaneuverable US tank, followed by thick black smoke billowing into the sky.

"Run," the sergeant's voice blared. "Run!"

The machine-gunners jumped up and ran as fast as they could to join their comrades.

Privat Author: Deepai iqhE6ApZ

Privat Author: Deepai l4mhIjS7

The US forces pushed into Vossenack with concentrated force. Every house was fought over. Downed US tanks blocked the streets. Acrid smoke filled the air. At times, visibility was completely obscured by smoke from burning ruins. Often the enemy could not be seen until he was right in front of you. Fierce hand-to-hand combat was the result. The firefights never stopped.

Despite being outnumbered, the Germans managed to hold part of the village until the evening. But the situation was beyond catastrophic.

"We urgently need support. The only self-propelled gun *(Author's note: A self-propelled gun = gun mounted on a partially armored vehicle)* that was here has been destroyed. If no help arrives, we'll have to evacuate Vossenack tomorrow at the latest," First Lieutenant Drexler shouted into the radio.

They were exhausted, tired, drained. Drexler almost gave the order to retreat, but fortunately the enemy had stopped fighting by nightfall.

Sergeant Keller and his squad were lying in one of the ruins. They had half a roof over their heads and good cover. Baar's wound on his cheek was being bandaged by the medic. The soldier with the Red Cross bandage on his upper arm was crawling from position to position, running from ruin to ruin. He had reached them a few minutes ago. Satisfied, he closed the first aid kit.

"It's a good thing you cleaned the wound ..." he said finally, "... because with the dirt here, you would have quickly caught an infection, and that's no joke."

The slightly wounded Hessian grinned, pulling back the corner of his mouth on the healthy side of his cheek more than the other. "That's what I thought, and I ruined the best handkerchief my Bärbel gave me."

"Is there anyone else here I can do something good for?"

"Look at my hand," Hassel whispered and moved over. "When I was changing the barrel on the machine gun, I held the asbestos flap the wrong way and burned my flipper. It hurt like hell."

"Let me see."

The medic let the pale beam of his flashlight glide over his hand. Two large blisters, the top layer already torn to shreds, immediately caught the eye. The pink flesh underneath was clearly visible. Every touch must have hurt Machine Gunner II.

"When did this happen?"

"A long time ago. Sometime during the day. I didn't feel it in battle."

"It hurts all the more now, doesn't it?"

Hassel nodded covertly.

"Don't be ashamed, comrade. You've held up well."

Keller had overheard the conversation and patted the young Landser on the shoulder. "Well done!"

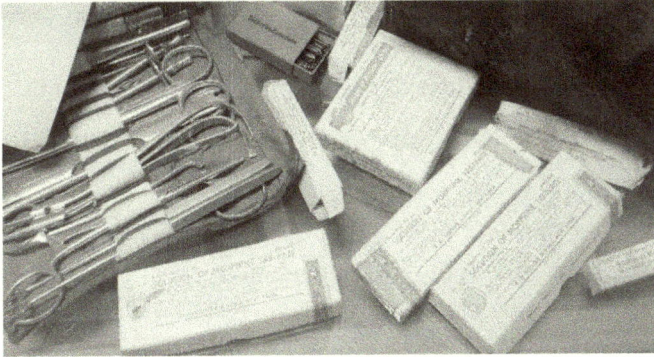

*Author's private archive: PA-N-0115 and PA-N- 0116 - medical kits
(german and US-m-kits mixed)*

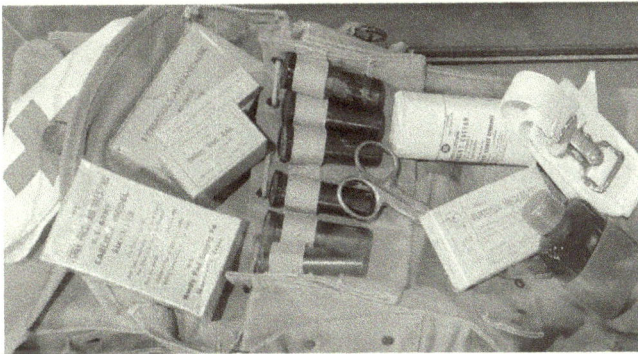

Proud that the highly decorated sergeant was pleased with his performance, he allowed himself to be treated.

Five minutes later, the medic packed up. "I put some burn ointment on it. Don't lose the bandage. I'll come back tomorrow and check the wound again. Do you need any painkillers?"

"No, I don't think so."

"Good, then I'll continue."

Baar patted the medic on the shoulder. "Make sure you don't accidentally walk into a ruin where the Yank is sitting!"

"As soon as the cheek is treated, the first stupid comments come in," the medic laughed.

"I was serious. It's easy to lose track of things with all that chaos out there."

"Do you know where Sergeant Giessenmeier or First Lieutenant Drexler are?" Keller wanted to find out.

"Giessenmeier? I think he's been hit. Drexler isn't far from here. Just go down the street and take the next intersection. That's where I just came from."

"Thank you."

"See you tomorrow, and take care," the paramedic said goodbye and disappeared into the darkness of the night.

"What's the situation?" Keller called to Grossmann, who was lying on the second floor of the collapsed house and had a good view.

"Everything is quiet. You can see stealth lights now and then. I think they're picking up their wounded."

"Then they won't attack again until daylight tomorrow at the earliest," the sergeant was sure. "I'll go to the company commander. Hofman, you take command until then. If I were you, I'd get something to eat and then find a reasonably comfortable place to sleep," Keller suggested, then left the ruins as well.

When the bucket truck had stopped, Major Retzer undid the leather strap of his steel helmet. He literally jumped out of the all-terrain vehicle and hurried into the requisitioned building that housed the regimental staff.

"Colonel," he began without mincing words after his commander had greeted him. "The situation is dire. The enemy is breaking through with..."

The regimental commander held up his hand. "Wait a minute!" he said, waving Retzer over. "Come here."

The Major walked straight to his superior's desk.

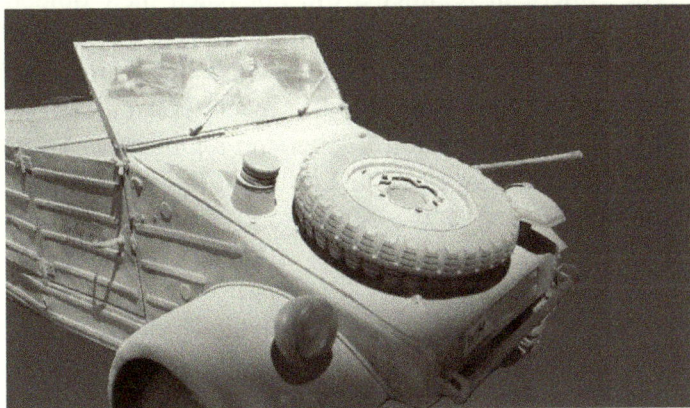

Private archive of the author: PA-N-0117 - bucket truck (VW)

"Look at the map. I was on the phone with the other battalion commanders. Since you and your unit are so close, I thought we'd talk in person, and I also wanted to congratulate you on taking over the battalion and being promoted at the same time."

"Thank you."

Major Retzer clicked his heels.

"Well," the high-ranking Wehrmacht officer began to report, "I had a briefing a few minutes ago. I can reassure you. The Americans have chosen a most inconvenient time for their offensive. I received a call from the division commander hours ago. Field Marshal Model has ordered General von Manteuffel to conduct a large-scale maneuver in the vicinity. I have been informed that two divisions are already on their way here. In addition, the Greyhound Division is coming as a third unit."

"The 116th Panzer Division?" Retzer asked immediately.

"That's right. They've already received their marching orders."

"I hope they arrive in time. My men have been hit hard. Vossenack can't be held much longer without support."

"The American regiments did not reach their objectives. They were repulsed at Ochsenkopf. Vossenack was held. Parts of the 112th US Regiment marched past to reach Kommerscheid and Schmidt, but they also failed to reach their objectives and were forced to retreat. A third American regiment was stopped by our mine belts. If we can just hold out long enough for our reinforcements to arrive, we can make it!

Retzer was relieved.

It began to rain again. Keller cursed inwardly as he walked down the road. Everything seemed cold and sinister. Two comrades carried a fallen soldier back on a stretcher. A still-burning piece of armor gave off an orange-red light. Every breath near burning oil stung the lungs.

"Sergeant Keller, you're just in time," said a delighted First Lieutenant Drexler. "Giessenmeier's been killed. You will take over the platoon."

"Me?" the Russian veteran blurted out, stunned.

"That's exactly what I said."

"By your command," Keller added, recognizing a questioning look in Drexler's eyes.

"I've already asked the battalion for reinforcements. Let's hope we get them. They'll take up position here with their platoon."

The officer's finger rested on a map. Keller was being briefed on the current situation. The company commander had occupied every house, every ruin, every pile of rubble that was remotely defensible. He was going to hold the village. To the last man if necessary. The war had now reached the homeland with its ground troops. The enemy was in Germany. Every inch of ground had to be defended to the last man.

The rain had not stopped. Patches of fog had appeared. They had settled over the land like little blankets of sky, seeming to bind the autumn chill to the ground.

Corporal Hofman stretched. He had taken the last watch and had been posted to the upper level an hour ago. It was getting light, but the fog meant that little or nothing could be seen.

"Damn continuous rain, damn fog," the Landser grumbled.

One by one they awoke. Breakfast was sparse. Water or cold tea from the canteen, yesterday's sandwiches and, depending on what was available, tinned sausage, cheese or jam. The faces of the soldiers looked dull. They were dirty, and most of them were covered with stubble.

"I can't see them, but I can hear the engine noise despite the miserable weather," Hofman called to his comrades.

The crack of a machine gun and the sound of grenades heralded another Allied attack.

"Everybody on guard," Keller yelled.

Huber couldn't see. All he could see ahead was rainwater and patches of fog, but he didn't care. Shooter I pulled the trigger, firing short bursts into the white wall of cloud over and over again. It soothed his conscience.

All the snipers of the battalion were assembled. Major Retzer, who knew how important this special type of weapon was, wanted to use his lone fighters in a targeted manner. The situation at the front was quickly explained and the objectives of the US forces were discussed.

"There is a fight for every house in Vossenack. Kommerscheid and Schmidt have already fallen. Help is on the way and some of it has already arrived. Gentlemen, the Americans have only one supply route along this part of the front. It leads steeply up through the Kallschlucht gorge. They have big problems there. We will give them even more."

The major looked into the men's eyes.

"I bet on you. In the year 9 AD, Hermann the Cheruscan used the forest to fight the legions of the Roman Emperor. He was victorious against Varus and his military superiority. We will also use the forest. Tree archers do immense damage. Go

153

into the forest, spread out along the supply route and wear down the enemy.

Georg Honnige still had these words in his head as he set off in the fog and rain. This time, the successful sniper had been given five days' rations. The lone fighters quickly parted ways. The man from Baden-Wuerttemberg moved alone through the woods, always on the lookout for the enemy. Although the private was out of the artillery's line of fire, it took him some time to get used to the almost constant thunder of the various guns.

He was in his element. Alone in no man's land and on the hunt. The only reminder of his fall was a large bruise on his knee. The swelling was long gone and the cold was gone. The dreaded cold with fever and sore throat had not come.

Thank God.

The tank was full, the line of march clear. Sergeant Georg Lannert's assault gun rolled through the night. The crew was well-rehearsed and had already been decorated for their successes. Johann Eck steered the steel colossus, concentrating on the route, while gunner and radio operator Thomas Kleimann had a heated discussion with gunner Arno Tiller about whether the military exercise at Gut Schlenderhahn was important or not.

"Shut up," Eck grumbled. "It's disgusting weather and I can't see ten feet. If I'm not going to put our assault rifle in the ditch, I need some peace and quiet!"

The others held on for a few minutes, then Kleimann had a question. "Where exactly are we going?"

"To the west wall," replied Sergeant Lannert. "The Americans want to take the Rur dam, and we're going to stop them."

"The comrades from the west wall are very lucky that we're close by."

"I would say it was extremely fortunate that we had our ammunition team with us during the exercise. We arrived as ordered, ready for battle, so to speak."

The conversation fell silent again. A good half hour later, the weather improved a bit.

"The rain is finally stopping. It's cruel to drive in this weather and only with camouflage lights," Eck grumbled and accelerated the assault gun III, which was armed with a 7.5 cm cannon and an MG 34.

The Maybach engine had six forward gears and one reverse gear. With a tank capacity of 310 liters, the assault gun could travel between 90 and 165 km at a maximum speed of 44 km/h, depending on the terrain.

A 10 watt VHF radio was installed for communication. However, only the vehicles above the platoon leader could transmit and receive. All other assault vehicles could only receive messages.

The terrain became more hilly. The rain started again. This time it pattered so hard that the speed was reduced to walking pace. The initial drumming of the water on the outer steel of the armored vehicle had become a staccato, the monotonous beat of which caused the crew to fall asleep.

Eck was quite pleased with that. When the tank was quiet, he could concentrate better on driving. The assault gunner loved driving the heavy steel colossus. The rattling of the tracks and the humming of the engine were his world. He whistled the tank song softly. It was only when the road became increasingly bumpy and Kleimann banged his head against the radio that everyone woke up to his scream of pain.

"Ouch. What kind of lousy gravel driver are you?" he taunted.

Eck took it in stride. Lannert yawned loudly and the platoon leader's voice creaked out of the radio.

"1st Platoon, head for the Falcon's Nest!"

Eck, who had discussed the route with Lannert before leaving, asked for a little help. "Georg, look at the map again! We're the first vehicle and I don't want to make a fool of myself."

"Falkennest is on the Brandenberg-Bergstein ridge."

After another 500 meters the tracked vehicle swung in and the rest of the train followed.

The wall of fog slowly dissipated, improving visibility in Vossenack to some degree. There was fighting all over the town. Soldiers ran through the streets in groups or platoons, engaging in relentless firefights and storming house after house. A merciless battle had broken out.

Hofman saw the top of a U.S. soldier's helmet emerge from behind the stone wall. Then another. With each step, they bobbed up and down like upturned cups. The men crept along the wall.

"They're coming from the right," he warned his comrades, pointing to the helmets, and Huber swung the barrel of the MG 42 around.

On command, the US soldiers jumped over the wall or ran around it. The target was the house where the soldiers were holed up. Within seconds, a fierce firefight broke out. Leiber caught the bullets from the rifles, winced, and fell to the ground.

Baar emptied the carbine and inserted a new loading strip. Crouching down saved his life. A hand grenade exploded in front of the window he was shooting from. Some of the shrapnel was thrown through the window opening and dug into the walls and ceiling, leaving cracks and scratches.

"They're already within grenade range."

Baar rushed upstairs and saw a US soldier get up and run to the wall of the house. His comrades were covering him with fire. Several rapid-fire rifles shot bullets from their barrels. The bullets crashed against the wall of the house, hitting window frames and tearing out splinters of wood.

Regardless of the hail of enemy bullets, the Landser took aim, aimed briefly, and pulled the trigger. The attacker fell to the ground, hit, and Baar immediately took cover. Instinctively, he pulled a hand grenade from his belt and unscrewed the breech cover. A quick glance out the window. Three or four Americans

156

were now charging the house. They fired without aiming. The German soldier pulled the safety cord, counted off and threw the hand grenade out the window. He yelled loudly to warn his comrades: "Attention! Hand grenade!"

Boom

Immediately after the explosion, he was ready to fire again.

"Sergeant Keller," the radio operator yelled, trying to drown out the noise of the battle. "We have orders to retreat. Vossenack has to be evacuated for now. The other two platoons have already been pushed out of the village!"

"Spark through that, we need a barrage!"

While the rearguard fiddled with the buttons on his radio, the sergeant immediately turned to the machine-gunner. "Huber, you take the road under fire, you retreat slowly, I have to go to the other two squads and tell them we're retreating."

As soon as he spoke, Keller ran out of the house and crouched down, regardless of whether Huber was already firing down the street.

"He's crazy," Hassel shouted, opening a new box of ammunition.

"That's just Josef."

Boom

The requested barrage came faster than expected. Three grenades, fired in quick succession, exploded between the rows of US soldiers.

"Get out," shouted the reporting soldier. "The anti tank gun only has five grenades left. They're covering us."

One by one, the soldiers retreated between the ruins. Sergeant Keller's platoon had also managed to break away from the enemy. His men's faces were blank and expressionless. They were dirty, some of them were shaking and were happy to have escaped death once again.

They reached the rest of the company exhausted. Keller had stopped, turned around and looked at the dying Vossensack. In the background, he thought he could make out a small column of tanks heading for Kallschlucht.

They could not be ignored. Honnige was amazed that he could get this far without meeting an opponent.

The forest allows it. It is too opaque. You can't draw a clear front line, was his conclusion.

He had been moving with extreme caution for almost an hour.

They must have outposts, the sniper was sure, as he retreated into the dense green of sprouting spruces to rest. He pulled a can of Scho-Ka-Kola from his pocket and bit off a piece of the caffeinated chocolate.

This will give me the energy I will need soon, he thought, and treated himself to a second piece. While he ate, the private kept a close eye on the area, listening for any sounds. Eventually he was sure he was completely alone. It was his habit to light a cigarette after eating. After smoking, he packed up, crawled out of the thicket, and continued on his way. Honnige used a compass to get his bearings and reached his destination around evening. He was now directly on the American supply line.

The terrain in front of him was steep. According to his map, he had to be right next to the Kallschlucht gorge. It was time to find a place to camp for the night. It would be dark soon.

Pitch black is a good weather to hide!

The sniper scanned the area. A natural hollow between two giant trees seemed like a good place to camp. In front of him was the forest, behind him, or rather below him, the slope. The experienced lone fighter was sure that no enemy would come from there.

The place is ideal.

Honnige unbuckled his backpack and the canvas of his tent. With a few practiced movements, he stretched the camouflaged canvas over the roof. He had found a reasonably dry spot, well protected from the wind. Nevertheless, the corporal placed additional leaves and a few pine branches around his camp until a small screen was piled up. He became invisible. He gathered more leaves to cover himself against the cold of the night.

Tomorrow my war begins, were his last thoughts, then he fell asleep.

Early in the morning, before the sun had fully risen, he got up. After a meager breakfast, he packed what he needed and left the camp. He wanted to continue using the space and walked an estimated three to four kilometers away. The rumble of artillery reached his ears in the distance. Pause for a moment.

No whistling, no howling means no grenades.

He was lucky. He was not in the line of fire. Finally he reached his destination. It was the forest road to Schmidt and Kommerscheid. The supply line of the US Army.

His camouflage was perfect. Pine branches were stuck in the wire mesh that was pulled over his steel helmet. He was also wearing a camouflage uniform. Now he had to find a tactic. He couldn't get too close, but he had to find a strategically advantageous spot. Honnige continued to climb. Despite the cold, sweat poured down his forehead. Finally, he reached an excellent spot. From here, the sniper had a good view of the trail in three places. All three locations were within acceptable range of his weapon.

There was already a lot of activity on the relatively well-maintained trail. Jeeps were driving up. The all-terrain military vehicles climbed the hill with ease, despite the rain soaking the ground. Trucks or even tanks, on the other hand, had a hard time making progress. The pioneers worked like mad.

Over the next fifteen minutes, the private tested several positions. He lay down in the firing position and looked through the scope.

Perfect!

The early morning fog had long since lifted, leaving behind the cold of the night. It was freezing, but the view was clear. That was all he cared about.

Three excellent positions.

At least two shots could be fired from the first position. Honnige checked the ammunition and the rifle once more, then took the first position and fired. The stock rested against his cheek and he watched the enemy through the telescopic sight. The hunter was looking for a worthy target. The soldiers swarmed. Man after man, vehicle after vehicle, unconsciously passed through the crosshairs. At some point, Georg Honnige got stuck on a person. He saw the GI only from behind. The American was waving his hands. He seemed to be giving orders. In any case, two pioneers dropped a wooden plank and ran away. Apparently they had to help because one of the vehicles was sliding in the mud.

My comrades do it the same way, he thought.

Author's private archive, PA-0-022 – German Pioneers build stick dam

Honnige decided to take the shot. Holding his breath, he found the pressure point and pulled his right forefinger through.

The shot cracked and the target collapsed. Now it wasn't just scurrying around in one spot, now the area in front of him resembled an ant hill that had been poked with a wooden stick. No one knew where the shot had come from. A few GIs fired volleys into the woods, but no one came close to firing in the direction of the sniper.

Should I change position? No! Not until after the second shot.

He stayed in position, watching the scene through the scope. They were looking for him. An officer was standing in his jeep with binoculars to his eyes.

I saw you first.

The shot rang out, the American collapsed, and the sniper rifle was immediately withdrawn. Change of position. Honnige rushed to the next selected position. Back in position, the private noticed that the American supply had stopped. They were avoiding the open areas. They were sure to send out a squad or two to look for him. He had a sergeant in his sights when something caught his eye. Among all the trucks, tanks, and jeeps fighting their way up the narrow path was a tank. The lone German fighter immediately drew his weapon. He pulled one of the explosive rounds from his jacket pocket and loaded it. Then he fired again. They stood still. It all had the character of a target practice. Honnige's shot at the tanker caused a huge explosion. The resulting fireball even shot over the treetops for a moment. Dark smoke rose. The sniper instinctively refrained from firing the fourth shot he had planned. He had to get away. Slowly, he crawled back. When he felt safe in the cover of the forest, he stood up and ran.

The supplies!

His thoughts kept circling around the gorge. Honnige decided to return to the troops and report his discovery. If there were two or three heavy machine guns and some grenade launchers at his position, they could stop the enemy's entire supply. He had to get to Major Retzer as fast as possible. He raced through the woods like a man possessed, finally reaching his own lines breathlessly and coming upon a platoon preparing for an assault. The man from Baden-Württemberg was so out of breath that he had to start three times before the lieutenant of the infantry platoon understood him.

The radio operator contacted Major Retzer, who sent a bucket truck to pick up Honnige.

The lieutenant waited until the radio call was over, then tried to talk to Honnige. "It's clear you didn't say anything over the radio. The enemy might be listening. Anyway, I have to get out there with my men now. Is there anything I should know?"

"No ..." the sniper shook his head. "... unless you go as far as the Kallschlucht."

"You were that far ahead?"

"Yes."

The officer looked respectfully at the lance corporal. "And what's there?"

"The Americans' supply route."

"You didn't encounter any enemy the whole way there and back?"

Another shake of the head.

"But it's possible some GIs have taken up positions there now. I blew up a tanker. They'll be looking for me."

"Thanks for the warning."

The lieutenant raised his arm.

"Forward!"

After Honnige calmed down, he did what he liked to do best. He smoked. It was only after the third cigarette that the bucket truck appeared.

"Are you the sniper I'm supposed to get?" the driver shouted, trying to drown out the sound of the engine.

The lone hunter nodded and got in.

"Pretty loud."

"The exhaust is in the a... ,uhh ... I mean, is broken and the repair shop has no replacement, so it has to go like this."

162

They rumbled down the street. Honnige noticed that the driver's uniform pants and boots were very dirty. "Stuck?" he pointed at the boots.

"Yes. This could be bad weather. Everything is muddy. There are places you just can't get through. I got stuck on a bend earlier, so it took a while. Thank God some pioneers came along. They put some wooden planks under me and pushed me along. I was free in a few minutes.

When the driver mentioned the wooden planks, the sniper remembered his first kill. He immediately pushed the thought out of his mind.

This is war. They are your opponents. They will kill you and your comrades if you don't move faster!

They passed the place the man behind the wheel had described earlier. The driver drove slowly on the wooden planks and passed the danger point without any problems. Shortly after, they saw the pioneers marching back to the shelters. Once again, the soldier in the bucket truck raised his hand in thanks and waved.

Arriving at the battalion command post, Honnige got out. His unkempt appearance made him look wild. The sniper rifle, its barrel wrapped in linen and greenery, had a magnetic effect on the clerk's office soldiers. The lance corporal was stared at, partly in awe, partly in disapproval. He stopped in front of a sergeant making a phone call. After he hung up, he looked up. "There you are. The Major is waiting."

Sergeant Lannert opened the hatch and stood in the opening. The cold morning air immediately made the assault gun commander wide awake. The icy wind blew into his face, chasing away any sign of sleep.

"You have a wonderful view from here," he said to his comrades and took a deep breath.

The heavy tracked vehicle jerked around a bend.

"It's damn tight up here. I hope you know how to drive," he shouted to the driver.

Johann Eck, his eyes slightly red, slowed down a bit and accelerated as soon as he rounded the bend.

"I'll drive you around blind."

"You are and always will be an old show-off," the Sergeant laughed. He was more than satisfied with Eck. Lannert was sure he had one of the best assault gunners in the Wehrmacht on board.

They had finally arrived at their destination. The battery commander's bucket truck stopped. Lieutenant Aumann got out. With a wave, he indicated where Lannert should position himself. Final instructions followed. Less than an hour later, the entire battery was in place.

"Our platoon has the best spot," said Kleimann, who stretched his legs with the others.

Tiller, the only smoker in the crew, immediately lit a cigarette. "Finally," he said with relief after the first puff, exhaling the blue vapor with relish. "I just didn't feel right without my morning cigarette."

"Where is Eck anyway?" asked Kleimann.

"I don't know. I thought he went to the meeting with Lannert?"

"What a load of rubbish. That would be a first."

"Then he does his morning ablutions in the woods. Did he bring the spade?"

While they were still thinking, the driver returned. He held his open canteen in his hand. Bright steam rose from the opening.

"Well, that's the advantage of knowing where the battery is," he said jubilantly. "How about some hot coffee?"

"Fresh coffee? Always a pleasure."

"Well, I said hot coffee, not fresh coffee."

The bakelite cups were filled. The hot drink did them good. The warmth brought a pleasant sensation to the exhausted bodies

164

of the assault gun crew. The sound of engines could be heard. Ammunition trucks were coming. A truck stopped. An older corporal jumped out of the cab. "Let's go!" he yelled in a rough Bavarian dialect. "The trailer's for you," he added, uncoupling the ammunition trailer.

Lannert returned at the same time. He still wore the standard field cap. The sergeant had pulled the camouflage blouse over his field shirt. He walked up to his comrades, stopped in front of them, and rested his right elbow slightly on the holster of his 08 pistol. "I see the ammo's already here. We're about to get started," he said without beating around the bush.

The corporal got back into his truck. "I'll pick up the trailer later," he mumbled, barely intelligible, and drove off.

"First things first," Lannert began to report. "We'll have a hot breakfast. Today it's scrambled eggs with bacon."

"They really mean well with us," said Kleimann happily.

"I can't believe it," said Tiller, tossing the stub of his cigarette to the ground. The embers hissed on the damp earth and within a few seconds the cigarette stub stopped smoking.

"I already knew that. When I went to get the coffee, the goulash cannon was already in operation," Eck grinned.

"And what happens next? That wasn't all, was it?"

"No! See that village down there?"

All three looked past Lannert into the valley.

"That's Vossenack. The American drove our men out of there and has been occupying the village ever since. We'll put the heat on him. Then the infantry will charge forward and kick the GIs out again."

Ninety minutes later, they sat in position with full bellies. The field caps had given way to steel helmets. An invisible tension crackled in the air. The assault cannon was ready to fire. Lannert stood in the hatch, scanning the area with his binoculars. Kleimann had his headset on, listening for the crucial radio message. The gunner also had the ammunition in sight.

The second battery was already thundering away.

"Now," the radio operator confirmed. "Fire at will," he added immediately.

"Fire!" repeated Tiller and fired the first grenade. There was a metallic click, followed by a muffled thud. The steel casing vibrated slightly. Kleimann heaved the next grenade into the barrel and slammed the bolt shut. Tiller glanced through the sight, made a slight adjustment, and yelled a warning: "Fire!" before firing the next shell. The obligatory look through the sight followed. It was on target. Now he was satisfied.

Gunner and loader began to work obsessively. Fire, load, fire, load. The entire battery fired its shells seemingly indiscriminately at Vossenack, enveloping the American occupiers of the village in a deadly storm of steel.

The assault gun battery mercilessly exploited its advantageous position. Shell after shell left the 7.5 cm barrels of the assault guns. A gigantic hellfire poured over Vossenack, mercilessly destroying and extinguishing streets, buildings and any life that stood in its way.

The second platoon of the first battalion was in the staging area. The incessant rain of the last days and weeks had taken its toll. Mud everywhere you looked. The ground was soaked to the bursting point and seemed to be overflowing. There was hardly a position or foxhole that was not under water.

The cannon stoves were burning in the shelters. Almost every space around the stove was covered with clothes hung out to dry. The soldiers, experienced in extreme weather conditions, had long since dug out their winter clothing.

"... and above all, you must be careful not to get trench foot," Hofman explained to young Hassel.

"Trench foot?" He rolled his eyes and looked at the Russian veteran questioningly.

"You don't know what trench foot is?"

"Where from?"

"Well, I know from my old man. My father warned me about it before I joined the Army. He told me that a number of comrades at Verdun had to have their feet amputated because of it," Grossmann interrupted.

"Don't keep me in suspense any longer."

Grossmann pulled his snuff box from his pocket, tapped it once on the chunky wooden table, then sprinkled a pinch on the back of his left hand. His nose wandered habitually over the brown pile of tobacco, sniffing it all in. The veteran soldier shoved the snuffbox back into his pocket, pulled out a handkerchief, blew his nose, and put on a serious expression. "When you're standing in water all the time, and your boots are soaked through like a wet rag, and your feet are constantly wet, your skin gets very soft. You automatically rub it off until there's nothing but raw flesh sticking out. The whole thing becomes infected because you can't find a dry place. The foot turns black, literally dies, and has to be removed. That's trench foot."

Hassel turned white as a sheet. "That's disgusting," he exclaimed in disgust. "You're kidding me, aren't you?"

"No, comrade! They don't do that," Keller clarified. "That's why our pioneers mostly laid wooden planks to serve as paths, and drainage channels and wooden planks were also installed in the trenches and foxholes. We learned not only from the 1914-1918 war, but also from our experiences in Russia. There we had muddy weather ad nauseam, followed by the iciest winters imaginable. If you didn't get trench foot, your toes would freeze off."

The door flew open. Günter Baar came in, moaning loudly. "It's freezing cold. If it keeps up like this, we'll have our first snow in the next few days."

He had only a band-aid on his cheek, and the wound was healing nicely.

"Close the door," Hofman grumbled. "There's a cold draft."

"You're upset about a little breeze? I've just seen a detector get off his bike, stiff as a board. And the poor guy was filthy

167

from top to bottom. A living lump of mud," the Landser laughed out loud.

There was a knock.

"Come in!"

A soldier stood in the doorway. "A message from the battalion, Sir," said the Motorcyclist soldier.

He looked very excited.

Drexler put down the cup of tea and stood up. "What's going on? When did the radio message come in?"

"No radio message! A reporter soldier! He just drove up."

"What?"

Voices outside the house. The door opened and a dirty-faced Reporter Soldier stood in the hallway. He pushed past the radio operator, entered the new company commander's room, greeted him shakily, and pulled a letter from his reporter bag. "Directly from Major Retzer, First Lieutenant."

"Thank you."

The officer took the message, tore open the envelope and read it. He sat down again and read the message a second time. "Radomski," he called after the Sergeant Major.

Rumbling, heavy footsteps. "I'm already here."

"Have all the pioneers come to me. Here we go again."

"By your command, First Lieutenant, Sir."

Thirty minutes later, the company's platoon leaders were assembled. Keller, who still held that position as an alternate, was also there.

"Vossenack will be recaptured," the officer came right to the point.

Silent faces. Many of them were old hands and knew what to expect.

"But this time the enemy will be shot softly. Tomorrow morning a hail of shells will fall on Vossenack. Our tanks and assault guns will take care of that. Then we'll retake the village."

"Just us?"

168

"No, Sergeant Graf. The first company will support us. As well as parts of the heavy company."

"There will be details later. I have to go to the briefing right now. I've only briefed you in advance so you can prepare your platoons. Tell the men to get ready for battle." He turned to the spike. "Radomski, make sure they have a decent meal and good rations for the packs. We don't know what to expect!"

"The kitchen sergeant has stew on the menu, First Lieutenant."

"Then let him see to it that he gets some real meat or sausage!"

"By your command."

They lay down in front of the village and waited. On the opposite ridge, there was a constant blinking and crashing. The deadly fire from the tanks and assault rifles still poured down from there.

Nerves were on edge. Everyone tried to deal with the situation in his own way. Grossmann talked nonstop. Huber and Hassel watched the road constantly. Sergeant Keller thought of nothing. At least he tried not to. Suddenly there was silence. The shelling was over. Now it was their turn. First Lieutenant Drexler sprang to his feet.

"Attaaaaack," he shouted at the top of his lungs and charged forward. The officer literally swept his men with him.

"Up, up! Move!" shouted Keller as he stormed off.

A billowing bell of gunpowder vapor hung over Vossenack. It smelled of smoke and burning. At first, the American defensive fire was extremely light. The US soldiers apparently had to realize that the shelling was over and that another enemy was charging them. Only gradually did the fire intensify.

The left attack wing was abruptly stopped by the barrage of a heavy machine gun.

"We've got heavy weapons against us! We are pinned down!"

The grenade launcher group was sent to solve the problem and moved up. No sooner were they in position than the dreaded *bang* was heard. Within minutes, explosive grenades were swirling through the air.

"They're heating up the Yank. The heavy machine gun stopped firing. Forward!"

They moved on.

Keller's platoon reached the first settlement in the village. It was apparently unoccupied. With a wave of his arm, one of his three squads charged into the house while the rest of the platoon secured it.

"Clear," the squad leader reported.

They moved on. From the back, across the gardens, they approached the next house. A few rounds whizzed past Keller. The sergeant ducked and zigzagged in front of his platoon. There was a scream of pain behind him. Keller fired a volley from his hip. He couldn't see a target, but it was good to at least return fire.

"Barrage," he yelled.

Huber and Hassel moved the machine gun into position. Shooter I quickly took aim and pulled the trigger.

Rrrrrrt

Empty shells were ejected. The rattle of the machine gun was Keller's signal to keep running. Huber went from window to window. Again and again he fired short bursts to provide cover for his comrades and to keep the enemy under cover.

The noise of battle grew. American artillery was firing and harassing the German rear.

Huuuuit ... boom

Again and again, shells landed between the ranks of the advancing Landser.

Keller pressed himself against the wall of the house. Hofman, Baar and a few other men had also made it. The others were still in cover, returning the defenders' fire.

170

"At least one of them is on the second floor. I also saw two rifle barrels by the window over there," he told the man beside him.

"What do we do?"

"We'll throw in a hand grenade and then storm the house."

Hofman nodded and gave the order.

Huber had just taken fire at the second-floor window when Keller detached himself from the wall of the house. Crouching, keeping close to the wall, he crept slowly toward the window. Leaving his submachine gun dangling at his side, he pulled a stick grenade from his belt with his left hand.

Author's private archive: PA-N-0120 - Stick hand grenades

He quickly unscrewed the breech, pulled the safety cord, waited a moment, and tossed the device into the window above him. Duck. He thought he heard the sound of the device hitting the ground. There were two warning shouts in English, followed by an explosion.

Wham

The sergeant waited a moment. Then he stood up and motioned for the others to join him. At his comrade's signal, Hofman stood with his back to the wall and clasped his hands. Robber's ladder. Corporal Keller climbed first onto his palms, then onto the lance corporal's shoulders. He held the barrel of his MP through the window and pulled the trigger as a precaution. Then he swung into the room. Baar and the others followed immediately. Hofman was the last to enter the room. The bodies of two GIs lay shredded on the floor. Blood and bone splinters covered the walls and floor. A picture of horror.

Quick steps in the hallway. Shots were still coming from above. An order was heard. An egg-shaped hand grenade rolled down the stairs and came to rest in the corridor. The soldiers realized the danger and pressed against the wall of their room.

Boom

They didn't hesitate a second after the explosion. They rushed out into the hallway to the stairs and ran up. A GI was charging them. A burst of machine-gun fire threw him backward and he crashed into a door that was pushed open. An American soldier stood at the window of the room and fired into the street. As the door flew open and he realized the danger at his back, he turned in a flash, now standing with his back to the open door, and three rounds from Huber's machine gun hit the soldier's back. He collapsed instantly.

The Landser suddenly stormed into each room.

"Clear!" shouted one of the men.

"Here too!"

"We've been through all the rooms."

Keller was sweating. His eyes fell on the dead Americans. The sergeant wiped the sweat from his brow with his sleeve. He walked slowly to the window and cautiously risked a glance out at the street. "Get the other guys!"

The rest of the platoon approached the building. From the window on the second floor of the building, Sergeant Keller noticed that the U.S. artillery howitzers kept hitting the lines of his comrades.

"They're shooting very accurately. That's no luck. They must have an artillery observer sitting here somewhere," he shouted angrily.

"In a tree at the edge of the forest?"

"A tall house," came the suggestions.

"In the church steeple," said one of the other group.

"That's it. We have to go to the church tower," Keller decided. "Everybody out of here!"

The sergeant's platoon left the house and advanced under the cover of houses and ruins. They spotted the company commander.

"Wait here," Keller told the men, and hurried crouching down to his commander.

He crouched behind a completely shot-up house wall and yelled at the radio operator to report back to the battalion command post. Keller crouched down beside the officer, gasped, and pointed to the church steeple. The artillery observer quickly reported back.

Drexler nodded. "I had exactly the same thought, and I'm on my way to the church right now. You'll take the flank with your platoon. If we make it to the nave, we'll have him, at least if he's up there."

"Where else, First Lieutenant. The church tower is the tallest building, and it survived the assault of the assault rifles."

Drexler had stopped listening. He checked his submachine gun and raised his hand. "Forward."

Rifle and machine gun fire rang through the village streets. Hand grenades exploded again and again. Some houses were clear, others had to be taken hand-to-hand. Fierce fighting. Bare steel in the hands of both sides. Many uniforms were stained with blood. Calls for medics could be heard on both sides. Fighters reared up in a final cry. Dying men huddled in corners, whimpering. The devil has thrown the gates of hell wide open.

First Lieutenant Drexler and Sergeant Keller's platoon reached the nave.

"We're going in," Drexler ordered without pausing, running purposefully toward the church gate.

A young private pushed ahead of the officer, opened the heavy wooden gate of the entrance, and collapsed in a hail of bullets from an American automatic rifle. The wooden gate swung back. The company commander instinctively swung to the side. Impacts could be heard. Splinters of wood ripped from the oak door. For a few seconds, the first lieutenant was paralyzed. He finally regained his composure. "Look out! Machine gun!" he shouted in warning.

Hofman, standing next to Drexler, looked frantically for Huber. When he spotted the machine gun, he first waved and then gesticulated wildly toward the back of the nave. "They're shooting out. You need to shoot through the windows."

Huber understood. He placed the bipod on the church wall and felt the stock against his cheek. Hassel was ready, too. Again and again, Shooter I fired his volleys through the already shattered windows of the church. A few bullets hit the walls and continued to whistle as dangerous ricochets. But most of the projectiles found their targets and flew through the window openings into the interior of the church. At the same time, Hofman pulled aside one of the heavy wooden doors, and Baar threw two hand grenades into the church.

Boom

Immediately after the explosion, Hofman tore open the wooden door again and the first Landser of the platoon charged into the building. A bullet whistled past the corporal's cheek. He felt the hot draft and jumped behind a wooden bench. A comrade collapsed in the doorway, mortally wounded. It quickly became clear that the enemy was firing down from the portal.

Hofman took aim and opened fire. He simply aimed at the flashing muzzle flashes. More and more Landser entered the church. Baar ran down the center aisle, almost made it to the portal, and threw a hand grenade up.

Boom

Screams. A badly wounded man fell over the railing and lay groaning with twisted legs in front of Baar.

"Surrender" shouted First Lieutenant Drexler, first in German, then in English.

The officer's voice echoed loudly through the church.

A burst of machine-gun fire was the answer. Meanwhile, Keller and three other men had reached the side staircase. He slowly made his way up the stairs. A wooden door blocked the entrance to the portal. He pushed it open with a firm kick and looked at the portal. A shocked GI looked at him. The GI was bleeding from his face and shoulder. As he turned the barrel of his MP on Keller, the sergeant pulled the trigger. Several bullets pierced the American lieutenant's chest. He was thrown back and lay in a pool of blood.

"Don't shoot," someone shouted. "Don't shoot!"

The gunfire began to die down.

"Cease fire!" shouted Keller, and all weapons fell silent.

Two hands appeared behind the organ and were raised in the air. A young soldier, whom Keller estimated to be just under twenty years old, surrendered.

"One of you come with me, the others stay here," the sergeant ordered, starting to walk toward the bell tower. Then he heard First Lieutenant Drexler's words.

"You were right, Keller. There really was an artillery observer on the steeple."

He, too, had realized his hopeless situation and surrendered. He had come down with his hands up, while Hofman had gone all the way to the top. The lance corporal found the Ari observer's equipment.

The company reporter ran to Drexler. "A report from the twelfth company. Captain Fuchs is trapped. More and more American infantrymen are pouring into Vossenack from the direction of Kommerscheid. They're coming over the Kallschlucht! We must set up a defensive line!"

"Tell him to fall back and come here. To the church!"

Huber's machine gun rattled again.

"They're coming back!"

The pressure increased again. Reinforced by the reserves that had been brought in, the members of the 28th US Division regained support. The US soldiers streaming back from Schmidt and Kommerscheid were immediately taken to the rear. Their faces were blank, silent, and filled with fear. Their eyes showed the horror they had been through. Many of the GIs were in a state of shock.

Captain Fuchs returned to the village under cover of a few smoke grenades with only twenty soldiers left. They fought their way to the cemetery wall and dug in there and in the ruins of the adjacent street.

The situation was terrible. Vossenack was a place of devastation. Burning wrecks, destroyed houses. Thick smoke hung over the rubble. Dead and wounded everywhere. Paramedics ran through the streets with stretchers, fighting their way through and over the rubble. To make matters worse, the weather was bad. A cold front had moved in and enveloped them. The sky first spat out sleet, which gradually turned into thick snowflakes.

"Batten down the hatches," came the order to the assault guns as they appeared in front of the villages of Kommerscheid and Schmidt.

"The Grenadiers are here! The order to attack will be given shortly," announced the on-board radio operator, Thomas Kleimann.

The voice over the radio sounded crackly and tinny as the latest message was added. "... and here's a last message from Vossenack. Our comrades have entered the village."

"Hurra!"

"Attack!"

The clatter of the chains increased. The driver stepped on the gas and brought the assault gun into position. The gunner saw a flash in the same spot over and over through the sight.

"I think I've spotted an infantry gun. Probably about the size of a Pak," he drew the attention of the vehicle's commander, Sergeant Lannert.

"Range?"

"Set!"

"Fire!"

The gun cracked.

Clack ... wham

Catching the recoil. Muzzle flashes flashed down the barrel, powder smoke wafted on the wind.

Reloading. The bolt closed quickly.

"One more!"

Clack, again came the metallic click that preceded firing. The cannon roared again, ripping through the assault gun.

"Hit," said a delighted Tiller, the gunner.

But the enemy kept firing grenades at them as well. More and more shrapnel scraped the outer wall of the assault gun.

"On the right. A Sherman tank," came the warning.

They were still in the open in front of the village. The roar of battle had reached a deafening volume. The heavy tracks twisted and tossed the steel colossus around. A grenade landed close by, kicking up shrapnel and dirt.

"I see nothing ... now ... I got it ... fire!"

Clack ... wham

It took only the blink of an eye from launch to impact.

Boom

The cooperation between loader and gunner worked smoothly. The bolt clicked into place and the next grenade was fired.

Where did it hit?

Splinters scratched the steel casing again and flying stones hit the metal.

Author's private archive: PA-N-0121 - assault gun

The next impact could be fatal for them.

"Tiller, you damn sky dog! Shoot him," Eck yelled nervously.

"Hit! He's on fire," cheered Tiller.

Beads of sweat rolled down the gunner's forehead and cheeks. The air was stuffy. They had been in their steel cage for more than two hours.

"Look out! Tanks at one o'clock!"

Eck gave it his all. He stepped on the gas and pulled the joystick. The tracks ate into the ground. The fighting vehicle bucked and turned, and the barrel spat out its deadly cargo again. After three more rounds, the Sherman was down.

It moved on. Lannert held on to the scissor telescope. The houses came into view.

Were the Grenadiers still there?

They provided the necessary protection from enemy tank destroyers, who crept up to the assault guns in the blind spot and planted explosives.

Boom

A huge explosion was heard.

"For God's sake," shouted the assault gun commander, who could see the inferno unfolding next to him from the blind spot. "It's got Willy."

The armored fighting vehicle driving right beside them was in flames. Eck pulled everything out of the engine and raced into the village. The battle was fierce. They fired their shells from the cannon again and again, fighting their way through house after house, street after street.

Suddenly there was a crash to the right. Something hard crashed loudly against the steel shell. The blood of the crew froze in their veins. This is what it must sound like when the enemy shell lands a direct hit and the projectile triggers the deadly explosion. The assault cannon jerked lazily. The feared detonation, which tore open the armored vehicle's skin like a sardine can, did not occur.

Only Eck was shouting like a berserker. "We cannot maneuver. We broke the right chain!"

Breathe a sigh of relief. The chain was shredded, the fatal explosion had not occurred. A stroke of luck.

A panoramic view through the scope. Smoke, burning wreckage of all kinds. Destroyed houses. Lannert also saw two dead horses lying in the road. But the most horrible thing were the many dead and wounded soldiers. They were screaming for help, for medics, for their mothers, or for God.

"There are dead and wounded everywhere," he breathed out, barely audible. The sergeant saw the true face of war.

He opened the hatch and crawled out of the assault gun. The machine gun 34 was immediately manned as a precaution, but no shots had to be fired. The noise of the battle died down noticeably. The enemy had retreated.

Medical trucks rolled incessantly from the casualty collection points to the troop formation areas. Medics ran around restlessly. They bandaged wounds, administered painkillers, and offered comfort.

Johann Eck had no time for them. He was only interested in the broken chain. Cursing, he stood beside the assault rifle and inspected the damage.

"And now it's starting to snow! Bloody hell!"

"Bad?" came the question from Lannert.

Eck took a few breaths, then shook his head. "No! We'll get it under control."

"You're a lucky guy."

"Then get out and help."

The villages of Schmidt and Kommerscheid were also retaken, but at a high cost, as they were fiercely defended. Both the Americans and the Germans suffered heavy casualties.

The situation was becoming tense again. First Lieutenant Drexler looked tense. "Your orders, Major," the officer confirmed the radio message. Then he turned to Captain Fuchs. "We have to hold the line! Our guys have already taken Schmidt and Kommerscheid. The Americans are retreating through the Kall_Valley, but they're fighting like hell."

"I felt that bitterly myself. We were in position right next to the corridor there. More than half of my men are now lying in the rubble. The Americans were far superior."

"We should hold our position," Drexler repeated.

"I will ..." Captain Fuchs got no further. His body jerked up under the volley of an American machine gun. The officer's face took on a strange waxy color. Eyes wide open, he collapsed, panting.

"They're charging the church again," someone shouted.

Sergeant Keller feared the worst.

What is the citation for the Close Combat Medal? The white seen in the eye of the enemy.

He closed his eyes for a moment and took a deep breath. "Now you can show if you're soldiers," he said to the men beside him. "I can hear the melee struts growing. They'll sprout from the ground faster than you can imagine. Get ready!"

Keller checked his magazine and got the spade ready. "Who's got hand grenades?"

"I do," Hofman announced, sliding to the window and risking a look outside.

The last intact pane shattered. An American sniper's bullet missed the corporal by a few centimeters. Hofman immediately threw himself around, literally sticking to the wall, and suddenly turned white as a sheet. He took a few deep breaths, then took the safety off the stick grenade and threw it out. As soon as it detonated, he pushed the barrel of his rifle out the window and fired.

US infantrymen repeatedly attacked the thin HKL in Vossenack. One of the most fiercely contested buildings was the church. It was dusk when the church had to be abandoned.

"First Lieutenant, we are too weak. We can't hold out for long. Besides, we have hardly any ammunition left. What about replacements?" Sergeant Keller whined to his company commander.

Drexler was a few meters away, reloading. "I know! I've already contacted battalion headquarters by radio and I'm still waiting for an answer."

Hofman reported from the portal, "They're trying to go around us and block the road at the end of the village," he warned, pointing to the advancing American infantrymen. He could see them clearly from his elevated position. "In a few minutes everything will be closed. Even now, our medics cannot get through unhindered," he added.

The situation was beyond precarious.

The reporter soldier felt uncomfortable. The stench of gunpowder smoke, the moaning of the wounded and the sight of the corpses were getting to him. He took off his headphones. His expression relaxed a bit. He looked relieved for a split second as he relayed the last message. "The battalion command post ..." he said. He couldn't say any more. The whole situation overwhelmed the young soldier. He had to throw up.

Drexler answered the radio. "This is First Lieutenant Drexler."

Wham

The officer ducked as a hand grenade exploded near the church, sending shrapnel, dirt, and small rocks flying through the air.

"Understood! Fall back! Over!"

He took off his headset. "Retreat!" he yelled loudly.

"1st Platoon is taking cover! The machine gun will be supported by the 2nd Platoon! The rest will move out in fifteen minutes. The signal will be a green flare! Pass the word!"

The order to dismount was given. Exactly 15 minutes later, when the green magnesium flare was fired into the dark sky, the soldiers rushed out of the church and from their cover around the building. They followed First Lieutenant Drexler. Machine guns rattled behind them.

Barrage! We can make it!

Including the first platoon, there were 65 men left. Happy to avoid a battle in which the enemy was vastly superior, they rushed through the night that had fallen. Shortly after leaving the village, they encountered the leading edge of the advancing US soldiers, who were about to encircle the German soldiers.

The two sides clashed with a loud clatter.

"Hurray, comrades," someone shouted, and the Landser followed the call as if it were automatic.

Hofman had emptied his magazine. He had the presence of mind to throw his weapon to the ground, grab his combat knife, pull it out, and lunge at a burly GI who had just shot a German.

The American swung his rifle in Hofman's direction. A shot rang out. At the same time, the lance corporal rammed the knife into the American's chest. Both fell to the ground. The Russian veteran's opponent was gasping and spitting blood. Hofman had rolled to the side. In a flash, he lifted his body up, lunged forward, and the compatriot's hand reached for the knife still lodged in the American's torso. As he tried to pull it out of the enemy's body, he felt a sharp pain in his right shoulder. The arm would not work.

What is that?

He looked at the painful area and saw that he was bleeding. "He got me," Hofman said, then his eyes went black.

The brutal hand-to-hand combat demanded the deepest inner conquest. There was only one goal for each. To survive! The man in the uniform of either side had to become a ravening beast, or he himself would die. They were not standing at the gates of hell, they were in the middle of it.

Keller swung the spade full force at the helmet of the enemy standing in front of him. The GI staggered. The sergeant struck a second blow with lightning speed. "Ahhh ..." he exclaimed, as if he was putting his last reserve of strength into the blow.

This time he struck his opponent on the right side of his face. The sharp side of the spade penetrated deeply, leaving a gaping gash. White bone was visible for a split second, then blood gushed out. The U.S. soldier collapsed unconscious. Keller stood there, panting. The war sickened him at that moment, but he had survived the battle. He was a victor without feeling like a victor. In fact, the opposite was true. He felt abandoned, alone and like a loser.

Baar had charged into the melee with his bayonet at the ready. The last bullet had been fired and there was no thought of reloading. He had just managed to fend off an attack and get into a better position. The Soldier rammed the bare steel into his opponent's stomach. He had pushed so hard that the blade had almost completely penetrated the GI's body. When he pulled it out, he saw a face contorted with pain. The mortally wounded American soldier pressed both hands to the stab wound and fell to his knees. He finally collapsed, panting. The German would never forget that look.

The powerful and persistent attack caused the Americans to retreat. They had been caught off guard by the ferocity of the battle.

"They're leaving," was shouted.

Everyone seemed to be waiting for the order to follow, but First Lieutenant Drexler hesitated. He looked at the faces of the survivors, examined the wounded, and then at the bodies of the fallen. He felt an oppressive emptiness.

Two American prisoners raised their hands. One was crying bitterly, the other seemed to be in shock.

"What's next?" he snapped, coming to his senses and catching himself. "Gather up," the company commander ordered in his usual confident voice.

They had defeated the enemy. That much was certain. For the moment, at least, the path to their own ranks was clear.

Keller looked around hastily.

Where are my men?

The Russian veteran was reminded of the Eastern Front. There they had been forced to retreat under heavy fire. He knew the feeling of helplessness. He had to act and bring structure to the chaos. "Take care of the prisoners," the platoon leader ordered, counting his men. Three were missing.

Huber came up to Keller. He leaned against the machine gun 42. The private looked tired and exhausted. "Hofman's got him. The medic's over there with him."

Keller was glad.

Not to lose another good comrade, he thought.

"What about him?"

Shrugged.

The sergeant ran in search of his wounded friend. At last he saw him, and beside him a soldier wearing a white armband with a red cross on it. The Samaritan in the field knelt beside Hofman and fiddled with him. The sergeant was with him in an instant. "What's wrong with him?" he asked.

The medic glanced around, then pressed cellulose onto the exposed wound. The medic's hands were bloody red. "Help me," he urged Keller.

"What do you want me to do?"

"This one was shot right through, but an artery was nicked. He lost a lot of blood and is only alive because I happened to be standing next to him when he collapsed. I clamped the artery. You have to put cellulose on the front and back of the wound so that I can apply the bandage tightly. Then get him to the military unit as soon as possible!"

Keller knelt down. Hofman was unconscious. As instructed, the platoon leader pressed the cellulose on the entrance and exit of the wound. His concerned look did not go unnoticed by the medic.

"He was conscious by now. I gave him a painkiller. Like I said, he lost a lot of blood."

"Will he ..."

"I have no idea. I've done everything I can."

The medic stood up and looked around.

"Porter," he called loudly.

A paramedic arrived and Hofman was placed on the stretcher. As the rescuer tried to lift him up with the medic, Keller offered to help. "You take care of the other wounded. I'll go with you."

"All right."

Things got hectic again. Single shots could be heard.

"Faster! We have to get back, the Americans are pushing on!" ordered First Lieutenant Drexler.

The first platoon ran up. Panting, a sergeant and a lieutenant stopped in front of the company commander. "The ... retreat ... would be," the lieutenant breathed out, "... convenient now. They ... did not follow us."

185

Drexler didn't have to think long. "Gather up and move out!"

"And the prisoners?" someone asked.

"We've got a long way to go, Lieutenant," the first lieutenant said, drawing the attention of the senior officer.

"Go with the men. I'll take care of the prisoners," he ordered, looking for Keller. "Sergeant Keller," he called.

"He's carrying Hofman back, First Lieutenant," Huber explained to him, still leaning on the machine gun.

"Good, Huber. Then I'll give you the task of bringing up the rear with your squad. Do you have any questions?"

"No."

Drexler turned back to the lieutenant. "I've ordered my company to fall back. Go to Captain Fuchs. I'll stay here with the rearguard."

"Got it!"

The soldiers retreated into the darkness. When they were out of sight, the officer pointed to the two prisoners. "Let them go. Let them return to their men!"

"As you command," Huber grinned sheepishly.

That was what he loved about his former platoon leader. In spite of the war, he was still human.

The captured Americans stood up anxiously. They took their first steps backwards, their knees shaking. Then they turned and ran. Drexler waited another quarter of an hour, then the rear guard retreated as well.

While the 28th US Division suffered heavy losses and had to retreat in many places, Vossenack remained in American hands.

The retreat of the defeated 28th US Division into the Kalltal became a gauntlet for the American soldiers. First the German artillery pounded the woods almost nonstop, followed by the German counterattack.

Taking advantage of Honnige's observation, Major Retzer positioned two heavy machine guns and a group of mortars at the spot described by the sniper.

"Fire," came the command from Major Retzer, and the guns went off. Bullets slammed into the trees. Hit GIs fell to the ground. Wounded men cried out for help.

The retreating US units walked into a deadly trap. The MG 42s mounted on gun carriages rattled away again and again, tearing holes in the ranks of the exhausted and demoralized Allied troops. The impact of the grenade launchers finally caused chaos. Vehicles were abandoned, smoking and burning wrecks blocked the narrow path, and many GIs continued their escape through the woods. But the German infantry was waiting, ready to fight and deliver the final blow to the enemy.

"Close the flanks," echoed the order through the forest.

"Follow me," shouted a company commander as he charged forward. His men followed in a wedge.

Eyes wide open, the fleeing Americans stared at the Landser and shouted, "Hurray!

The assault was a military success. The villages of Schmidt and Kommerscheid were liberated. In Vossenack, however, the US Army held out. Only part of the village was occupied by German forces, and the HKL in the village was moved accordingly. Vossenack became the epitome of hell on earth, and every soldier sent there had to live in fear of death.

From the point of view of the Landser, they managed to retake half of the village, or in some places just a few houses, only to lose it again afterwards. Hard-fought counterattacks meant that the hard-won territory had to be relinquished. Fighting was fierce and intense on both sides. Hand-to-hand combat was the order of the day.

The battles of early to mid-November 1944 went down in history as the Battle of All Souls.

With over 3,000 killed and wounded, the German losses were a high price to pay for the partial victory achieved.

Even more bitter was the defeat of the 28th US Division, which suffered 6,200 casualties, twice as many as its opponent.

This severe blow to the U.S. Army had a demoralizing effect on the surviving GIs. General Eisenhower had miscalculated and was forced to call a brief armistice.

Author's private archive, PA-0052 Landser - pioneer after deployment

The military disaster was compounded by bad weather. Winter had arrived while the calendar was still in fall. The cold and wet were especially hard on U.S. soldiers, who were still fighting in summer uniforms. Weather-related illnesses skyrocketed.

After General Eisenhower personally visited and inspected the troops at the front, he knew that the exhausted 28th US Division had to be withdrawn immediately. It was no longer capable of leading another attack.

While new US units were sent to the front, the OKW only reinforced the 275th Infantry Division with a few available reserves.

Although the Landser had been at the front for months, the unit was not recalled. Although the soldiers were not told the reason for this, rumors began to circulate.

The fact was that the planned Ardennes offensive, code-named "Watch on the Rhine," could not be jeopardized. The army command insisted on keeping the tried and tested Russian veterans in action, who had so far held their own against the enemy.

Despite the increase, the 275th Infantry Division had not reached its target strength. Only the lull in the fighting mandated by the US forces could be used to recover.

With the 1st, 4th and 8th U.S. Divisions, they were immediately confronted with experienced U.S. soldiers who had already participated in the D-Day invasion on June 6, 1944.

Author's private archive, PA-H-106 March to the Front

"Did we drive them out properly?" Hassel asked a few days later. "Since they were driven out of Schmidt and Kommerscheid, there's been peace and quiet."

"First of all, they're still there, and secondly, this is the calm before the storm," Josef Keller immediately dispelled any illusions.

The sergeant got up and went to the cannon stove. He opened the door and put two logs in.

"What do you mean?"

"They have endless material. They'll be back, you can count on it. They could hold Vossenack anyway."

"It's going to get tougher," Huber hissed between them. "More tanks, more men, and more Ari!"

"I don't think so! They can't get through the terrain with tanks," Hassel countered. "We've seen that."

"They'll come," Keller shot off unequivocally. He wanted to end the discussion. So he didn't allow any more objections. "And now let's talk about other things, otherwise you'll get a case of frontal fever!"

"I saw pioneers marching up to the HKL with piles of equipment."

"They'll fix the holes."

"What holes?" Grossmann asked.

"Mines and so on."

"What do you say to the German doctor who kept the truce in the Kalltal and treated the wounded on both sides?" Keller changed the subject after the discussion had clearly not died down.

"That was a great thing. The wounded are the poorest bastards, because they often have to lie on the battlefield for hours without help because their division is retreating or advancing."

"When they advance, the medics follow. That's quite normal."

"But the Americans are said to have gone crazy. A rumor from the latrine tells of lost GIs being led back to their own men by our people."

"You mean out of pity?"

"Rubbish! They would have taken them prisoner," Keller interjected.

"I didn't get the feeling at Vossenack that we got along so well with the Americans that we'd take them by the hand and bring them home," Huber thundered.

"Oh no! And what did we do?"

"Well, we sent the two prisoners back, but that was the exception."

"Otherwise you would have had to kill them."

"I'm still a soldier, not a murderer!"

"The doctor will surely get a medal," Hassel changed the subject, bringing calm back into the discussion that had become heated.

"I know an example from Italy. During the fighting on the Gustav Line, a sergeant was awarded with a medal for bringing about a cease-fire after the Americans had been shot up on the Rapido. It was a big story in the papers."

"Speaking of the wounded, how is Hofman doing?" asked Baar.

"He should be better. I'm going to visit him today. Who's coming with me?"

The whole group stepped forward.

"Great, then I'll quickly let the rest of the train know that I'll be gone for a few hours. Just in case. Being a platoon leader isn't as easy as it used to be," Sergeant Keller explained. "I would suggest that we leave after lunch. We'll take it easy today. Weapons are cleaned and ready to go, there's nothing special on the duty roster. Besides, the meal distribution for our unit is scheduled for half past ten."

"So early?"

"It doesn't matter. I'm hungry as hell already."

191

Laughter. When it came to grabbing food, the soldiers were always ready for it.

The next piece of news came while they were eating. Keller had met Radomski, the Master Sergeant, and sat down with his old comrade from the Eastern Front.

"Good to see you," Radomski began, mouth full. "I have good news for Baar. He's with you now, isn't he?"

The sergeant nodded. The Sergenat Major chewed the bite and swallowed. "Pretty tough, this meat," he grumbled briefly, then speared a potato. But before it reached his mouth, he continued to speak.

"Baar was promoted to Lance Corporal on November 1st. But he was lost in the fighting. You can send him to me later and he'll get the letter."

"He will be pleased."

"You just want to get something out of him, don't you?"

"A promotion like this deserves to be celebrated," grinned Keller.

Radomski knew his way around. After all, he was an old hand. A professional soldier who had been in uniform for more than ten years. "What does he have to jump for?"

"Just a little something for the group, including me, of course," Keller grinned. "Baar will be Hofman's successor and will lead the group as long as I'm the reserve platoon leader."

"How is Hofman anyway?"

"We're going to visit him this afternoon. I can tell you how he's doing later."

"This afternoon, you say?"

"Yes. Isn't that good?"

"Very well, actually. If you come to my house first, you won't have to walk. At least the way there. Our medics are just getting supplies of bandages delivered. The truck will definitely go back to the field hospital. Of course you can ride along. But you'll have to hurry and leave by noon."

"Great. We'll be on time. When does it leave?"

"Before one, I guess."

Keller looked at his watch. "We can easily make that. And what about Baar and the party?"

"Oh yes, ... ha ... ha ..." laughed Radomski, "... I've stashed away some market goods. Three bottles of wine and one bottle of grain. When you're celebrating, Baar can buy the stuff."

"All right, but you'll give him a good price."

"Do you think I want to get rich?" grinned Radomski.

"I remember when we did a thing or two in Russia. I know you," laughed Keller.

"Don't worry, Josef. He'll pay the usual price."

"When shall we be there?"

"Best right after dinner. The old man is with the battalion, then I'll be alone in the office."

"Is he gone for something special?"

The face from the sergeant major suddenly became serious.

"We've had a lot of casualties, Josef."

"I know. We lost half the company at Vossenack alone."

"The regiment, ah, what ..." he made a disparaging gesture, "... the whole division has only a third of its combat strength left. Reinforcements have arrived, as far as I've heard, but the comrades don't relieve us, they're just thrown into the HKL."

"I was afraid of something like that. Half of my platoon was made up of young soldiers. For many of them, it was their first contact with the enemy."

"But they faced it bravely."

Keller pondered. "I agree, but for how long? I already had to break up a discussion in the dugout today. I know this excitement. It brings nothing but trouble. If we hadn't drawn a line, I could have sent one or two of my comrades to the field doctor with front-line fever by the end of the day. How many more sacrifices do we have to make?"

193

"I asked the boss a similar question."

"And what did he say?"

"We are not fighting for Moscow, Rome or Paris, we are fighting for Cologne, Munich and Berlin. We are on German soil."

"He could make Minister of Propaganda."

Radomski looked around frantically. "Man, are you stupid? Watch what you say!" he warned urgently. "People have been court-martialed for far less dangerous statements."

"It's just us," Keller reassured him. "Besides, I'd like to know why we can't go on stage."

"We are so important because half of our people are still battle-hardened Russian veterans. Soldiers like you. And for God's sake, I'm one," thundered the Master Sergeant.

A couple of Landser from the next table turned around. Then the sergeant major with the butt rings on his sleeve lowered his voice again. He even began to whisper. "I heard something else."

The professional soldier's upper body bent over the table. His mouth was now very close to the sergeant's ear.

"In the hinterland, they are rearming for a huge counterattack. We just have to hold our positions so that our comrades can prepare for an offensive in peace. There should also be a lot of Tiger tanks. You'll see, the turning point everyone is smiling about is coming. We will drive the Allies back into the sea. It will be like Dunkirk. Only this time they won't escape, they will pay for the destroyed German cities."

"Theater of operations? Where will all the divisions come from? When I look at our new generation..."

"Remember my words! Stand always in front of your man. For them you are a hero."

"Hero? What a load of garbage. I can't listen to this crap anymore. Do you know how much pain I went through? It wasn't fun being in the hospital for months. I'm not a hero, I was lucky!

That's all. And for all the suffering I got a piece of metal stapled to my chest and the sergeant's braids as a thank you."

"I know how long you were gone. It was almost ten months to the day. And that includes the NCO course. I know exactly, Josef. I'm the Master Sergeant."

Keller leaned back at first, then leaned forward again. "When will this offensive take place?"

"I'm no psychic, but it can't be long now. Hang in there."

The company sergeant paused for a moment and took a deep breath. "And you know what?" he continued in a good mood.

"No?"

"I'm going to add a carton of cigarettes to the market goods later. I'll give them to you and your platoon. You can distribute them as you wish."

A smile came back to Keller's face. Radomski couldn't help the situation. He was a good comrade and very well-behaved. The sergeant shook his hand.

"It's a deal! And I'll be standing in front of your office with my old group shortly. You make sure the truck doesn't leave without us."

"All right, old house. See you soon."

Baar received his certificate of conveyance and bought the marked goods to celebrete with his comrades. Sergeant Keller received the promised Juno-Cigarettes ration. In front oft the company command post a truck was parked. The red cross on a white background was clearly painted on the doors. The truck was a foreign model and the bed was empty.

"Looks good. We'd all fit on it. Where's the driver?" Huber wanted to know.

The group was standing outside the door while Keller and Baar were still in the Master Sergent´s office.

"I'll be there. Don't worry."

The sergeant and Baar, who had just been promoted to lance corporal, came out. An older soldier accompanied them.

195

Keller grinned. "Good old Radomski wasn't exaggerating," he groaned barely audibly as he walked to the truck.

He carried the cigarettes in his left hand, for all to see.

Hassel poked Grossmann in the side. He couldn't take his eyes off the older soldier. "He must be over forty now and still just a soldier. Surely he's done something wrong, hasn't he?"

"No, comrade. He was too old for the army and only had to enlist now. After all, he's just a driver."

"You think so?"

"Why don't you ask him, if you're so curious?"

"Well, it's not that interesting. I don't really care. It was just a thought," Hassel waved him off.

The driver opened the door. "Up you go, comrades," he said to the group standing around. "When it gets cold, think warm thoughts," he added jokingly.

As everyone climbed onto the flatbed, Keller sat down in the cab.

"What kind of car is this?" he asked curiously.

"It's a Chevrolet. 1.5 tons, built in 1940, to be exact. Why do you ask?"

"From the Americans?"

"No. A captured vehicle from the Dutch. Their army was equipped with them."

He started the engine and the truck roared. Dark blue clouds of exhaust came out and danced in the wind until they finally dissipated completely.

"A little more mud and we'd be stuck every twenty yards," the driver began a conversation.

"The pioneers did a pretty good job here, don't you think?"

"You could say that. It was a good thing to fill in the dirt access roads with gravel."

"At least around the dugouts," Keller confirmed.

"There anyway. Prevents wet feet. But I think the action with the guns was even more important. The ammunition drivers are grateful. Do you have any idea how much those things weigh?"

"A lot, for sure, but you know what surprises me even more?"

"Like what?"

"I'm surprised the Allies haven't sent in their planes yet. They usually bomb all kinds of things together."

"You mean the air raids that don't actually take place because otherwise someone at the top would be called Meier?" the truck driver alluded to Göring's *(Herman Göring = German politician, military leader, and convicted war criminal.)* statement and asked the question sarcastically.

"That's exactly what I mean!"

"Because of the bad weather. That's as clear as mud."

"But the weather wasn't bad for flying every day."

"But where would they go? Just drop ten tons of bombs on a forest? Surely they would have done that if their supplies were inexhaustible. But they're not. I think they're finished. They would have sent out a couple of squadrons of planes by now."

"I haven't even looked at it from the side."

"You see. You can still learn something from old Bohltmann."

"Your word in God's ear."

Sergeant Keller pulled out his pack of cigarettes. "Do you want one?"

"No, thanks. I don't smoke. And I don't like people smoking in my cab. I can't stand it very well."

"No problem."

The cigarettes went back into the pocket of the field blouse.

"How far is the military hospital?"

The driver frowned briefly, thinking. "They've set up a field hospital a good six kilometers from here. That's where your friend should be. I know the people in the ambulance column well. Most of the transports in the last few days have gone there."

"Then let's hope Hofman is there."

197

It was November 16, 1944, and half the way had been covered when the sky darkened. It began with a distant roar that grew louder and louder. The men on the flatbed were already pounding on the roof of the cab.

"Airplanes! Hundreds of planes!" they shouted.

Bohltmann braked. They were in the middle of the road. By now, the roar of the planes' engines had grown into a persistent rumble. The truck driver opened the door and stood in the door frame. Keller followed. They all stared up, unable to take their eyes off the countless Allied bombers and fighters above.

"Speak of the devil ..." Bohltmann exclaimed in amazement, the first to regain his composure. "We must get off the road."

He immediately got behind the wheel and slammed the door.

"Hang on!" he shouted as loudly as he could to the back of the truck and stepped on the gas. "We've got to get this thing off the road. We're safe in the woods!"

His powerful arms whirled around the steering wheel. The engine howled.

Sergeant Keller held on with both hands. He realized the armada was splitting up. Bombs were being dropped.

"The area ahead of us is being bombed. We have to turn around."

The truck rocked back and forth. Bohltmann took his foot off the accelerator and braked abruptly.

"Ouch," came a scream from behind.

A few soldiers had been thrown forward onto their comrades by the sudden braking.

The driver saw a suitable place to turn. He turned the wheel and groaned like a hard worker. Reverse, crank again, accelerate. Detonations tore through the air. The shadows of the bombers flitted over them. Huber sat wordlessly on the platform, transfixed. His mouth was wide open, but no sound escaped his lips. Only when the bomb bays opened did he react.

"We've got to get out of here. Into the forest!"

He jumped out during the turn. The other Landser didn't hesitate a second and followed Huber. As several bombs hit the road, tearing holes in the pavement with an incredible roar, Bohltmann and Sergeant Keller also knew they had to get out of the vehicle.

"Get out!"

The driver let go of the steering wheel and jumped out of the cab with the engine still running. Keller jumped out of the truck as well. The landing was not too hard, thanks to the rain-softened ground. The sergeant rolled off, jumped on and looked up. The number of planes seemed to be increasing.

"That's impossible," he wondered.

Just a short time ago he thought the enemy had no reserves, and now the largest fleet of aircraft he had ever seen was overhead.

They ran into the forest as if stung by a tarantula, throwing themselves to the ground and holding their hands over their heads. The earth seemed to shake.

Huuuiiiit ... wham ... boom

Thoughts came flooding back. Breathe a sigh of relief, it came down far away from us.

Huuuiiiit ... Wham

Dear God ... please help ... just one more time!

Individual bomb blasts could be heard again and again. Sometimes they were quieter and farther away, sometimes they thundered right next to them. After less than a quarter of an hour, the scare was over. For some of them it was probably the longest fifteen minutes of their lives. The bombers flew a loop and returned to their home airfields. Only a few fighters were still circling in the sky.

Bohltmann stood up, pale and shaking slightly. He walked to his truck, which was still parked with the engine running in the small lumberyard next to the road. Twenty meters in front of him, a tree lay across the road.

199

"If we had turned around, we could have been under it," the truck driver pointed out.

Huber and the others came out of the woods one by one. Keller lit a cigarette. He saw thick clouds of smoke rising. Wordlessly, he held out his hand and pointed.

"That's where Düren is," she explained to Bohltmann, who guessed what question the sergeant would ask.

"That must be how our people feel back home when the air raids come. Sitting in their basements, powerless," Baar muttered.

"Is anyone hurt?"

The team leader counted them. They were complete. No one seemed to be seriously injured.

"What was that?" asked Grossmann, still in a slight state of shock.

"A bombing raid in daylight. Our air force can't do that," Baar fumed.

"I suspect the worst," said Keller, trying to bring some order to the chaos. "Can you drive?" he asked Bohltmann.

"Yes," he replied in a slightly shaky voice. "If the road ahead is clear," he added, pointing with his left hand to the tree across the road. "Back there, the road is closed for now. It will take either heavy equipment or a group of pioneers and half a day to clear that tree back there."

"Mount up!"

They complied with their sergeant's request. Bohltmann got behind the wheel and drove off. Again and again he had to dodge smaller and larger bomb craters. The closer they got to the rear position, the more hectic it became. Fires were being put out. Ambulances were driving away, gendarmes were directing traffic. The acrid smell of burning was still in the air.

"I don't like this," Keller said.

One of the chain dogs stood in front of them, raising his right arm. When Bohltmann had stopped, the field gendarme came up to the truck driver. "Where are you going?"

"To the field hospital. I'm dropping the comrades off there and loading another load of supplies for the II Battalion."

The military policeman looked first at the cot, then at Sergeant Keller. Before he could say anything, the Russian veteran spoke.

PA-N-0122 - Uniform and metal sign Field-gendarme (german military police)

"Keller, I Battalion, 2nd Company. We're off duty this afternoon and want to visit a wounded comrade. He should be in the field hospital here."

"Seriously or lightly wounded?"

"What does it matter?"

"The seriously wounded have been transferred to the hospital in Düren."

"Where can I find out more?"

"Not today. First we have to find out what was destroyed in the attack."

A second fieldgendarm came running up. He stopped excitedly beside the other military policeman. "Hans! The Americans are attacking. We should send all off-duty soldiers back to their units immediately!"

"I knew it," groaned Keller.

"You heard?" the field gendarme asked.

The sergeant nodded. "Dismount," Keller ordered.

The men jumped off the cot. Now they could hear the enemy artillery. The wind carried the sound of detonations all the way to the stage.

"Can we at least find out what happened to our comrade?"

"I can call the field hospital, that's all," the friendly chain dog *(Author's note: Kettenhund = nickname for Feldgendarme - based on the gorget (metal shield) they wear)* offered.

"Please!"

"Karl ..." he said to the second field gendarme, "... why don't you run to the field telephone and call the military hospital? Ask for a ..."

"Hofman. Lance Corporal Eduard Hofman, I. Bataillon /2. Platoon," Keller added.

Bohltmann pulled up. "I have to go," he said goodbye.

After the truck pulled away, the Landser waited for a word from the field hospital.

"The road is no longer passable. There's a tree across it. About two or three kilometers from here," they told the field policeman.

He took down the message. The other one came back. He shook his head. "Hofman came to Düren yesterday. There is a big hospital. I tried it, but in Düren no one answered the phone call. The town was also a target for the bombers."

"Thank you very much for trying," Keller replied disappointedly. He turned to his man. "Let's get back before some officer catches us and takes us to a rendezvous point."

Disappointed faces. Nod in agreement

"I would advise you to do the same," said the field policeman.

American troops had launched Operation Queen, the largest
air assault in support of a ground offensive in World War II.

Well over 90 percent of the cities of Jülich and Düren,
considered vital to the German supply lines, were destroyed.
More than 4,000 bombers and fighters participated in the raid.

German positions were also bombed, but excellent camouflage, good fortifications, and poor Allied reconnaissance kept
losses to a minimum.

Heavy artillery fire replaced the bombing. Newly developed US rocket launchers, modeled after the Russian Stalin organs, were also used.

Once again, the Landser were caught in a barrage and had
to endure a gigantic storm of steel before American infantry divisions, freshly deployed to the HKL and supported by armored
forces, stormed the German positions.

When the group reached their quarters, the company was
abuzz with activity. On alert! They had to rearm immediately.
Cold rations and ammunition were issued. The soldiers stood
around, ready to march, waiting for orders from their commander. They were in reserve and would be deployed where the fire
was greatest, that much was certain.

"I don't like it at all with Hofman," said Huber, the machine
gun slung over his shoulder, both arms casually draped over it.

"Me neither. We only got a fraction of what came down on
Düren. When this is over, we've got to find out what's going on
with Hofman."

Huber nodded. "I agree. I just hope it doesn't go back to
Vossenack."

First Lieutenant Drexler stepped in front of the team. "We'll
stay on alert, but we're not moving out just yet. We'll be serving
hot food in an hour."

The situation eased somewhat. The prospect of a hot meal appealed to the compatriots.

"Then we'll move at night," Keller said, and he was right.

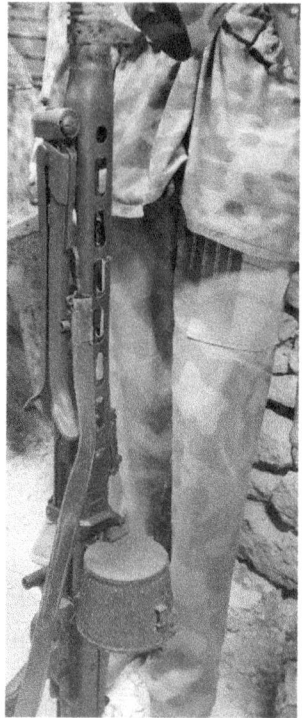

Author's private archive: PA-N-0123 and PA-N-0124 - MG 42 with attached belt drum (50 cartridges) - cartridge belt and stick hand grenades in the belt. Camouflage uniform

First Lieutenant Drexler held the receiver of the field telephone. He sat at his desk looking at the map in front of him. He was already mentally following the instructions he was receiving.

"Yes, that's right! I understand," he finally confirmed and hung up.

The officer took a deep breath, grabbed his coffee cup and emptied it in one go. "Radomski, here we go!"

The company sergeant had already heard parts of the conversation through the open door. He got up and entered his superior's room.

"Do you want me to compete?"

Without answering, Drexler pulled on his coat and buckled his belt.

"The Americans are attacking with full force. Tanks and fresh infantry units."

That was answer enough.

"Fresh troops again?" Radomski exclaimed in amazement.

"It's the third division we've had to deal with since we got here," the company commander confirmed. "This time they are advancing in two wedges. One attack will be on Hürtgen, the other will go through Vossenack to Simonskall. Their objective will again be the village of Schmidt. Our objective is Simonskall. Our comrades on the ground are still holding the village against the enemy, who is pushing up the serpentine road from Vossenack.

Radomski's face darkened. "When the men hear that we have to go back to Vossenack, they won't be happy."

"I know the name comes as a shock, but we are soldiers and we fight where we are needed."

"They'll wonder why our bunch has to go back there."

"Radomski! We don't ask, we don't think! We carry out orders!"

"Understood, First Lieutenant, Sir," the Master Sergeant barked, clenching his hooks.

"I'm not thrilled either, but we know the terrain and, most importantly, we're needed. As I said, the Americans are pushing up from Vossenack to Simonskall. Our comrades there can't hold out much longer and urgently need support.

"There's also a medical bunker there."

"That's right! It's being cleared now. There's no time to lose. Radomski, you lead the company," the officer ordered the sergeant major.

With temperatures near zero, the deployment to the main battle line began. An icy wind accompanied the soldiers as they marched silently through the forest. They had turned up the collars of their coats, wrapped scarves around their heads, and pulled woolly hats down over their ears. During the lull in the fighting, the uniforms were washed and the soldiers' battered bodies were freshly deloused. Those who had the opportunity had their hair cut, and the beards that had grown in the trenches were shaved off. Now things were moving again. No one knew how long it would take.

On the way to the front, the men's minds were filled with different thoughts. Fear combined with heroic fantasies. While some were excited and their pulse quickened with every step, others thought of how they would face the enemy, throw them back, and crack their armor. Afterwards, they would be decorated in Berlin. Straight from the Fuhrer's hands.

Only the battle-hardened among them had cold eyes. They knew what awaited them.

From the plateau, the soldiers climbed down narrow paths to join their comrades. The fighting seemed to have subsided. However, the battlefield was still hectic. Wounded soldiers were still being rescued and brought to the rear. Medics pushed themselves to their limits, dragging their comrades through the woods. Occasionally, a machine gun would rattle, drawing a bright, trembling trail of tracer ammunition through the moonlit night into the Kallschlucht gorge. It was usually followed by the artificial magnesium light of a flare. It flickered, illuminating the sky and earth for a while.

"Why do they keep throwing up flares?" asked Grossmann as the artificial light flickered in the sky for the third time in twenty minutes.

"I guess they want to keep enemy shock troops from getting behind the lines," Hassel said.

"Or just to give the medics some light," Keller interjected.

They reached their area of operations well after midnight.

First Lieutenant Drexler, at the head of the company, stopped. "Platoon leaders to me!"

A lieutenant, a sergeant, and Sergeant Keller stepped forward. Drexler lit up a map. "We're right here," he said, placing his left index finger on the map. "North of us is Vossenack. The Americans and their armored forces are coming this way," his finger moved over the map, "to the west of us is Simonskall and to the east is Mestrenger Mill. The Kall River forms a natural barrier between them. Southeast of us is Kommerscheid, then Schmidt. Assault gun batteries are on their way there now and will arrive soon."

Assault guns meant hope.

The officer continued. "The meadows are mined! We must be especially careful here if we have to retreat. Our real goal is to drive the enemy back to Vossenack and then out of the village."

"Where are the other companies deployed?" the lieutenant asked.

"The heavy company controls the serpentines, the other two companies are on the right flank. Our squad is near Kommerscheid. This is also the location of the troop assembly area. Our medics should set up a suitable casualty nest. There is a medical bunker in Simonskall. If we can push the enemy back, we can use it. Everything clear so far?"

The lieutenant cleared his throat again to ask another question. "The battalion command post ..."

"... is also in Kommerscheid," Drexler added.

The platoon leaders took over their commands. The men spread out over the terrain. The area was densely wooded. Only a few individual paths, laid and used by humans and animals over many years, cut through the sloping terrain. The mixed forest had become sparse. While the deciduous trees towered naked into the sky, the sparse green conifers provided shelter from enemy aircraft. Above, on the plateau, were Kommerscheid and Schmidt; below, in the ravine, flowed the icy Kall.

Huber and Hassel found an ingenious position for their MG 42 and the equipment was set down. In addition to the two compatriots, two other comrades had carried boxes of ammunition.

"We have an excellent field of fire and sufficient cover here," said the private happily, placing the machine gun on the bipod.

Grossmann agreed with his Gunner one. "If I add a few thicker branches or small logs on this side, even the weather side is covered."

"Well, I'm not worried about the weather."

"But it's freezing cold."

Keller came by. "Good spot."

Meanwhile, Grossmann had placed the ammunition boxes where he could get to them quickly. The replacemeant barrels fort he MG 42 were ready. So were the asbestos rags and tools.

"Thank you, Josef," Huber replied.

"Try to dig in a little. I know it's hard with the roots. The ground's frozen in places too, but you know how valuable a good foxhole is," the assistant platoon leader suggested.

The two machine-gunners grabbed their spades and started digging.

Just two hours later, First Lieutenant Drexler's company was in position. Those who could tried to squeeze out another two or three hours of sleep.

Sniper Georg Honnige had also gone to bed. He had gone to the company commander earlier and asked if Lieutenant Drexler had a special assignment for him. However, his experience told him that he would participate in the upcoming battle as usual.

"You already know who or what you are investing in," was the curt reply.

Honnige was amazed to see that the company troop had also come a long way. Radomski had even hit him. The Master Sergenat, equipped with a steel helmet and a submachine gun, was in the middle of the front line.

"We are fighting for every meter of land, for every centimeter of soil," was the motto.

After the last battalion meeting, the officer had exchanged ideas with the other company commanders and talked about the open secret of the upcoming offensive, which was leaking out more and more in officer circles.

"We must hold the Siegfried Line! No matter what the cost," Major Retzer had said. "If we give up, the flank for the theater of operations will be open and everything will have been for nothing."

"Do you think the offensive will succeed?"

"I don't know the details, gentlemen, but as far as I know, everything is in place for a strong push. I suspect the result will be similar to the blitzkrieg. The enemy will sacrifice itself. We've already wiped out two divisions. They have no strength and no reserves. If we give it our all, the Winter Offensive will hit the Allies so hard that we will be able to negotiate a separate peace.

"That wouldn't be bad. Just the thought of the Russians invading germany makes me sick," said First Lieutenant Drexler, and everyone agreed with him.

"We still have the strength, so go to your men and show them how a German officer leads, namely from the front!"

A unanimous "Yes, Major!" rang out.

The cold of that night seemed to have reached its peak in the morning. Even in the thick winter uniforms, it was frosty. Günther Baar, who had just been promoted to Lance Corporal, stood up and wrapped his hands around his chest to keep warm. A muffled rumble, followed by a whistle, suddenly filled the air.

All of the Landsers internal alarm bells immediately went off and he threw himself to the ground again.

"Artillery attack," he shouted as loud as he could, crouching down and waiting for something to happen.

Huuuiiiit ... boom

The first shells lowered their flight path, zoomed downwards and hit the ground. Luckily, the volley was too short. Only occasionally did a stray shell come dangerously close. Trees were splintered, some falling with a cracking sound. Shrapnel raced through the air, shredding everything in its path.

After agonizing minutes of hoping and fearing, the fire was moved. Their worst fears had come true. Now the german soldiers were in the center of the steel storm, and the grenades exploded in the midst of them.

The company commander literally barked into the radio: "We're right in the line of fire! You have to take out the enemy artillery forward observer! ... What? ... They're not coming!"

Boom

Heads were pulled in. An injured man screamed as loud as he could in hellish pain. Panicked cries for a medic whipped through the ranks.

Drexler was convinced that the cries had not gone unnoticed by the man on the other end of the radio link.

"You can hear for yourself! If nothing happens, the Americans can march right through here. And that's because we're all dead! ... Yes, indeed! ... Good! ... Got it, over!"

Angrily, he put the radio down and raised the binoculars. The waiting began. Every minute seemed like an hour. How were they going to take out the forward US artillery observers?

Huiiit ... Boom

Less than ten minutes later, the hills opposite were shrouded in artificial fog. Since the Allied artillery observers could not be turned off, their view was obscured. This tactical measure saved many soldiers from being killed by artillery fire.

Then suddenly there was a huge crash on the other side of the ravine, on the enemy side. The echo of the gigantic impact reverberated several times.

"What was that?" asked a young soldier.

"Sounds like the heavy railroad guns. Our artillery answers."

A machine gun rattled. Bullets bored into tree trunks and blew off the bark. The sound of the bullets grew louder. The German guns fell silent. The infantry fire had not yet been returned, there was still no order to fire. Hold out!

"They're coming," was whispered.

Infantry fighting broke out all along the front. On the left flank there were heavy explosions.

"They're coming in tanks at Simonskall," Huber whispered to the man next to him.

He and Hassel lay at the MG 42, waiting for a good opportunity to fire. Soldiers in dark green uniforms approached the Kall, a small tributary of the Rur that could be described as a stream. But after heavy rains, the water level of the fast-flowing river had risen sharply and posed a serious obstacle.

Again and again, the GIs fired seemingly aimlessly into the wooded area as they took up positions on the banks.

"Fire only on my command," the company commander repeated.

Adrenaline coursed through the bodies of the lurking defenders. Their weapons were still silent. The enemy suspected, no, they knew they were here. What must be going through the minds of the US soldiers?

At the moment when a second American machine gun was set up to cover the pioneers who were running with bridge-building materials to the banks of the two-meter-wide torrent, the command echoed through the ravine, which was a relief for many of the soldiers. "Fire!"

Huber had taken aim at the enemy machine gun nest and pulled back the trigger. The heavy infantry weapon fired its rounds. The recoil was absorbed by the shoulder, as usual. Huber pressed the butt firmly against his cheek and shoulder. He kept correcting the direction of fire, firing burst after burst.

Hassel let the ammunition belt slide over his hands. Again and again he peered over his cover.

The American Browning machine gun lay on the ground, the shooters beside it. They were dying heroic deaths. Huber had swung the barrel. Pioneers carried a wooden footbridge to the rushing stream. Bullet after bullet left the barrel oft he machine gun. One of the US Pioneers fell tot he ground fataly wounded. Another GI immediately grabbed the end of the footbridge, but this soldier also fell victim to the machine gunner.

Wham

Shells exploded on the hillside. Shrapnel and wood splinters whizzed dangerously through the air. Keller ducked his head. A young soldier in the third squad could not avoid death. As he fired his carbine, a piece of shrapnel tore open his carotid artery. Blood gushed from the wound. The soldier immediately dropped his weapon and grabbed his neck with both hands. His eyes widened as he looked at Sergeant Keller. The wounded man tried to scream for help, but no sound came out of his mouth except for a gurgle. Blood was being pumped out of his body with every heartbeat. Keller reached for his first aid kit, but by the time he had it in his hand, the soldier was dying next to him with a waxy expression on his face. The sergeant knew there was nothing he could do. With a glazed look of anger, despair, and the will to survive, he looked down at the Kall. In the meantime, the American pioneers had managed to build two footbridges across the two to three meter wide river. The heavy planks buckled under the boots of the soldiers walking across them and jumped up.

Keller saw an American slip and fall into the creek. The GI struggled to get up and wade to shore. When he finally reached dry land, he grabbed his chest and fell backward into the water. The body floated away, leaving a clearly visible trail of blood.

More and more American soldiers crossed the Kall and took the hill under fire. The battle was on. Hassel opened a new ammunition box.

"Change the barrels," Huber whined, pulling back the machine gun.

Hassel grabbed the hot barrel with the asbestos flaps. In no time, the replacement barrel and new belt were in place. Not a minute too late, Shooter I was ready to fire again. This time he fired at one of the pedestrian bridges. Two GIs fell into the water and were hit. Bullets bored into the wood. The remaining soldiers at the crossing immediately jumped into the water. They preferred the cold, raging water to certain death.

Boom

Earth and wood splinters covered the German machine-gunners. A shell had landed not far from their position.

Wham

The next shell died near them.

"They've got us," Hassel cried in panic. "We have to change position!"

Huber didn't seem to hear him. He kept firing at the attackers. Then a grenade exploded so close to the machine-gun nest that a few shrapnel grazed the gunner.

"Ouch! Damn," he groaned, grabbing his cheek.

Blood slowly trickled into the neckline of his collar. Instinctively, the private ran his hand over the injury several times. Then he looked down at the bloody, red palm. He looked at Hassel, who was obviously talking to him, but Huber could only make out muffled fragments of words. His left ear was numb, but he felt no pain. He saw Hassel grab two ammo boxes and prepare to jump. One last eye contact, then the machine gun shooter II jumped up and ran to the back. Huber didn't think twice, grabbed the machine gun and followed his second man. About thirty meters away, they dropped to the ground again. Gunner I immediately brought his weapon back into position.

"Medic," he heard Hassel's muffled voice. "Medic," was repeated. He also waved.

The Samaritan of the field came running. Crouching and repeatedly taking cover behind trees, he approached the two machine-gunners. Deadly rounds whistled through the air. The medic's chest rose and fell rapidly. Waiting for a favorable opportunity, he jumped up and covered the last fifteen meters in one bound. When he reached Hassel and Huber, he dropped to the ground and gasped for air. Then he opened one of the two medical bags he carried, grabbed Huber's chin with his left hand and said, still visibly out of breath: "Turn ... your ... head toward me."

Shooter I turned his head slightly to the left. A questioning look followed.

"Just three small flesh wounds, nothing serious."

"What?" The machine-gunner was still slightly deaf in his left ear.

"Not so bad," the medic repeated, dabbing at the wounds. He took a pair of tweezers from his pocket and pulled a small splinter out of his cheek.

"Ouch," Huber let out a short cry.

"It was still in there, everything else is cuts! Here ..." he handed him the small splinter, "... you can keep it as a souvenir."

The private took the splinter, looked at it briefly, and threw it to the ground.

"I'll put some tincture of iodine on it so the wound doesn't get infected. We won't get far with a plaster, the splinter wound is too big for that. I'll have to put a compress on it and secure it with a bandage."

Huber looked at the medic questioningly.

"It looks bad, but it won't help. If you're lucky it'll heal, if you're unlucky you'll have to have stitches in your cheek."

Huber nodded. He had only understood half of it anyway.

By the time the medic was finished, the machine-gunner felt like a badly wounded man. "With the white thing on my head, I'll be instantly recognizable," he said, gritting his teeth.

214

"If you don't like it, you can go straight to the battalion. That's where the doctor is."

Hassel tapped him on the shoulder. "Hurry up! A second wave is coming."

The medic jumped up and ran to the next wounded man. Meanwhile, Huber lay back down behind the machine gun, pressed the butt against his shoulder, took aim, and pulled the trigger.

First Lieutenant Drexler changed the clip on his MP 40. "Honnige," he called to the sniper.

The Lance Coropral was in position not far away, crawling to his company commander. "First Lieutenan?"

"Find a good spot and aim at the officers and NCOs. If the Americans are headless, they will retreat!"

"Yes, Sir," the sniper groaned and crawled away.

Honnige looked around. He jumped up and ran to a fallen beech tree. There he took cover and crawled along the ground to the former top of the tree. Peering through the branches, the corporal had a good view of the Kall and the slope. He was also difficult for the enemy to spot in the tangle of branches. He took aim. He looked at the GI's faces through the scope. He closed his eyes quickly. He had to suppress any thoughts that immediately popped into his head.

This is the enemy! Open your eyes.

Looking through the scope, he swung the barrel of the sniper rifle around. A sergeant waved his squad over and gave tactical signals. The index finger had already pulled the trigger to the pressure point and was crooked for the shot. The American sergeant collapsed, mortally wounded.

The barrel of the gun continued to move. An officer was being treated on the banks of the Kall. A medic applied a tourniquet to the wounded man's leg as the officer barked instructions to a radio operator kneeling beside him. Honnige took a quick breath, held it, and pulled the trigger. The shot cracked and mingled with the normal roar of battle. The sniper was pleased to see the radio destroyed. The medic, the radio operator, and the officer lay on the ground, making themselves as small as possible to avoid being a target. A moment later, they looked at each other in confusion.

Keep moving!

Medics carried the wounded to the rear. Two GIs were dragging an apparently unconscious comrade behind them. A third stood in front of them. They set the wounded man down and seemed to be discussing something. The third waved his arms wildly. Honnige shot him in the back.

Then an officer came into the sniper's crosshairs. The sniper recognized the two white lines on the soldier's helmet.

A captain! Just in time for me, he thought.

He had him in his sights. Just as Honnige was about to pull the trigger, the captain disappeared behind a tree. The hunting instinct was aroused. Where would he reappear?

There he was again!

He saw the right side of his target. The officer kept swinging in front of and behind the tree. A machine-gun shell whirled past close to the enemy. The captain and his companions stayed behind their cover. They were lying on the ground behind trees. Honnige could see only their legs. He knew the soldier in the middle was the officer. The sniper aimed for the knee and pulled the trigger. Twitching movements. The target writhed in pain.

A hit.

The men beside him called for a medic. The captain rolled to the side. Honnige could see him now. The American's face was contorted in pain. The next shot would save him.

Boom

A grenade landed next to the sniper's position. A shower of shrapnel from leaves, dirt, pieces of wood and metal swirled around. Keep your head down, take cover, don't be a target. Seconds later, Honnige felt the wood of the rifle stock against his cheek again. A glance through the scope.

Away!

Swiveling.

Nothing. They already took him out.

Next, a machine gun nest came into the lone fighter's cross-hairs. He pulled the trigger. Gone. The shooter had moved at the last moment. A second shot followed immediately. Too fast. The bullet grazed the American's steel helmet. The sharp-eyed US soldier had seen the muzzle flash of the second shot and knew the sniper's position. He swung the machine gun around and fired a few rounds at the fallen beech tree Honnige lay behind.

Bullets whistled over him, shredding branches.

Take cover! They've got me!

The first volley was too high, the second too far to the right. The sniper was about to retreat when the third volley rattled off. This time, the bullets landed directly in front of, next to, and above him. Honnige felt a sharp, hellish pain in his side. He pressed as close to the ground as he could. Centimeter by centimeter he crawled back. He moved at a snail's pace.

Just don't stand out! It hurts like hell. This hellish pain.

The man from Baden-Württemberg gathered all his strength. When he finally got out of sight of the machine-gunner, he was dragging himself away more than he was running. Soon he realized that his strength was dwindling and the pain was becoming unbearable.

Honnige spotted a foxhole, made his way to it, and dove in with the last of his strength. Goose bumps covered his body as he saw two decomposing bodies. They were GIs who had been lying here since the first heavy fighting around Schmidt and Vossenack. The war showed its cruel face once again. Honnige crouched a few inches from the dead. The smell of decay crept into his nostrils. It didn't help. He had to survive this. The lone warrior closed his eyes and collected himself for a moment. A glance to the side. Blood. A closer look revealed that he had an entry wound and an exit wound.

One bullet through, he breathed a sigh of relief and leaned back. A bullet doesn't need to be taken out.

He took a deep breath.

That damn stench.

It was then that the twenty-something realized the madness of war. The images in front of his eyes blurred. Honnige unbuckled his belt and slipped out of his camouflage shirt. Then he fumbled in his pocket for bandages. Take a break. Gather his strength. He opened his coat and took it off. Carefully, he removed piece by piece until his upper body was exposed. As he lifted his left arm again, he clenched his teeth to fight the pain. Finally the wound was exposed. Shivering with weakness and cold, he applied compresses to the injury and then wrapped a makeshift bandage around his torso. His hands trembled. Once again, full concentration. He tucked the loose end of the bandage into his pants. Suddenly he got scared. If the two dead US soldiers weren't found here, he wouldn't be found either.

I don't want to die like this!

The lone fighter pulled his clothes back on with the last of his strength. Two attempts to button up the warming cloak failed. Then Honnige crawled out of the foxhole.

Where are my comrades?

Eventually his eyes went black and he collapsed unconscious.

When Lieutenant Drexler realized that his company could not hold the position much longer, he radioed for reinforcements, but the reserve was already deployed elsewhere. The enemy was superior all along the front.

"What?" the officer shouted into the radio, "Simonskall has been abandoned? Then the Americans are already behind us! ... To the Mestrenger mill? ... Repeat, please! ... Understood! We're retreating to Mestrenger Mill! Over!"

The company commander immediately relayed the order to his men and informed them of the rendezvous point.

"The first platoon will cover the retreat. The machine gun of the third platoon will provide support. A squad each from the

218

first and third platoons will support the medic. Since the enemy has broken through behind us and is attacking Kommerscheid and Schmidt, the road to the rally point should no longer be passable. We will therefore take our wounded with us, provided they are fit for transport.

One by one the company withdrew. They had fought bravely.

The Mestrenger Mill was northwest of Kommerscheid and Schmidt. Outposts were set up. Drexler reported his new location and announced the number of troops. He was told to hold until further orders.

To everyone's surprise, Radomski showed up in the evening with his company. They, too, had been involved in brief skirmishes, but were able to make their way to the mill.

"Nothing can stop an old warhorse like me so quickly," said the Master Sergeant, greeting his comrades with a broad grin despite the deadly situation.

The company commander was relieved to find Radomski leading the company. He greeted them and immediately gave instructions. "Outposts change every three hours. Rest and take care of your weapons. Radomski, I'm glad you made it to us. Please see that the men are supplied with ammunition. We'll dig in here and hold the hedgehog position until new orders are given, but that's nothing new for us, comrades."

Someone shook him. The pain immediately returned.

Where am I?

Honnige came to slowly. A group of American soldiers were standing around him. A GI wearing a Red Cross bandage looked at the wound. A sergeant searched the German's pockets. The wounded sniper was alternately hot and cold. He had a fever. The sergeant found the Zippo storm lighter given to Honnige by the wounded GI. The soldier's name was Brian Lordson and he was a member of the 9th Infantry Division.

I'm sure you think I killed him and then picked his pockets. How can I best explain that I'm not a looter?

The wounded soldier tried to speak, but he was too weak and could only stammer out incoherent fragments of words.

The lighter went into the pocket of the grim-faced US soldier. He angrily uttered a few sentences that Honnige couldn't understand. The medic, on the other hand, seemed unimpressed and continued to treat the German. The sniper was finally given an injection and collapsed.

When he regained consciousness, he was lying on a cot in a tent. It was heated. His torso was exposed and an IV needle was in his arm. The soldier tried to remember.

What had happened?

He looked at the situation again. He was under the beech tree. Gunfire was raining down. Retreat after machine-gun fire. One hit. Then he took cover in a foxhole where two half-decomposed bodies lay. He had taken a bullet. Shot through. An enemy medic had treated him.

"Are you awake?" a voice asked in broken German.

Honnige looked at an American medic.

"You lost a lot of blood. We didn't think you'd make it, but you're a tough guy."

"Thank you," the patient croaked. He had a very dry throat.

"Here," the Army doctor said, handing him his Zippo lighter, "this is yours. The sergeant who found it on you did some research. Yesterday he informed me that PFC Brian Lordson of the 9th US Division is alive. He spoke with him and learned that you helped him."

Honnige nodded.

"The war is over for you. As soon as you are healthy again, you will be sent to a prison camp and return home after the war."

The doctor left.

The sniper opened the lighter and snapped the lid shut.

Zip-po.

Thoughts circled.

Did it save my life?

He didn't know. It was over. He would survive and return home after the war. No more sneaking up, aiming and shooting. Over and out!

Honnige closed his eyes and was thankful. As he thought of his childhood home and the pictures of his family, tears of joy ran down his cheeks. At that moment, the man from Baden-Württemberg had no idea that it would be two long years before he would finally be able to hug his parents again.

The assault rifles were ready for battle. Camouflaged by the dense green of pine branches, the battery, including Sergeant Lannert's gun, stood at the edge of the forest, waiting for the enemy.

Lannert looked through the commander's hatch. Nothing was visible yet. There was an eerie silence in the air. They knew the enemy was approaching. It had long since been announced over the radio. The hours and minutes of waiting tore at their nerves.

How will the battle end this time? How strong is the enemy?

Questions to which there were no answers at the moment. Hoping and praying was all they could do.

At first there was only a faint hum, which grew to a buzz, then to a roar. The sound of engines. The US tanks were inexorably approaching the high plateau in front of Schmidt.

Wham

There was a bang.

"They're coming across the mined meadow again," the assault artilleryman said to his team. "Did the Americans think our engineers wouldn't lay mines a second time?"

Boom

The mines detonated again. The sergeant got behind the scissor scope. "What's taking them so long?"

Wham

Finally he saw the silhouettes of the tanks. "There they are! And now I know why the mines are going off and the Yank is moving so slowly."

"Don't make it so exciting. What's going on?"

"They've got a couple of Sherman crabs up there."

"Mine sweepers," Eck groaned.

"Fire only on command! The order just came through," said Kleimann, the ship's radio operator and gunner.

"Can you see what else is coming at us?" asked the gunner, Arno Tiller.

"I see mostly dust and clouds of exhaust. There are at least three or four crabs ahead, clearing the way."

The APC's mine flails, made of heavy chains, swung around the axle and hit the ground hard. They dug deep and hard enough into the ground to detonate the T-mines.

The Sherman Crabs were modeled after the British Scorpions, which were based on the Matilda main battle tanks. The decisive advantage of the Sherman Crabs was that the threshing drum, which was mounted on two long cross struts, did not require its own engine, as was the case with the rear-mounted Matildas; instead, the drum of the flails was driven by the chain drive wheel at the front of the American tank. In addition, unlike the British prototypes, the tank retained the turret and all of its armament.

Both the 75mm cannon with up to 97 rounds and the 7.62mm coaxial MG with 4750 rounds were ready for use during the evacuation.

"I can see them. It's getting dicey now," the gunner complained. "I've got one in my sights! When's the damn fire team coming?"

"Relax, Arno, the boss knows what he's doing."

There was an eerie silence inside the assault gun. Despite the November chill, drops of sweat ran down the foreheads of the assault gunners.

Wham

Enemy tank guns fired and shot their shells out of the barrels.

Kleimann checked the radio again to make sure it was set correctly.

The war of nerves was eased when the main gun fired and Kleimann yelled at the same time: "Fire at will!"

The shot rang out. The loader immediately fired the next tank shell. The breech closed quickly. Fire.

"Hit," Lannert announced proudly.

At the same moment, an enemy grenade crashed to the ground near the assault gun. Splinters and stones hit the side plating.

"Range 1200 - 1 o'clock," Lannert yelled.

This angle could just be reached with the cannon without turning the assault gun. The sergeant could already see the next flash of the American tank in the scope.

Wham

The gunner worked precisely, preferring to take a few seconds longer. For the other occupants, it was pure nerve-wracking. "I got him!"

Click

Launch.

"Crap! The grenade hit at the wrong angle and bounced off!"

Suddenly things got extremely hectic. Another tank shell hit close to the gun. This time, it banged even harder against the outer wall of the steel colossus.

"Fire!"

There was a dry crack before the grenade was fired.

Ignition, it shot through Lannert's head.

The tube ejected the explosive. The projectile whirled toward the target, hitting it and unleashing its deadly effect.

Boom

The Sherman exploded with a thunderous roar. A jet of flame shot into the sky. Dark smoke of burning oil followed. This time the gunner had scored a direct hit.

"Explosive grenades! US infantry attacking!"

Machine guns rattled away.

Rrrrrrrt ... rrrrrrrrrrrrrrrt

Rings of sweat formed under the gunner's armpits. The air in the assault gun grew warm and stuffy. The breech slammed shut.

"Ready!"

"Fire!"

The first three explosive grenades were fired in quick succession, exploding in the midst of the charging enemy infantry, tearing bloody holes in the attacking ranks.

Human bodies swirled through the air. Torn arms and legs fell to the ground. Some soldiers had bloody bone ends sticking out where their limbs had been.

A huge explosion shook the assault cannon. A burning tree crashed to the ground next to the armored vehicle.

"The person next to us got a direct hit!"

"The position has been discovered! The order to attack has just been given," the radio operator announced.

The engine howled. The driver stepped on the gas and the assault gun began to move.

"Range 900 - 3 o'clock! Tanks!"

Kleimann, who already had an explosive grenade in his hand, switched it back and grabbed an armor-piercing grenade at lightning speed. The breech closed quickly.

Fire.

"Another one!"

The grenade hissed out of the barrel again, with billowing muzzle flashes. The next fight to the death had begun.

More grenades were fired. Three rounds later, the enemy tank was in flames.

"Stay to the left! Explosive grenades!"

Johann Eck, the driver, slammed on the brakes and the steel monster came to an abrupt halt. Three Shermans had appeared directly in front of them. Immediately recognizing the situation, Tiller aimed the barrel and fired. The explosive grenade hit the middle US tank. The breech closed again. This time there was another tank shell in the barrel.

Boom

Direct hit on the turret top.

Now the other two Shermans fired their cannons. Eck immediately turned hard right and gave full throttle. The heavy tracks jerked and pushed the steel hull around. The air pressure caused by the detonations of the tank shells could be clearly felt. Shrapnel scraped loudly across the steel. The assault cannon narrowly missed.

Something exploded. Lannert panicked and swung the scope around. Thick smoke obscured the view of the American tanks. The gunner breathed a sigh of relief when he spotted his assault gun mates. They were providing massive fire support. Shot after shot was fired. Finally, the relieving third powerful detonation sounded.

The flank was held. The attack was repulsed. Landser jumped to his feet and cheered as the Americans retreated.

"Men, we need ammunition. Back to the point of issue."

Eck turned all the way around and followed the tracked vehicle in front of him. The link to the battery had worked.

Soldiers ran past them, reinforcing the front lines. Lannert opened the hatch. Fresh air crept into the assault gun. He breathed a sigh of relief.

"It's never been as tight as it is today," the commander said to his comrades.

"My field blouse is all sweaty," laughed Kleimann.

The ammunition trucks were already waiting for the guns. Shells were loaded. No time for a break. The battery commander put the pressure on.

"Mount up," the command finally echoed through the ranks. "There are tanks at Kommerscheid! We have to play the fire department and knock out our infantry buddies!"

Lannert closed the hatch. Everyone was in his place. The atmosphere in the steel box was tense again. Eck followed the platoon leader's gun, which was clearly visible through its antennas.

As they approached the fighting compartment, projectiles from infantry weapons scraped the steel wall again and again. It also began to rain. The driver cursed. "If this keeps up, we'll be stuck in the mud before we get to Kommerscheid! Besides, the visibility is pretty bad ..."

"Keep calm, Johann! The Yank has the same weather," Tiller grumbled back.

"Don't argue! Are you ready? Looks like we're here."

The assault guns scattered over the ground. Grenades exploded all around them. Eck dashed past an infantry position. Out of the corner of his eye he saw an officer giving orders to his men. They were preparing for a counterattack.

"Our boys were going to push the Yankees back," he said quickly.

A crashing sound made the assault artillerymen's blood run cold.

"We were hit by a grenade that must have ricocheted," Lannert thundered.

"Who fired? Where is the enemy?"

The scissor telescope rotated.

"11 o'clock - 700!"

Eck braked and steered. The rear of the steel colossus shifted. The multi-ton vehicle slid into the desired position in the sodden earth. The gunner took aim.

"Fire!"

At the same time as the gun fired, they heard a loud bang. The assault cannon shook. Something hard hit the outer wall.

Eck was the first to catch his breath. "We've been hit. The left track is hit."

He played with the gears. "We can't maneuver," he added.

An acrid smell permeated the cabin.

"Fire! We're on fire!"

Lannert pushed open the hatch.

"I've got him in my sights," Tiller insisted, firing again.

"Gone," Lannert warned. "Everything out! Get out of here! Quick, before it all blows up in our faces!"

The sergeant got out and knelt down beside the hatch. He helped Kleimann, who was the next to get out of the stricken vehicle. Dark smoke rose from the rear. Small jet flames could be seen. Rain pelted down on them.

Bang

Directly in front of the assault gun, another grenade hit the ground. Lannert felt pressure on his back. A sharp pain took his breath away. He was thrown forward.

"Grit your teeth," he heard his comrades say, then Kleimann and Eck grabbed his arms and jumped to the ground. They pulled Lannert down with them.

"Ahhh," the wounded man roared.

Hell opened its gates again. Lannert felt his strength ebbing away. Everything blurred. He felt the fainting coming on. Suddenly everything was dark and still.

"Get out of here," yelled Tiller, taking the lead.

The other two dragged Lannert along. The earth shook. A frantic look over his shoulder.

"Infantry attack!"

A minute later, the assault cannon took a direct hit and exploded. The bang was so powerful that the fleeing Landser threw themselves to the ground.

Eck raised his head and turned around. "Madness," came from his lips. "We were just sitting in there!"

"Into the woods," Tiller shouted to his comrades.

More than two hundred meters had to be covered. Eck slipped. Lannert fell with him. A quick glance at the motionless sergeant followed. His chest was still rising and falling.

"Go on," Kleimann said immediately.

Eck stood up, grabbed his gunner's right arm again, and ran on. Bullets whistled through the air. Machine guns rattled incessantly. Hand grenades exploded. In between, the engines of tanks and assault rifles roared.

Hectic breathing. Stinging lungs. Legs getting heavier and heavier. Eck fell to the ground again. Tiller replaced him.

"I'll ... take over," he rasped and grabbed hold.

Fifty meters to go. A grazing shot tore Kleimann's uniform. He didn't feel it in his panic. All they could see was the forest. The moment they reached the sheltering trees, the assault gun crew collapsed, exhausted.

"What ... what ... is wrong with him?" Tiller was the first to catch his breath.

"Don't ... know."

Cautious patting of the cheeks. No reaction.

"Let me have a look," Kleimann gasped, sitting down beside the unconscious Sergeant.

His palms slapped the injured man's face left and right. A wince.

"Georg," Kleimann addressed him and patted him lightly on the cheeks again.

By now it was pouring. The attack on Kommerscheid seemed to have stalled. The weather conditions affected both sides, reducing the visibility of the tank drivers and gunners. The overhanging tree under which they sat offered little protection. Their uniforms were dripping wet. They didn't care yet. The crew's concern was for their gunner.

"He's conscious again."

"This ... hurts ... like hell," the injured man complained in a weak voice.

"Let's take a look at your back. Don't tip us over again!"

228

They turned Lannert onto his stomach, exposing his back.

"For God's sake," Eck remarked when he saw all the blood. "Georg caught some shrapnel."

"The little things are just flesh wounds. The blood is deceptive ..." he pointed to a gaping wound under the shoulder blade, "... but this one seems to be deep. Judging by the entry wound, this is quite a real big one."

Tiller looked back. We need to go deeper into the forest and head northeast. We can't go back through Kommerscheid!"

Lannert groaned. "Bandage me up and leave me here."

"You must be mad," Kleimann scolded.

"All or none," Eck interjected immediately.

Tiller agreed with the other two. "We'll take you with us."

"My map bag ..."

"It's here. You had it with you. Now take it easy."

Eck and Tiller took out their bandage packs and bandaged the guard.

"It should hold until we get to a medic."

Meanwhile, Kleimann studied the map. "There's a medical bunker in Simonskall, but the Americans should be through there by now. Then there's the Mestrenger Mill and ..."

"We'll go there," Tiller decided.

"I would have suggested it, too. It's not too far."

They put the severely weakened Lannert back into his uniform and propped him up. When they put him on his feet, he groaned loudly. "Ahh, that hurts!"

"Grit your teeth! Either you come with me or you'll die here," Kleimann snapped, his words deliberately harsh.

Lannert nodded. "I can do it!"

The rest of First Lieutenant Drexler's company had dug in around the Mestrenger mill. The wounded were being treated on the property itself. The intelligence officer tried to contact the battalion, while the company commander took note of the casualty list.

"Let's hope some of them were captured in good health," he whispered to himself.

"They put up a good fight," Radomski remarked.

The rifleman replenished his reserve magazine. "It'll be dark soon and it's raining cats and dogs. I think we'll have our rest until morning."

"I hope so! The men are exhausted."

"With all due respect, First Lieutenant, but they've been that way for weeks."

"I know how long we've been on the front line here. I'm also incredibly proud of the troops," Drexler replied, taking a deep breath. "When this is all over and I'm still alive, I'm going to make sure there's a shower of tinsel. And I'll personally present every award."

"Good," the Master Sergeant replied, putting the filled reserve magazine in his pocket.

"By the way, I also assume that the Americans will not attack again today. They have lost so many men that they will inevitably have to take a break."

"How often did we think the same thing in Russia?"

"This is another front and another opponent."

"You're absolutely right."

"Are the men in position?"

The Sergeant Major nodded. "All set, First Lieutenant. The medics are at work, some of the men are freshening up as best they can, and Keller's platoon has taken the first watch."

"Thank you."

It was just before dawn when Günther Baar saw shadows in the woods. The lance corporal warned the man next to him with a low whistle. Grossmann peered through the branches.

"They're not gum chewers, they're some of us," he said.

"But they're coming from the wrong side."

"They're carrying a wounded man."

"Let's take a look at him. Cover me," Baar replied, getting to his feet. His gun was at his hip, his finger on the trigger. He cautiously approached the incoming troop and finally spoke to them in a firm voice: "Stop! Stop!"

"Don't shoot! We are Germans! We have a wounded man with us."

"Come over here!"

The four assault artillerymen had made it to the Mestrenger Mill. Sergeant Lannert was immediately treated by a medic. He was given painkillers and then his wounds were treated.

While the small shrapnel was removed, the large shrapnel had to be left in the wound. "We have to operate here. We have to make sure we get to a field doctor. He's already the third wounded man to suffer like this. Something has to be done soon," the medic said.

"But he'll make it, won't he?"

"Looks like it's a tough one. We'll get him through!"

"And then we ran into the woods," Tiller finished the report to First Lieutenant Drexler.

"Kommerscheid and Schmidt are probably in enemy hands," he realized, punching his fist into the palm of his hand. "Damn!"

"Are we trapped here?" the gunner asked.

Radomski patted the assault gunner on the shoulder. "Don't worry, comrade. We've fought other battles. Now go back to your men and warm up. A hot cup of tea or coffee will do you good. You're soaked to the skin."

Tiller left the room.

Although a few candles were still burning, Drexler studied the map by flashlight. "If we're lucky ..."

There was a knock. The company commander stopped in mid-sentence. Radomski called out loud: "Come in!"

The medical sergeant entered the room. "First Lieutenant, you wanted a report as soon as I have an overview."

"Please."

"Seven lightly wounded have been treated and are back in the trenches. Five hospitalized wounded are over in the room, and three of them, including the sergeant, need surgery as soon as possible. We only have the small first aid kit. Our resources are limited."

"Would the men survive being transported on foot?"

The medical sergeant shrugged. "I don't know, Sir. Maybe they would, maybe they wouldn't."

"We need to put together a task force, Radomski. I need to know if this narrow corridor ..." the first lieutenant pointed to a spot on the map, "... is clear of the enemy and passable."

"The terrain along the Kall is difficult," the company sergeant replied immediately.

"If it's the only way to get the wounded back, we have to try."

"I'll lead the assault myself. How many men should go?" suggested the Sergeant.

"Take seven men. That should be enough."

"Understood."

At that moment, the newsman came into the room excitedly. "First Lieutenant, I've reached the battalion."

"Very good!"

"The Americans have asked for a ceasefire for two days. They have so many wounded lying in the woods and meadows that we have offered to stop the fighting for 48 hours on humanitarian grounds."

"That saves the day," said the company commander happily.

"Radomski, tell the men about it."

"Will be done immediately."

"Have orders been given for us?" he continued, but stood up at the same time. "You know what? I'll talk to the battalion myself!"

Sergeant Keller reacted calmly when it was announced that the transport of the wounded through enemy lines was permitted, but that they themselves had to remain in their positions.

The company was reinforced through a narrow corridor next to the Kall, which was flooded by heavy rain.

The assault artillerymen returned to their unit.

After the ceasefire, the counterattack expected by the Landsers followed. The death dance of Schmidt, Kommerscheid and Vossenack continued.

In the first three days of Operation Queen, two US regiments suffered above-average casualties. The German artillery and machine gun fire from the well-developed defensive positions repeatedly cut large gaps in the lines of attack.

Although the U.S. Army blasted additional tank tracks into the woods to reinforce the infantry with tanks, the defenders' minefields ultimately caused enormous casualties among the attackers.

The US Army needed the ceasefire on November 19, 1944, both to recover their wounded and to regroup.

The OKW, on the other hand, reinforced its defensive forces during this period with two divisions from the offensive contingent for Operation Wacht am Rhein. *(Author's note: Code name for military operation)*

The northern Eifel front had to be held at all costs.

General Eisenhower relentlessly pursued his regiments into the Hürtgen Forest. The U.S. Supreme Commander was determined to overcome this obstacle and advance into the Rhine Valley. But the German resistance could not be broken. Each village had to be taken by infantry with great effort and loss of life. Counterattacks were the order of the day.

The two villages of Großhau and Hürtgen were fought over for two weeks. By the time they were taken by American forces in late November 1944, more than 3,000 U.S. soldiers had been killed.

Despite the massive American superiority, the German troops were able to prevent the US units from advancing to the Rur dam.

The Ardennes Offensive, launched on December 16, 1944, ended the fighting in the Hürtgen Forest for the time being.

The villages of Schmidt and Kommerscheid did not fall until February 1945.

The Rur dam was reached too late by US infantrymen. It had been blown up by German engineers. The flooding delayed the American advance into the Rhine Valley for another two weeks.

The Battle of the Hürtgen Forest is still considered one of the worst defeats ever suffered by US troops. Casualties were estimated at 33,000 on the American side and 28,000 on the German side.

The completely exhausted 275th Infantry Division was merged into the 344th Infantry Division in December 1944 and reorganized as the 33rd Infantry Division in Flensburg in early 1945. It was finally destroyed on the Eastern Front in the Halbe Battle.

Josef Keller, who was promoted to first sergeant for bravery in the face of the enemy, was one of the soldiers who managed to fight their way through to the lines of the 12th Infantry Division. Shortly before the end of the war, they crossed the partially destroyed Elbe bridge at Tangermünde and were captured in the west.

Of Keller's Russian comrades, only Radomski and Huber, the machine-gunner, were still alive. All the others had been killed.

The End

Additional information about snipers:

(Excerpt from my book: Sniper of the Waffen-SS at the Eastern Front)

Sniper equipment (in addition to standard equipment)

- Rifle with rifle scope (telescopic sight)
- Ammunition (see following article)
- Container for the rifle scope
- Tools and care utensils for the rifle scope (partly re-gulated
- in service regulations, e.g. for the ZF 39, D134 dated
- January 22, 1940)
- Cleaning device for the gun
- Binoculars with auxiliary apertures
- Combat knife
- A compass
- A little mirror
- Camouflage helmet cover
- Camouflage sniper jacket
- Camouflage tent awning
- Camouflage-net with mosquito net
- Camouflage Mask
- Camouflage string and nails
- Fork (padded branch fork) for rifle rest
- Winter camouflage for weather conditions

Rifle

The most common rifle used by German snipers was the Karabiner 98 k. It was also preferred to the later Rifle 43 because of its longer range and better accuracy.

Ammunition used - 7.9 mm (8x57IS):

- · S. Pointed Bottom
- · l. S. Slightly spitzer bullet
- · s. S. Heavy spitzer bullet
- · S. m. E. Iron-core spitzer bullet
- · S. w. K. Pointed steel core bullet
- · S. w. K. (H) Hardened steel core pointed bullet (see note)
- · S. w. K. L`spur Pointed steel core bullet with tracer (see
- · note)
- · S. m. L`track Pointed bullet with tracer
- · (see note)
- · P. w. K. Phosphor with steel core
- · Pr Cartridge Phosphorus / incendiary projectile
- · (see note)
- · B. Cartridge Observation cartridge (see note)
- · Various practice pellets

Note:

The hit (impact) of the observation round could be observed as both a small flame and a small cloud of smoke could be seen on impact. Behind a phosphorus charge was a capsule containing lead azide or nitropenta. The projectile usually had a silver tip.

Note: Although the use of the B cartridge as an explosive projectile is repeatedly mentioned, it was probably not very common, as the effective range of the projectile ended at about 600 meters.

Another incendiary projectile used was the Pr (phosphorus) cartridge.

The pointed bullet with a hardened steel core was only produced until 1942 due to the lack of tungsten.

Tracer ammunition combined the projectile with a tracer charge. This was ignited by burning nitro powder. The burning time reached up to 900 meters. A glow mark was visible.

Telescopic sight (ZF)

There were several models of telescopic sights, which differed in mounting, magnification or light intensity. Depending on availability, the rifleman selected the scope (e.g. ZF 39, ZF 41, ZF 4) according to his needs and preferences.

Sniper badge:

The sniper badge, donated by Adolf Hitler on August 8, 1944, was awarded in three stages.

- Level 1 (3rd class) = 20 kills
- Level 2 (2nd class) = 40 kills
- Level 3 (1st class) = 60 kills

It was forbidden to include shots fired in close combat. The enemy was also not allowed to show any intention of defecting or being captured.

All kills had to be confirmed. Snipers sometimes kept a notebook in which they recorded their successes. The following had to be noted: Shot number, place and time, a brief statement of the facts and a witness.

The badge is made of greenish-grey fabric, embroidered several times and oval. It shows a black eagle's head turned to the right with white plumage, an ochre eye and a closed beak. The body is covered by an oak leaf fragment consisting of three leaves and an acorn arranged on the left. The edges of the badge are stitched. The individual levels can be distinguished by the cord sewn around them, in silver for level 2 or gold for level 3.

Snipers were hated and feared by the enemy. On all fronts, snipers who were captured were mistreated or even tortured to death. For this reason, precision marksmen generally refrained from wearing the sniper badge. Notebooks and equipment that could be used to identify a sniper were disposed of when capture was imminent.

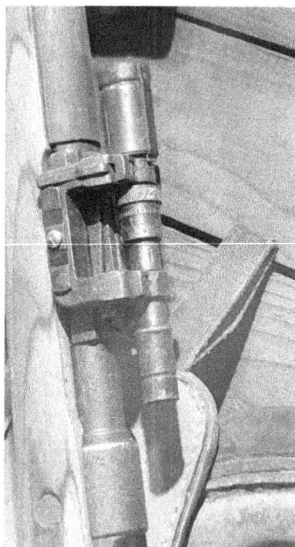

Author's private archives: PA-N-0125 - rifle scope on K 98

Glossery and Landser-Jargon (Landser-Slang)

MP 40 *also called "Schmeisser" because the name of the weapon's designer was applied to the magazines.*	Submachine gun 40, successor to the MP 38, standard submachine gun of the German Wehrmacht and Waffen-SS, bar magazine, 32 rounds, 9 mm Parabellum
PaK	Anti tank gun (cal. 3,7 cm or 7,5 cm)
MG 42 *Nickname among the enemy: "Hitler's saw"*	Universal machine gun model 42, (also year of introduction in the Wehrmacht/Waffen-SS), very effective weapon, caliber 7.92 x 57 mm
HKL (Hauptkampflinie)	Main battle line
OKW (Oberkommando der Wehrmacht)	High Command of the Wehrmacht
Siegfried-Linie (also called Westwall)	630 km distributed military defense system along the western border of the German Empire during World War II
Scho-ka-kola	Caffeinated, round chocolate packaged in a tin can.
Sanka	Medical vehicles – signed with a red cross on white ground
Concentrated charge (original)	Prefabricated explosive in cuboid form, dimensions: 7.6 x 16.4 x 19.5 cm, weight with carrying ring: 3 kg explosive
Concentrated charge (several hand grenade warheads are bound around a stick grenade)	Emergency aid for blowing up obstacles, shelters or for defense against armored vehicles (the latter usually for blowing up chains or when attacking immobile vehicles)
z.b.V.	military abbreviation for: for special use

Eight-Eight	german anti-aircraft gun (FlaK), caliber 88 mm, which could also be used for ground targets
Age	Nickname for: Superior officer (usually company, battalion or division commander)
Thunderbolt	Latrine / field toilet
Medic	paramedic
Goulash cannon	Field kitchen
"Sore throat"	Someone would like to receive an award (Knight's Cross, Iron Cross, etc.)
Dog tag	Identification tag (usually worn on a chain around the neck)
Chaindog	Military Police = Field gendarme, recognizable by the tin sign he wore
Suitcase (also heavy suitcase)	heavy grenade
Kübel o. Kübelwagen	Light, all-terrain military car (Volkswagen)
Kitchenbull	cook
Landser	German soldier's name (Landsknecht = mercenary fighting on foot 15th/16th century)
tinsel	Medal/als/also insignia of rank
Latrine slogan	rumor
Spieß (Spiess) (Master Sergeant)	Company sergeant (usually a senior sergeant in the position of a sergeant major - he was recognizable by the two piston rings sewn onto his uniform sleeve)
String puller	Radio operator (soldier)
S-Mine	Abbreviation for shrapnel mine, fragmentation mine or spring mine. When triggered by a kick or tripwire, the body of the mine is propelled to

	about hip to shoulder height and explodes with a fragmentation effect. This weapon was so effective that it has found many imitators to this day.
Aunt Ju	A nickname for the Junkers Ju 52, a type of aircraft manufactured by Junkers Flugzeugwerk AG, Dessau. The most successful model was the three-engine Junkers Ju 52/3m from 1932, which evolved from the single-engine Ju 52/1m model.
Twelve-engined	Professional soldier (service period was at least 12 years)
TVPl	Military association place
UvD	Abbreviation for: Unteroffizier vom Dienst /Sergeant on duty (usually a special service to supervise the internal service, the UvD followed the instructions of the company sergeant (Spieß) and ensured compliance with military order at the end of the service. Among other things, he was responsible for waking up the soldiers, supervising the performance of cleaning duties and observing the night's rest)
WuG (weapon an equipment)	Weapons and equipment sergeant, usually a member of the combat team

Source reference

Wikipedia:

https://creativecommons.org/licenses/by-sa/4.0/deed.de

https://de.wikipedia.org/wiki/275._Infanterie-Division_(Wehrmacht)

https://de.wikipedia.org/wiki/Schlacht_im_H%C3%BCrt-genwald

and

Memories and records provided by veterans and contemporary witnesses (in writing or in personal conversation with the author) and the author's own knowledge.

More Books by W.T. Wallenda:

Now in English – the German bestseller:

W. T. Wallenda

THE SNIPER FROM
STALINGRAD

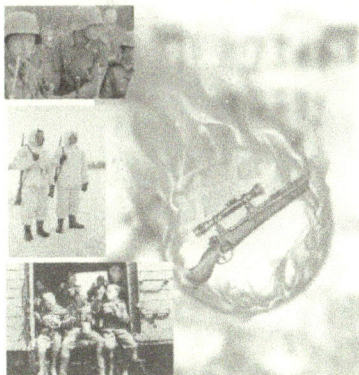

The Sniper
from Stalingrad

W. T. Wallenda

Publisher:
Books on Demand, 2024
188 Pages
ISBN-13: 978-3759720580

Paperback: € 9,99
E-Book: € 6,99

Stalingrad, 1942 - 19-year-old Alfred Miller, a member of the 100th Panzer Division, comes to know and hate the cruel horrors of war during the fierce and costly battles for the "Red October" factory. Thanks to his marksmanship, he becomes a sniper.

After the encirclement of the 6th Army, the young Austrian wanders through the ruins of the dying city on the Volga during the coldest winter in years, both hunter and hunted. Hunger, cold, misery, death and fear are his constant companions.

The war hits hard and merciless every day. The soldiers are brutalized, the hope of salvation dies. Ultimately, there are only two ways to escape suffering and a grim fate: either get on one of the planes out of the cauldron, or die.

Shocking, thrilling, exciting ... from the diary of a war veteran

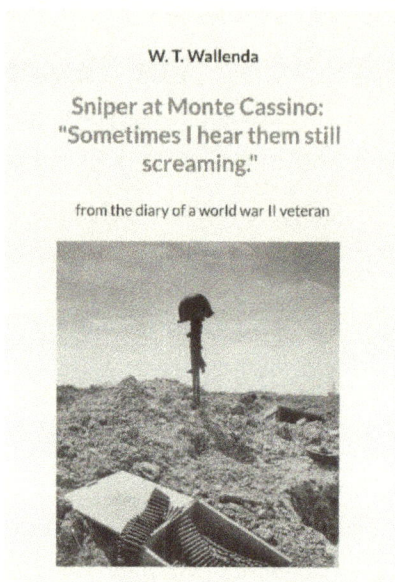

W. T. Wallenda

Sniper at Monte Cassino:
"Sometimes I hear them still screaming."

from the diary of a world war II veteran

Sniper at Monte Cassino: „Sometimes I hear them still screaming."

from the diary of a world war II veteran

W. T. Wallenda

Publisher:
Books on Demand, 2024
200 Pages
ISBN: 978-3757845223

Paperback: € 11,99
E-Book: € 6,99

As a member of Regiment 361, the former foreign legionnaire witnessed the merciless fighting on the Gustav Line and around Monte Cassino. The war had reached an unimaginable level of cruelty, and death struck mercilessly every day.

Altmann was quickly trained as a sniper and immediately sent to the front. He recognizes the faces of his victims through the telescopic sight. His hands start to shake, his heart races. Goose bumps covered his body. Fear, misery, the loss of his closest comrades and the screams of the dying made him pull the trigger despite his initial doubts.

Josef Altmann tells his story without pathos, free of heroism and frighteningly close to reality. This book is an unflinching factual account and should serve as a memorial against war.

www.ingramcontent.com/pod-product-compliance
Ingram Content Group UK Ltd.
Pitfield, Milton Keynes, MK11 3LW, UK
UKHW021036260125
454178UK00001B/41

9 783769 315509